NINE
LEVELS DOWN

Books by William R. Dantz

Hunger
Nine Levels Down
Pulse
The Seventh Sleeper

WILLIAM R. DANTZ

NINE LEVELS DOWN

A TOM DOHERTY ASSOCIATES BOOK   NEW YORK

NINE LEVELS DOWN

Copyright © 1995 by Rodman Philbrick

A Forge Book
Published by Tom Doherty Associates, Inc.
175 Fifth Avenue
New York, N.Y. 10010

Forge® is a registered trademark of Tom Doherty Associates, Inc.

Design by Lynn Newmark

Library of Congress Cataloging-in-Publication Data

Dantz, William R.
    Nine levels down / William R. Dantz.
        p.   cm.
    "A Tom Doherty Associates book."
    ISBN 0-312-85483-8
    I. Title.
    PS3554.A583N56   1995
    813'.54—dc20   95-15451
                                            CIP

First edition: July 1995

Printed in the United States of America

0 9 8 7 6 5 4 3 2 1

For Lynn, always.

MSD, or Microcomputer Sedation Device:

A surgical implant that detects psychopathic rage and interrupts the cycle of violence by rendering the subject unconscious. Developed and implemented on an experimental basis by Dr. Anna Kane, a behavioral psychiatrist with the New York State Department of Corrections.

PROLOGUE

First Trial

Adirondack Correctional Treatment and Evaluation Clinic
Dannemora, New York

Norman couldn't help it, he was a psychopath.

"Sit down, shut up," said the guard.

When Norman settled all three hundred of his pounds, the chair creaked. Mildly retarded and prone to spasms of fugue-state violence, Norman had voluntarily undergone a psychosurgical procedure that was supposed to control, as the nice lady doctor explained it, his "bad temper."

Norman didn't know about that—he understood only that he would get extra dessert. He and Tiny Tim, a ninety-pound check forger who smelled of bubble gum and hair tonic, were seated on folding metal chairs in a small windowless room, awaiting appointments with the nice lady doctor, Anna Kane.

"Stop fidgeting," the guard said.

Norman had three moods that played like alternate speeds on a phonograph: catatonic, paranoid, and rage. Right now he was stuck in the paranoid groove, convinced that Tiny Tim was thinking bad thoughts about him. Ugly thoughts that flitted through the stale air like dimly perceived bats.

His chair creaked: *eek eek,* almost a bat sound.

Norman's hands twitched—he wanted to crush the bad thoughts that were flying out of Tiny's head, but the guard was armed with a Taser that would, Norman knew from experience, drop him cringing to the floor if he made a wrong move.

Beside him, within easy reach, Tiny blew a pink bubble, held it, smiled nervously at the guard.

"Don't even think about it," the guard said to Norman.

But Norman wasn't thinking, exactly, he was feeling, and what he was feeling now was rage. Rapidly expanding rage. Hold it inside and he would blow up like Tiny's pink bubble gum. Deny the rage and the bat thoughts would nest in his hair. Norman was terribly frustrated, but a small part of him was frightened of the guard.

What to do? In a moment he would have to act, regardless of consequence.

The guard groaned, folded his hands across his ample belly.

"Cramps," the guard muttered. "Sick," as he stumbled from the room.

Norman was alone with Tiny Tim.

On the monitor the subject looked blank and Buddha-like. The only visible indication of uneasiness was the slow clenching and unclenching of the fists.

"Does he realize the guard has left the room?" Dr. Kane asked. She had been working with the subject for only a few weeks, and relied on an ACTEC staff psychologist to help her interpret behavior.

"Sure he does," the staffer said. "Norman's not *that* retarded."

Dr. Anna Kane glanced at the computer indicators that monitored the subject's level of anxiety. Increased blood pressure, heartbeat, hormonal changes, they were all rising. "The subject is hot," she said. "These levels indicate PTR. He should be reacting."

"Yeah?" The prison shrink had been working with killers and psychopaths for most of his adult life, and he made no secret of his skepticism regarding Dr. Kane's work. "Well, Norm is slow, it'll take a while for his body to catch up to his brain."

Anna ignored the sarcasm and studied the monitor intently. What, exactly, was happening in there? The giant convict was finally starting to move, getting up from his chair. The fists were clenching faster now, but there was no other visible indication that psychotic trigger reaction was taking place. The huge, infantile face remained expressionless. Numbingly blank.

"Norm likes blunt objects," the staffer said confidently. "Last three victims he did with a table lamp. Mom, Dad, and Gramma. He'll go for the chair, it's the only blunt object in the room."

Sure enough, the giant was reaching for the metal chair.

Tiny Tim reacted by racing to the door, where he struggled frantically with the handle, unable to accept the fact that the only exit was locked.

The giant lifted the chair over his head.

"Okay, this is it," Anna said, glancing at her computer indicators. "The MSD is evaluating input. Any second now . . ."

At that moment the microcomputer sedation device implanted in Norman's brain sensed that a psychotic episode was taking place. The chair tumbled from his upraised hands. The huge man collapsed like a felled tree and slumped to the floor, unconscious.

Dr. Kane turned to the staff psychologist. "It worked," she said. "Damn it, it *worked.*"

"Check the monitor," the staffer said. "You got a situation developing."

"What?"

"Check the monitor, Dr. Kane."

Tiny Tim knew an opportunity when he saw one. Norman lying there unconscious, saliva bubbling from his lips, this was a dream chance to make the big creep go away.

Tiny peeled off Norman's prison slippers. No laces because laces were a weapon. Tiny didn't need laces, he knew a better way. He peeled off Norman's mouse-scented socks, balled them up, and shoved the socks deep into Norman's fat wet mouth.

There. Choke on it you beast.

He used the toe of the slipper to jam the gag deep into Norman's throat, cutting off his air. Simple but effective.

Tiny went back to his seat, sat down, examined his fingernails. Out of the corner of his eye he could see Norman's fat, expressionless face turning blue. So the big loony was about to become a suicide. Tsk, tsk. There would be a moment of silence on the cell block, followed by wild applause. For the first time in his life, Tiny would be a hero.

The door burst open. Taser-armed guards swarmed into the little room.

Medics dug the socks from Norman's throat and began resuscitation.

"Careful," Tiny advised. "I heard he bites."

The guards cuffed Tiny, who did not resist. He was not, after all, prone to violence.

MEMO

TO: Dr. Anna Kane,
Psychiatrist
New York State Department of Corrections

FROM: Albert C. Darling, Ph.D.,
Chairperson, Advisory Board
Behavioral Modification Programs Oversight
Committee
New York State Department of Corrections

SUBJECT: Project funding,
Trials, Microcomputer Sedation Device

Dear Dr. Kane,

Notwithstanding your reservations concerning the suitability of convict John Marlon, the so-called "Subway Killer," as a candidate for inclusion in the second-stage MSD trials, the Board has concluded that his application should be approved, for the reasons I reiterated during our recent telephone conversation.

Your concerns about security precautions have been duly noted, and forwarded to Security Chief Henry R. Portis at the Forensic Psychiatry Annex in Manhattan. As you are no doubt aware, the Annex is a sealed, maximum-security environment designed to contain and control seriously disturbed offenders. The Oversight Committee has concluded that even if your experimental device should prove ineffective in controlling Marlon's behavior, there is no possibility of him harming other inmates, or the Annex personnel.

Good luck, Dr. Kane. If the implementation trials go as planned, MSD may revolutionize the way we control violent offenders.

DAY
1

Theory

CHAPTER ONE

There was something wrong underground.

It began as a vibration, carried up through the rails and into the car where Anna was seated. Just another of a myriad of subway sensations, no more or less apparent than the rhythmic swaying as the train sped through the tunnels, or the whisper of displaced air, or the rattle of the car couplings, or the metallic squeal of the wheels.

The vibration increased. Anna glanced at her fellow passengers. All avoided making eye contact. Nobody showed any sign of concern. Nothing less than a bomb going off was going to pierce their personal cocoons, that narrow, inviolable space of privacy maintained by city commuters.

Anna took a deep breath and closed her eyes. Why was her pulse suddenly pounding? She wasn't afraid of the subway or the trains, and certainly not this busy line in Manhattan. The cars were relatively new and clean, the stations had all been recently refurbished, and Transit Police made regular patrols. Violence still occurred, of course, but she herself had never been menaced in the underground. Nothing to be afraid of down here.

And still her heart pounded.

Don't be ridiculous, she told herself, you're a behavioral psychiatrist, you *know* about anxiety. It wasn't the subway that was bothering her, it was anxiety about the new project. Had to be. Look at it objectively, and the panic will subside. Calm, be calm . . .

Dr. Anna Kane had almost succeeded in willing away her irrational fears when the brakes suddenly locked. The track screamed, the cars began to shudder and buck violently. The lights went out. In absolute darkness the train finally lurched to a stop.

There was a moment of silence, then a sharp, steam-charged hiss, as if some great mechanical creature had just died.

In the darkness someone sighed and said, "Ah, shit, not again."

Weak lights began to glow in the tunnel. Passengers started banging impatiently on the exit doors. In the dimness Anna noticed an old woman staring at her. Mad, glittering eyes in an ancient face. "The devil," the old woman muttered, striking her cane against the floor of the car. "The devil lives in the underground. You must pray."

Anna glanced away. Just her luck, to be accosted by a religious fanatic when she couldn't easily get away.

At that moment an exit door jerked partway open. A uniformed man stood in the tunnel, holding a flashlight. "Sorry, people, we got a break in the track and the doors are jammed," he announced. "You got a choice. You can wait until they get a repair crew here and jack up the car, I got no idea how long that will take. Or you can walk to the head of the train. Thirty yards, you'll be at the station."

"What about the third rail?" someone asked.

"Power's off on this whole section of line," the uniformed man said, sounding bored. "You'll be okay, just keep to the path."

Anna knew about the third rail—step on it and you'd fry. For that reason, passengers were usually banned from the track area, but now an exception was being made. She made her way along the gravel-strewn area beside the track, keeping well clear of all the rails, power or no power. Be grateful you're not trapped on the train for hours, waiting for the repair crew, she told herself. And watch your step.

She was relieved to see the station platform right ahead, bathed in faint yellow emergency lights. Another uniformed man helped the passengers climb a short ladder up to the platform.

"Uppa ladder," he kept repeating. "Uppa ladder, uppa ladder."

Anna was glad she'd worn her sensible shoes. The ladder was creaky but that wasn't the problem. The problem was the blood, or what looked like fresh blood on the platform. A puddle of dark liquid dripping over the edge to the tracks below. Under the emergency lights it looked almost black. Had someone died here? From the quantity of blood it seemed likely.

"What happened?" she asked the man with the ladder.

"Don't ask," he said. "Move along, lady, please."

Anna obeyed numbly, following the others up the long, dimly illuminated stairway. The escalators, no surprise, were not functioning. Halfway up the steps she began to feel strangely out of breath, suddenly aware of the great weight of the earth above her. Tons and tons of iron and dirt pressing down, held up by crumbling tunnels. It made you think.

When she finally came up into the light Anna felt as if she had been trapped in a huge labyrinth deep under the city and had by some miracle clawed her way out.

What a crazy idea. Totally irrational. What had gotten into her?

The real miracle was that when she raised her hand a yellow taxicab appeared out of nowhere and pulled to the curb.

The driver rolled down his window. "You okay, miss?" he asked with genuine concern.

"Fine," she said, getting into the cab. "Just fine."

Ten minutes later her hands finally stopped shaking.

CHAPTER
TWO

The inmate John Chester Marlon was transported by high-security van. He lay facedown on a thin foam mattress, his hands and feet chained to steel rings on the floor of the van. The rear door was padlocked shut from the outside. An electrified steel mesh screen divided the front compartment from the rear. The van was equipped with full electronics: a police radio, a CB unit, a cellular phone. Precautionary measures.

Two New York State marshals rode in the front, along with a driver. Each marshal was equipped with a Mace cannister, a baton, and a hand-fired Taser. By order of the warden there were no firearms in the van. The marshals were keenly aware that on a previous occasion a prison guard had inexplicably surrendered her handgun to the prisoner. That guard, now paralyzed for life with a lead pellet in her spine, claimed to remember nothing of the incident, other than a vague recollection that Marlon had been "very persuasive."

The transport van, en route from the Ossining Correctional Facility for almost two hours, had been stuck in gridlocked traffic on lower Broadway for the last twenty minutes.

"Hey Marlon," said one of the marshals in a taunting voice. "How's that foam taste, huh?"

The marshal did not look at the prisoner when he spoke. Looking at the prisoner was bad luck, no doubt about it. The other marshal chimed in: "You know that pothole we hit, crossing Twenty-third. I bet he tasted *that.*"

The prisoner did not reply. The prisoner could not reply, had he so desired, because the prisoner was gagged. This was not an officially sanctioned transportation policy—the rules expressly forbade the gagging of inmates—but was a precaution taken by the marshals on their own. Guard in the wheelchair, what had she been thinking, handing over her sidearm? What did it mean, that Marlon could be, quote, very persuasive, unquote?

Persuade you to death, as he'd persuaded his victims, down there in the subways of Manhattan. As a gold-hatted city engineer, a resident expert on underground excavation, John Chester Marlon had led a secret life, preying on young women he lured into dark tunnels. Three victims they knew of—probably dozens more, they ever located the bodies. So why take chances? Gag the man. Have a little fun, knowing he can't reply.

"Hey Marlon? I heard they're gonna give you a brain transplant, that right?"

"Yeah," said the other marshal. "They're gonna give him a *human* brain this time."

They broke up laughing.

"Hey, we're just kidding, huh? Sorry about getting stuck in traffic here, Marlon, but it's not like we can turn you loose, give you a subway token."

This *really* broke them up. The idea of the notorious Subway Killer being given a subway token, it was hysterically funny. As the nervous laughter died away they heard a rhythmic tapping sound.

Tap, tap, tap, very steady.

Hands on their Tasers—thirty thousand nonlethal volts—the marshals turned warily, peering through the wire mesh screen. John Chester Marlon remained chained to the floor of the van. All you could see was the back of his close-shaved head, his face buried in the gray foam mattress.

Marlon was tapping the fingers of his right hand. Tap, tap, tap, as if expressing impatience.

The marshals shut up. They said not a word as they inched through the traffic, and when the van was finally backed up to the concrete loading dock of the New York State Forensic Psychiatry Annex, they left the inmate's final transfer to the hospital security guards.

Share a space with John Chester Marlon, even the bound and gagged version, it spooked you.

CHAPTER
THREE

The cop was in the Annex lobby when Anna Kane finally arrived. He was hunched in a chair, chewing gum and filling in the *New York Times* crossword puzzle. In pen, she noted, with nothing crossed out.

"Detective McRay?"

He looked up, snapped the paper shut. "Yo," he said with a smile.

"I'm Dr. Kane. I was supposed to be here an hour ago. Sorry to keep you waiting."

The detective had dark brown eyes, glossy brown hair combed back from his forehead, a solid chin. Good-looking without being preening-perfect, Anna decided. A ready smile revealed several slightly crooked teeth. She liked the smile. He stood up, a man of medium height and build, and offered his hand. No bone crusher, just a normal handshake.

"Hey, this city," he said. "Hope you didn't get mugged."

"No," Anna said uneasily. "Just a breakdown on the subway." She decided not to mention the possibility that the train had been derailed by a jumper, if the blood-spattered platform was any indication.

The detective hadn't let go of her hand and she didn't want to yank it free, make it seem like she was recoiling from his touch. Some people were touchers, needful of physical contact. Anna was not a toucher. Definitely not.

"Oops! Sorry!" he said, when he realized he was still holding her hand. Genuinely embarrassed.

"Coffee?"

"You got decaf?" McRay asked, following her through a door marked *Annex Staff.* "I had about six cups already."

Dr. Kane hadn't as yet had time to set up an office at the Annex. That was second on her agenda, right after this meeting with Detective McRay. She had been assigned a temporary cubicle that contained a metal desk, a telephone, two chairs, a work table. In one corner was a stack of cardboard boxes, files that had been shipped down from Dannemora.

"Have a seat, Detective," she said, and returned a few minutes later with two coffees.

"Cheers," he said, raising the paper cup.

Anna settled behind the unfamiliar desk, leaving her coffee untouched for the moment.

"So," he said. "You're a prison shrink, is that right? Excuse me, I mean psychiatrist."

"Behavioral psychiatrist," said Anna.

"Yeah, but criminal behavior, right? What makes these guys tick?"

"That's one way of putting it."

McRay seemed to understand that his bluntness might be offensive, and he sought to make amends. "Hey, what do I know? Ten years on the cops, I still got no idea why they do what they do."

Wanting to put him at ease, Anna said, "I'm supposed to be an expert, but the only thing I'm sure of is that nobody really understands what makes an otherwise normal human being become a killer."

McRay smiled. "I've been reading about this thingamajig, the gizmo you put in their heads. Does it really work?"

"That's what we're here to find out. And actually, the device is installed in the back of the neck, under a fold of skin."

"Oh yeah?" said the detective, rubbing the back of his own neck.

"It's really very simple. A tiny computer chip detects violent impulses. It then sends a very weak electrical signal to a specific area of the brain, rendering the subject unconscious."

"That's it?"

"That's it," Anna said. "Think of it as a switch. A sophisticated switch."

"Knocks 'em out, huh? For how long?"

"Depends on the subject. Usually no more than a few minutes."

"And if he's still feeling violent when he wakes up he gets another zap?"

Anna nodded.

McRay said, "Hey, I like it."

"The implant is tailored to each individual. Some have thresholds of violence that are quite low."

"Tell me about it," McRay said. "Look at 'em cross-eyed they go nuts, am I right?"

"Some of them, yes," Anna said. She cleared her throat. "Detective, I don't want you to take this wrong, but I'm not really clear on why you wanted an appointment with me."

McRay put his coffee cup on the edge of her desk, leaned forward in his chair. His eyes were bright and intelligent, looking right at her. "My buddy Marlon," he said. "That's the connection."

"You know Mr. Marlon personally?"

McRay grinned. "In the first place, nobody calls him 'mister.' Believe me on that. He's Marlon, period. What happened is, I used to be with the Transit Police, back when Marlon was still a city engineer. Ran into him a few times, checking permits, strictly work-related stuff. In those days, you wanted to drill or dig underground, it had to be approved by Marlon. He was the resident genius, knew where every pipe and conduit was buried."

"You became friends?"

McRay looked appalled. "I didn't say that. This was strictly professional, just small-talk stuff. The weather, the Mets, whatever."

"I see."

"I never really knew the guy, but it was enough to get me on the Special Task Force after he got nailed."

"Special Task Force?"

"To locate the Doll House, Dr. Kane. Where we think he stashed the bodies. I guess you know we never located most of his victims."

Anna pawed around on the desk until she came up with a notebook and opened it to a blank page. "I've studied his evaluation files," she said, uncapping her pen. "But the 'Doll House' reference doesn't ring a bell."

McRay chuckled. "You've been upstate, out in the boonies, I guess you don't get the tabloids, huh? They played it big for a week or so, until the next gory crime came along. You do know Marlon is still a suspect in at least twelve other murders? Excuse me, 'disappearances,' since we haven't located any bodies."

"I did, yes," Anna said. "I'm not sure I knew precisely how many."

"Could be a lot more," McRay said, "you count all the possible match-ups. All we're listing is the most probable. Missing persons last seen in the vicinity of a city subway or tunnel, or in one case near an open manhole. We narrowed those down to victims who fit the profile: young attractive female, long hair, professional or studious type. For instance, of the three victims we *do* know about, two wore glasses and carried briefcases. All three had shoulder-length hair. Average height, slender build." He stirred uncomfortably and glanced away, breaking eye contact.

"Is there a problem?" Anna asked.

"I couldn't help but notice. You, uhm, sort of fit the profile yourself."

"So do millions of other women."

"Good point," McRay said, sounding relieved. "So you really think it'll work on Marlon? This implant thing?"

Anna took her time answering. "Can you keep a confidence, Detective?"

"Keep a . . . yeah, sure." He made the sign for zippering his lips.

"He's not my first choice. So far we've tested the device on trigger-reactive psychopaths. Frenzy killers. I'm not at all sure that Marlon is a trigger-reactive."

"Frenzy killer? You mean like he goes nuts, can't help himself?"

"That's not how a psychiatrist would describe it, but yes. We know Marlon is a serial killer, and most serial killers tend to be fairly methodical. Some are quite emotionless. Or *seem* to be emotionless. Also, Marlon was a socially integrated psychopath—he held an important job, functioned with his coworkers and so on. Which makes it less likely he's a trigger-reactive type."

"So you're not sure it'll zap him?"

"We'll find out, one way or another. He's a high-profile case, a celebrity serial killer, if you will, and my superiors think that if his behavior can be controlled the state will approve funds for a much wider implementation plan."

"They want the publicity. And you don't."

Anna smiled. "That's about the size of it, yes. So anything you can tell me about Marlon may help with the evaluation."

"I can tell you this much, Dr. Kane. He scares the hell out of me. I've been cleared to question him three times so far, and I got exactly nowhere."

"He's unresponsive?"

"Oh, he loves to hear himself talk. Ask him about the Doll House and he just smiles and keeps on talking. His theories of life and death, his theories on politics, on baseball, you name it. But he won't tell us about the Doll House. We wouldn't even know that's what he called it, except he confided in a cellmate the first day he was arrested. The cellmate was a plant, of course, and Marlon's smart enough to know that, so it's like he *wanted* us to know. Like he's taunting us."

"Many serial killers are quite intelligent," Anna pointed out. "And most are convinced that everyone else in the world is terribly stupid."

McRay nodded. "That's him. Only he doesn't think we're human beings. He thinks we're bugs."

"He said that?"

"It's how he acts. The way he looks at you. Not always, just when he wants to make an impression. When he wants to scare you." McRay paused. "Have you met him face to face?"

"Not yet. Later today."

"Be sure to keep your distance. You know about that prison guard?"

"Yes."

"Shot with her own gun. And she gave it to him. Just handed it over. Like she was hypnotized."

"I read the reports," Anna said. "They didn't mention hypnosis."

"Yeah, well, not everything goes in reports. All I know is, he's got this ability to persuade people. The day he got caught he talked three different women into accompanying him into an unlighted repair tunnel. He killed the first two, and if the third one hadn't played dead and then smashed him on the head with a brick, he'd *still* be down there taking victims. That's the only reason we got him, because he was knocked unconscious. A lucky shot."

"I saw the skull X-rays," Anna said. "No permanent damage."

"Too bad," McRay said. "So what happens if this MSD thing works? He gets to walk?"

"Not a chance. If it works he, or others like him, may be able to circulate in the general prison population. Certainly he'll be less dangerous to other inmates. That's the scope of the program, trying to find a way to make violent offenders less dangerous to fellow convicts, and to prison staff."

"Glad to hear it," said McRay, sounding relieved.

Anna was steadfast—after five years of dealing with convicted killers, her convictions were firmly held. "Let me be very clear on this. I have not advocated and would not advocate that such an individual be released from prison. I never, ever want to see this guy on the street. Or under it, for that matter."

McRay seemed satisfied. "Okay. But you've never actually met him."

"That's correct."

"All I'm saying, be careful. Be very, very careful. He's a monster, Dr. Kane, but you'd never know it to talk to him. That's what he did for years. He fooled people. Those last three he grabbed, I gotta tell you they were all of them very sharp New York ladies. Commuted every day to work, never had problems. Street smart, okay? And yet this guy was able to convince them it was okay to follow a stranger into a dark tunnel."

Anna Kane smiled. She decided she liked the detective, appreciated his empathy for victims. "Don't worry," she assured him. "I won't be following Marlon into any dark tunnels."

CHAPTER
FOUR

After the detective left, Anna checked the clock, decided she had time to unpack a few file boxes. Funny how easily the conversation had flowed with the policeman. Normally she found it difficult to communicate with cops—most of them had an attitude about psychiatry. They believed it was a crackpot profession, a way of making excuses for criminals. Kevin McRay had been different—he was genuinely interested in the MSD project, sincerely concerned about her welfare, with all his warnings about John Chester Marlon.

Anna found herself wondering if he was married, not because of any romantic inclinations—the relationship would have to remain strictly professional, of course, absolutely, no question—but because of, well, simple curiosity. No wedding band, she'd noticed that much. Purely an observation, didn't mean that she was interested. She'd decided in medical school that marriage would make her life too complicated, and since then she hadn't met anyone who'd changed her mind on the subject. Her life was full, so busy she could barely keep up with her research and reading; there was no place for more demands on her attention.

Put him out of your mind Anna, get down to business.

For the next twenty minutes she stuck to the alphabet, transferring file folders from the boxes to the metal drawers.

* * *

The ride up to the Isolation Unit was smooth, uninterrupted. As she exited the elevator she was met by a security guard. A tall, gangly man with a deceptively boyish face and soft blue eyes. His hair was clipped very short, in color somewhere between blond and gray, which made it even tougher to judge his age.

"Henry Portis," he said, offering a pale hand. "I'm in charge of the day shift security detail. Welcome to the Isolation Unit, Dr. Kane. I gotta little spiel they like me to deliver the first visit, if you don't mind."

"Please go ahead."

"Okay," he began, consulting a clipboard. "First, the only access to the unit is via this elevator. We monitor that from the lobby. The switching is controlled from over there in that bullet-proof booth. You'll notice there are no windows in the Unit, and every room and cell, including toilet and shower facilities, are under constant fiber-optic video surveillance. Don't ask me what 'fiber-optic' is, all I know is we get great pictures. As to the security rules, they're similar to what you have up in Dannemora. Basic is that no member of the staff can be alone with any of the inmates. Physical proximity, there has to be a guard present."

"Of course," said Anna. "I wouldn't want it any other way."

The guard presented her with a photocopy of the Isolation Unit security regulations. "Just sign here, acknowledge you understand and agree to abide by the floor rules."

Anna scrawled her initials. She knew the rules.

"Welcome aboard, Dr. Kane. Any problems, ask for Hank."

"Thanks, Hank, I will."

John Chester Marlon was stored in a small padded cell equipped with a flame-proof mattress, a stainless steel commode, no lid, and a television mounted out of reach. Monitoring was available directly, through a six-by-ten inch Plexiglas viewing port, and via the sophisticated fiber-optic video monitors.

When Anna arrived at the special holding cell, Marlon was sitting on his bunk, watching television. In that posture his shapeless, bright orange prison overalls made him look almost hunchbacked. He heard the Plexiglas cover sliding away from the wall opening and glanced over.

"You have lovely eyes," he said instantly, smiling. "Are you female, by any chance?"

"I'm Dr. Kane, a psychiatrist with Department of Corrections. Thank you for volunteering."

Marlon stood up from his bunk. In his early forties now, he was long-limbed and powerful, and had maintained his physique during three years of confinement, much of it in segregation. His skull was shaved close—a personal choice—and the dark stubble of a curved widow's peak bisected a broad, unlined forehead. He had small, colorless eyes and a warm, pleasant smile. Ignore the shaved head and the prison overalls and he looked like a mild-mannered shop teacher, or maybe a gym instructor.

Marlon stepped forward, raising his right hand.

"Stay behind the white line, please," Anna said, ready to back away from the slot.

Marlon paused, looked with amusement at the white line painted on the cell floor, several feet from the small opening in the wall. His right hand, held palm out, dropped to his side. With an air of resignation he returned to his bunk, where he lay on his back, his eyes focused on the television screen.

"I get a kick out of this," he said without turning his head. "They're watching me watch Phil Donahue. You know he wanted me on his show? Only it was on serial killers, the latest flavor, so obviously I couldn't make it."

"Why is that?" said Anna.

Marlon cranked himself up on one elbow, looking at her. He had such mild, almost gentle eyes that if she hadn't known better she might have believed him when he said, "Because I'm not a serial killer," he said. "I'm not a killer at all."

"You're innocent."

"Oh come now, Dr. Kane," he said. "No one is completely innocent. Even a sweet, caring young female like yourself is guilty of *something*."

"Mr. Marlon," she said, changing the subject. "Do you understand what you've volunteered for?"

He nodded. "For the advancement of science. For the good of mankind. And also, I have to be honest with you, to relieve the boredom. Up there at Sing Sing everybody is dull abnormal, including the guards."

"I mean the specific procedure," Anna said. "I know you signed the paperwork, but I need verbal verification that you have voluntarily agreed to participate in the experiment, and that you fully comprehend what we're asking you to do."

Marlon rubbed his nose, squinting. "We?"

"The Annex staff. And myself, of course."

"But this is your thing, right? You invented this clever little device you want to install in my head?"

"I helped with the computer program that makes it function," Anna said. "The device itself was developed in a medical research lab."

Marlon shook his head, disappointed. "Please," he said. "I read your original article in *The American Journal of Forensic Psychiatry*. You postulated the development of a microcomputer sedation device at least a year before it was invented. The thing is yours, Dr. Kane. Take credit where credit is due."

Aware of the heat rising in her face, she backed away from the viewing port. Mustn't let an inmate see you blush. And Marlon was correct, the MSD implant had been developed as a result of her speculative article. She was in the habit of playing down her role because beating your own drum was frowned on in the serious scientific community. Particularly for a woman, where simple ambition was often treated as a form of sexual aggression.

When the blush faded she moved back to the slot and said, "I didn't know you had access to professional journals, Mr. Marlon."

"Just Marlon," he insisted. "What happened is they tried to deny me access to library materials, the ACLU went to bat for me. So now I can request anything I want, except for pornography, which doesn't interest me."

"Do you understand what an MSD implant is, what it does?"

On the bunk Marlon closed his eyes and recited, as if from memory: "A microcomputer sedation device monitors neurological and psychological activity. If the activity indicates a psychotic episode is taking place the subject is rendered unconscious by means of a weak electrical charge to the limbic area of the brain." He opened his eyes and smiled at her. "Did I get it right?"

"Word for word," she said. "In addition to the implant, you've agreed to participate in a behavioral study with five other inmates. There is no secret agenda here—the other inmates will be aware of your implant, and how it may affect your behavior. Is all that clear?"

"Yes," he said. "May I call you Anna?"

Anna had been through this with other inmates on several studies, and knew it was best to keep things on a professional basis. "I prefer Dr. Kane," she said.

"Maybe later," Marlon said, smiling slightly. "After we've become good friends. Intimate friends."

"That's not going to happen."

"You never know," Marlon said, lying back on the bunk. "You just never know what might happen."

CHAPTER
FIVE

Detective Kevin McRay worked out of Midtown South, the precinct headquarters on West 35th Street. Entering the bullpen area, which he shared with numerous other detectives, he couldn't help wondering what Dr. Kane would think if she really knew how the so-called Special Task Force operated.

First place, "task force" implied a whole team of detectives, and the fact was that after three years of coming up empty on the Subway Killer and the rumored "Doll House" where he stashed his victims, the Special Task Force had been reduced to a single, low-grade detective. McRay was it, he was the whole show, and he was hanging on to the assignment by his stubby, well-nibbled fingernails. Lose this and he'd be back in the Transit Police, just one of thousands, many of whom were better connected, had better chances of meaningful assignments and possible promotions.

No doubt about it, if McRay didn't catch a break here, develop solid evidence that the Doll House actually existed, he'd get bounced to general assignments. The boneyard. Without connections or an influential rabbi, his career would be in the dumpster. The signs of erosion were everywhere, and getting worse by the shift. Fellow detectives joked about how he was milking the case, how not one missing person file had been resolved.

The task force had been created when Marlon was still hot news. At one time forty-five detectives had been on assignment, loaned from other divisions. Subway lines and utility tunnels had been searched; Marlon's work assignments had been run through computers, looking for patterns. The software spit out probabilities—the dozen or so cases that most closely fit his profile—but it was like chasing ghosts. There were no bodies, no proof, no physical evidence to tie Marlon to the missing women. Marlon himself had successfully stonewalled the investigation, maintaining his complete innocence, insisting that the Doll House was an invention of the tabloids or a crazy cellmate, that it would never be located because it had never existed.

Gradually the task force was reduced. McRay's lucky résumé—he'd worked with the Transit Authority, had a knowledge of the subways, knew City Engineer John Marlon slightly—meant he'd be the last to go, but for the last few months he hadn't even had an office to call his own, merely access to a desk and phone used by several other special assignment detectives working more current crimes.

Dr. Kane's study was his last shot. Somehow he had to get her cooperation, use the situation to his advantage. There was a possibility that Marlon, with his huge ego, might try to impress the pretty young psychiatrist by alluding to his crimes. Talk about them in the third person like Ted Bundy had, or Son of Sam. If that happened, would Dr. Kane pass on the information, or was she one of those soft-headed shrinks who insisted on maintaining confidentiality with a convicted psychopath?

Kane hadn't come across like a softy. That hadn't been his impression, but you never knew. Get on the right side of her, that was crucial. For reasons having to do with the case and maybe for other reasons as well. For instance, the way she pushed her glasses up on her nose, tapped a pencil against the fullness of her bottom lip, you couldn't help but notice that she was unintentionally sensual.

Get to work, McRay, he chided himself. Keep it on the up-and-up. This is crunch time, your job is at stake.

Hunched at his borrowed desk, he punched up files on the computer. What he had in mind was compiling a dossier of suspected victims, letting the good doctor see that they were real human beings, much like herself. Maybe get her to drop a few victim names to Marlon, show him photographs of the missing women, see if he reacted.

"Kevin, you lazy bastard."

"Yo, Lenny."

Len Jakowski was a detective with Safe and Lofts, had a few years' seniority on McRay, and was somewhere in that gray area between acquaintance and friend. Rather than settle the issue, they bantered. "Don't 'yo' me," Jakowski said, perching on the edge of the desk, coffee in hand. The paunch was deceptive—Len was strong as an ox. Wiry, pale red hair receded from his high, freckled forehead, and his deep-set eyes tended to bag, making him look older than his years—the plight of many a cop. "Do I look like a guy responds to 'yo'? Come on, Kev. You been watching too much MTV, it's rotting your brain."

"I saw you at a disco once, Len. You had on your white patent leather shoes."

"Right. Me and John Travolta. What's this I heard, they transferred your buddy to the city?"

McRay gave Jakowski a thumbnail sketch of the situation, and his impression of the shrink in charge. Len made no secret of his amusement. "I love it," he said. "Anybody wants to drill a hole in that bastard's head can't be all bad. Sounds wacky, though. Brain surgery is going to make Marlon a good little boy again? No way."

"It's not like that," McRay said. He felt the need to defend Anna Kane. "It's not really brain surgery as such. She says it won't directly affect his personality, or any brain functions—or mess up his memory. All it does is knock him unconscious if he gets excited and tries to kill someone."

Jakowski grinned. "I'd like to install one of those implants in the captain. He'd be out cold most of the time, keep the son of a bitch off my ass."

"I think she's okay," said McRay.

"Who?"

"Dr. Kane, the one in charge. I thought she'd be a flake, wanting to mess with a creep like Marlon. She's not. What she wants to do, make psychos like him less dangerous to the rest of the prison population. Not to mention the guards."

Jakowski made a face, got up from the desk. "I got a solution in that regard. It's called the death penalty. Fry the son of a bitch, he can't hurt anybody."

"This is true," McRay acknowledged.

Jakowski waggled a finger, cocked it like a gun. "Do that, ice that mother, you'd be out of a job."

"Also true," McRay said. "And it gets more obvious every day."

"So what are you going to do, Kev?"

He shrugged. "I guess I'll just have to be creative."

"You mean lie?"

"You said it, not me."

CHAPTER SIX

Anna was there in the Isolation Unit when Ned Cody arrived in the company of a prison transport guard. The way he carried himself, the handcuffs looked like jewelry.

"Fabulous," he said, looking around at the stark facility. "A Lunatic Hotel. Do we get little chocolate mints under our pillows? And more important, is this another audition or do I finally get a starring role?"

Two years in a state pen had aged Ned Cody. There were dark circles under his expressive eyes. He no longer had the blow-dried haircut or the bronze tan. Maybe he never really had the tan, Anna decided, maybe it was just makeup.

Before pleading guilty to aggravated homicide—throttling his girl-friend while under the influence of alcohol and drugs—Cody had been an actor. He still had the moves, at times still exuded the confident charm of a man who had once had a role, albeit a minor one, as a handsome blond heavy on the soap opera "Days of Our Lives." But for his brief career as a television actor, Ned Cody's story was like a thousand other inmates. Male kills female in drunken rage, finds himself making a new life in prison, surrounded by men who have committed similar crimes.

"Who else is in the cast?" Cody wanted to know. "The usual suspects, I assume. Bad actors and heavies and walk-ons."

"You'll meet them later," Anna said. She couldn't help smiling when Cody was around, which was one reason she had picked him for the Marlon study.

Her interest in Cody was originally sparked by watching him conduct a theater workshop in which inmates were encouraged to reenact their crimes, playing the part of their victims. It was harum-scarum stuff, the kind of prison encounter group that could easily have gotten out of hand, but Cody pulled it off somehow, and managed to skirt the edge of violence without surrendering to the impulse.

When Anna had challenged him, asked if he ever felt compelled to reenact his *own* crime, Cody had turned to her with an expression of infinite melancholy and said, "Every night, Doc. Every goddam night." Then, breaking into a wry grin, he'd added, "And matinee on Tuesdays."

This combination of anguish and insight made him an obvious choice for the study. Aside from the puzzle of how a known serial killer like Marlon interacted with other inmates, there was the question of how best to handle prisoners convicted of so-called passion crimes, who make up a significant portion of the prison population. Cody definitely fit into that category, and there was something about him that convinced Anna the passion hadn't quite burned out.

"Hey, I'm auditioning here, Doc, and the casting director is staring off into space. Damaging my fragile ego."

"Sorry, Cody."

Cody raised his hands, displaying the cuffs, while the accompanying prison marshal leaned against a wall, in no hurry, enjoying the show. "So what's the role, Doc?" Cody asked. "I read the script—volunteers to interact with psycho. So what else is new, huh? I been up there at Dannemora tap dancing around *hundreds* of psychos. What makes this different?"

"Have you heard of John Chester Marlon?"

Cody, reacting, made his big blue eyes bug out. "Oooh-ee. Big time. Major talent. Mr. Subway Charm himself."

"Be glad you're not the star of this one, Ned."

Cody dropped his pose. "Hey, I'm happy to be in the city, even if it's under lock and key. I'm thinking of this as regional theater, you know? Close the show here, it's back to bad old Broadway." He paused for effect. "So what happens next. More tests? You want to plumb my depths, wring out my psyche, what?"

Anna shook her head, bemused by his performance. "Are you ever not on?" she asked. "Is it always an act?"

"You're the shrink," he said. "What do *you* think?"

"I think you should settle in, try and relax. We'll get started tomorrow."

"No chocolate mints on the pillow, huh?"

Anna hesitated. "No pillows, Ned. This is a hospital environment, but it's still part of the prison system."

Cody's mood, ever changeable, darkened. His emotions always seemed clearly reflected in his expression, but was it real or part of his act?

"You'll excuse me, doctor," he said. "The bellhop wants to show me to my room."

The marshal, vastly entertained by Cody's blarney, chuckled as he led the actor away. "Man, you are full of it, Cody, you know that?"

That, in essence, was the question Anna wanted answered. Was there a real man beneath the actor's facade? If so, could he explain why he killed another human being, a human being he had supposedly loved?

The bus from Attica arrived soon after Cody was shown to his cell. The group of inmates looked around wide-eyed, impressed with the Isolation Unit, the high-tech environment that was a world apart from their dank prison cells and the shabby prison clinic where most of them had participated in other voluntary medical or psychological experiments.

Anna was there to check them off, make them welcome. More to the point, she wanted the Annex guards to understand that these particular inmates were trying to be cooperative.

"Leander Jones?"

Narcotics. Assault. Rape. Deriving income from prostitution. Transportation of pornographic materials.

A large black male with imposing, intelligent eyes grunted, staring at her, not the least intimidated by her presence.

"Thank you for volunteering, Mr. Jones."

"Hey, it's my pleasure, sweet thing."

Anna ignored the not-so-subtle taunt and went on. "Mr. Nussbaum? Carl Nussbaum?"

Vehicular homicide. Borderline retarded.

"What?" said a small, soft-looking man with gray skin pallor.

"Do you understand that you've volunteered to participate in a behavioral modification study, Mr. Nussbaum? Do you recall that I interviewed you a few months ago? And you expressed an interest in participating?"

Nussbaum glanced fearfully at his fellow inmates, then nodded.

"I'll discuss this with you later, Mr. Nussbaum."

"Nussy," he said in a small voice.

"We'll talk later, Nussy." Anna put a question mark next to his name. "Joseph H. Garvey?"

Mail fraud. Check forging. Prior conviction for rape.

A fleshy man with deep-set eyes and a small wet mouth, Garvey licked his lips and said, "At your service, Doc. Like I said before, I'm very interested in modifying my antisocial behavior. Only make sure the parole board knows about it, deal?"

"I'll do my best, Mr. Garvey, and thank you for volunteering." She turned to her last file, and the last inmate in line, who had been hanging back. "You must be Arthur Glidden."

Thirteen counts of sexual assault on a minor child.

"Huh? How'd you know that, my name?"

"Because you're the only one I haven't called. And because I interviewed you briefly several weeks ago."

"Oh."

Anna put a question mark by his name. Was Glidden simply uneasy in this new environment or had he, a child molester, been threatened or intimidated by the other inmates?

" 'Scuse me, Doc, is it true what we heard?"

"What did you hear, Mr. Garvey?"

"Subway Killer," he said importantly, puffing himself up. "The one they say messed with all them dead women."

Anna hesitated. "Mr. Marlon is also a volunteer."

"He's a crazed psycho-killer, is what he is. You intend to mess with his head?"

"Mr. Marlon will be participating in the experiment," said Anna. "I'll fill you in on the details as we proceed."

Leander Jones lifted up his head and smiled. "This man Marlon thinks he is a god, ain't that right?"

"More like the devil," said Garvey.

"Thank you for your comments. That will be all for now." Anna signaled the security guards, who had been standing by. "We'll begin evaluations tomorrow morning, right after breakfast."

Leander Jones chuckled softly. "Look out he don't have *you* for breakfast, Dr. Kane."

CHAPTER SEVEN

The return trip to the hotel where she was temporarily housed was uneventful, save that the cab ride took twice as long. Rush hour. The taxi, piloted by a silent, glowering gentleman who muttered in a language Anna guessed might be Arabic, inched through the City Hall area before entering the molten trickle of Sixth Avenue north. She disembarked at Waverly Place and walked a short block east to Washington Square. She had wanted to stay in the Village because it was relatively close to the Annex, and because it had a neighborly feel that was absent in the concrete canyons of midtown. Walking along the tree-lined street, admiring the brownstones, she was convinced she'd made the right decision. And she remained convinced even when the elevator failed to answer and she had to walk up five winding flights.

The hotel was turn-of-the-century, recently renovated, and the ancient claw-foot tub remained the focal point of the small, white-tiled bathroom. Anna drew a deep, hot bath and settled in. Sounds of the city were audible through the cracked-open window: the beep and squawk of traffic from Sixth Avenue, distant sirens, dogs barking in the park—the sounds all blended together and were oddly soothing.

Anna sighed deeply as she added more hot water to the bath, manipulating the brass faucet with her toes. Ahhh. It was a kind of bliss, this water therapy, a nightly ritual. This evening she was washing away the uneasiness, the sheer nervous funk of meeting John Chester Marlon face to face. Would her reaction have been different had she not known who he was, what he had done? Impossible to say, because she did know, and therefore everything the man said and did, his very posture, his tone of voice, all of it seemed to allude to his crimes, the terrible things he had been convicted of, the even more monstrous appetites he was suspected of indulging.

The Doll House. What an odd, suggestive name for a secret hiding place. A cache somewhere in the tentacled systems of subways, trains, submerged highways, conduits, sewers, and waterways deep under the city. A world Marlon knew better than any other living man.

The security guards had warned her, Detective McRay had warned her, even the other inmates had warned her about the danger of getting close to Marlon, exposing herself to his power. Did she really seem so vulnerable, or was it simply because she was female and Marlon was known to have preyed on females of a certain type?

With her body thoroughly relaxed by the warm, soothing water, Anna tried to scrub Marlon from her mind. Put him out of her thoughts for now, deal with him tomorrow, and then only within the context of the implant experiment. Think about something else—Detective McRay, for instance.

Anna had been around law enforcement officers for long enough to know that cops don't fit any particular type or category, they come in all flavors, and in their brief encounter McRay had impressed her as being different, somehow apart from the crowd. The way he had snapped the newspaper shut, as if he hadn't wanted her to know he was filling in the crossword puzzle. Was he embarrassed by the activity? No, she decided, it was something else, an inner privacy exerting itself. They had that, at least, in common. Later there was the impression he held something back, information or conjecture about Marlon—oops, she was back to Marlon again. Impossible to think about the cop without having the killer intrude.

Don't think of either man, don't think of anything. Anna breathed deeply, slowly, lulled by the discordant symphony of city sounds and the gentle lap of water, and found herself drifting into a place that was almost like sleep.

Floating in the comfort of her own private place, she knows the dream will come again. The dream, like the distant city siren, is always there in the background. Even when she is awake it is there, disguising itself, resonating in everything she does, everything she thinks.

The dream of the woman with no face.

The woman in the room with one window. The woman with the long, long mane of white, white hair. She has been in the room for years. For eons. Forever. Her hands, nervous hands, reaching out, and the words coming out of the no-face, words that Anna senses rather than hears. The words are alive in the dream, alive in Anna's mind always, forever and always.

Hide. You must hide, Anna. He's coming back. He's coming back!

And the blood. . . .

Anna startled herself awake. The water was cool and she shivered climbing from the tub. Toweling herself dry, she realized that the faint chirping noise was crickets. Crickets in Washington Square Park. A familiar, comforting sound—strange to hear it here in this huge city. Anna draped the towel on the rack, headed for her bed. She was not disturbed by the dream of the faceless woman, not anymore.

It was almost, but not quite, like an old friend.

CHAPTER EIGHT

The lights had been dimmed in his cell and John Chester Marlon lay on his flame-proof mattress, feigning sleep. The truth was, he rarely slept. What he did was lull his body into a state of relaxation while his mind ticked over, idling.

There was much to consider. For nearly three years he had been segregated to the maximum security wing of the ancient and barbaric Ossining Penitentiary. His only human contacts had been the guards, his several lawyers, and a parade of shrinks who poked and pried at him with various theories and strategies. The lawyers, appointed by the court, petitioned for his transfer to another facility, or a psychiatric ward, or failing that for his integration into the prison population.

Marlon assumed that his lawyers would fail. He had a keen appreciation of his situation. A man convicted of a double murder, suspected of serial killer activity, and again convicted of deadly assault on a prison guard, was unlikely to be paroled. Not merely unlikely, he reminded himself; it would never happen. The best he could hope for, working within the system, was entry into an enclosed world of violent offenders. Blade-crazy Latinos, race-angry blacks, brain-damaged white trash—the truth was, given the choice, he preferred the relative peace and stability of solitary confinement.

This interlude at the Psychiatric Annex was a gift. An opportunity that might never again be repeated. Lying here in this sterile cell he was a mere seven stories from freedom. Just seventy feet.

In the dimness Marlon allowed himself a smile. He would find a way. Through the woman to freedom. He could taste it, yes, and then he realized, amused, that he had bitten his tongue. The lovely taste in his mouth was his own blood.

DAY
2

Implant

CHAPTER
ONE

Marlon was sitting up on his bunk, wearing a thin, green hospital gown. He leafed through a *National Geographic,* licking his thumb before he turned each page. He seemed to be aware that Dr. Kane was watching him through the window slit, but did not respond until she spoke his name.

He looked up brightly. "Good morning, my dear," he said. "How did you sleep?"

"Fine," she said. "And you?"

"Peachy. Just peachy. Have you seen this one?" He held up the magazine. " 'Tahiti, Troubled Paradise of The South Pacific.' Lovely photographs. That's where Gauguin went, to paint the beautiful natives. In exile from all he knew, and from all who knew him."

"Are you interested in art, Mr. Marlon?"

He closed the magazine, put it on the mattress. He sat there facing her in his thin hospital gown, hands on his knees, shoulders back, chin up. The posture of an attentive, obedient student. "I'm interested in everything," he said. "Right now I'm interested in knowing precisely when my surgery is scheduled. The guards find it amusing not to tell me. But since I have not been fed, and this silly little gown was provided, I assume it's this morning."

Anna said, "A detail of security guards will come for you in about thirty minutes. You'll be given an intravenous sedative here and then taken to the OR."

Marlon nodded, satisfied. "Will you be assisting in the surgery?" he asked.

"No. The operation will be performed by a neurosurgeon. It's a very simple procedure. The implant is about the size of a dime, slightly thicker, and it is slipped under the skin at the back of the neck. The only thing that actually touches the brain is a strand of platinum wire thinner than a human hair. The insertion takes about fifteen minutes. You should be in Recovery by nine o'clock, and back up here by early afternoon."

"So I don't get to linger in a hospital bed? No pretty nurses to empty my bedpan?"

Marlon smiled. He was joking.

"We'll start calibrating the implant tomorrow morning," Anna said. "You should be fully recovered by then, and any residual anesthesia will be out of your system."

"Please be more specific," Marlon said. "Define 'calibration.'"

"The implant is adjusted for each individual. We determine the threshold of violence, and set the activation level."

Marlon smiled brightly. His teeth, she noticed, were small and even, as white and regular as a row of Chiclets. "Ah," he said. "So you'll try to induce anger and then see if I knock myself out? Is that it?"

"That's it."

"Might not be so easy," Marlon said. "I'm a gentle person, Dr. Kane. I don't anger easily."

"The implant is extremely sensitive. The microchip is able to detect very small fluctuations in metabolic levels."

Marlon nodded happily, as if he'd anticipated this particular response. "Is it sensitive enough to detect my innocence?" he asked. "Because I'm an innocent man, Dr. Kane. I never hurt anybody."

Anna decided she couldn't let that pass. "What about the guard at Ossining?" she asked. "She's in a wheelchair for the rest of her life."

Marlon shook his head and sighed. "She did it to herself. That's what nobody seems to understand. The poor woman did it to herself."

CHAPTER TWO

The volunteers, excluding Marlon, were allowed to take their meals and socialize in a common room. The room, like the cells, was constantly monitored by video, and by direct observation of at least one security guard.

Dr. Kane waited until the breakfast trays had been collected before entering.

"Good morning, gentlemen. How's the chow?"

The quality of the chow was enthusiastically proclaimed. Although institutional—the Isolation Unit was, after all, an annex to a psychiatric hospital for the criminally insane—the food was several levels above anything available in the state prison system. The only volunteer with a complaint was Ned Cody, who looked as if he hadn't slept well. Dark circles under his eyes, his blond hair matted against his temples, a slight tremor to his hands.

"Not bad but a little salty, Doc," he said. "Are they dosing us with saltpeter, by any chance? Or the modern equivalent?"

The Taser-armed security guard who had entered the room with Dr. Kane stiffened, focusing his attention on Cody. Potential troublemaker, or just a mouthy wise guy?

Anna wasn't amused by the saltpeter inference. "If any of you require medication, it will be delivered in the usual way," she said. "The food here is not contaminated or drugged."

Cody eyed the guard. "Hey, I was kidding, Doc," he said uneasily.

Anna was firm. "I know how rumors get started, Ned. And I think I understand something about institutional paranoia. I just want all of you to understand that we are *not* engaging in testing drugs or medication in this program. Are we clear on that?"

She looked around the table. Some of the volunteers nodded, others shrugged or indicated indifference. Arthur Glidden, the child molester, stared at his folded hands and did not respond.

"Mr. Glidden? Do you understand?"

He managed to nod without meeting her eyes. Anna noted his tension—one or more of the other convicts was getting to him, that seemed obvious. She decided to notify the security detail, tell them to pay special attention to Glidden, who, as a "skinner" or child molester, was at risk for attack, as well as for suicide.

For now, however, she had a program to run.

Anna took a seat at the table and opened a file folder. "We'll begin by describing the parameters of this study," she said. Behind her the guard shifted his stance, keeping all the inmates in view. "First let's define 'psychotic trigger reaction,' for those of you unfamiliar with the term."

All of the volunteers were attentive. Ned Cody asked for a paper and pencil. He wanted to take notes.

"You'll have to settle for a crayon," Anna told him. "No sharp objects allowed in the Unit."

"A crayon is fine," Cody said. "Can I have red? Red's the best flavor. Just kidding."

He'd started something. With the exception of Arthur Glidden, all of the men requested paper and crayons. Some, like Cody, actually took notes.

"May we continue?" Anna said. "We've got a lot to cover here, gentlemen, and I want to conclude before we break for lunch."

CHAPTER
THREE

The subject arrived in the OR strapped to the gurney with canvas restraints. His ankles were shackled. Four security guards accompanied him, armed with Tasers, Mace, and batons.

"He's sure got a buzz on," said one guard.

"Buzz buzz," said Marlon. His head was lolling and his eyelids were droopy.

"See what I mean?"

"Float like a butterfly," Marlon said, slurring the words. "Sting like a bee."

A few minutes later Marlon was unconscious and the gurney straps were loosened. The security detail remained just outside the OR, keeping watch through the Plexiglas viewing port. Ready to respond if needed.

A surgical nurse prepared the patient. There was no need to shave his head, of course; she merely had to paint his skull with disinfectant.

Seven minutes later the neurosurgeon entered fully gowned and gloved. A hired gun, one of the few female neurosurgeons who freelanced from hospital to clinic in the New York area, she was accompanied by her personal assistant, a willowy young male who carried a small black plastic case. The case contained a selection of surgical instruments, as well as a battery-operated drill outfitted with a selection of sterilized, hair-thin drill bits.

"My my," said the surgeon as she examined the unconscious patient. "So this is what a serial killer looks like."

"I've got an Uncle Herbie looks just like him," her assistant quipped. "It's handy they didn't have to shave his head."

Four minutes later the anesthesiologist had the patient respirated, patched to the monitors, and correctly positioned facedown on the surgical table. The head was clamped in place. The target area on the back of his skull, a fold of skin where skull meets neck, had been outlined with a felt-tip pen.

"Ready when you are, Doctor."

The neurosurgeon picked up her scalpel, glanced at the CAT-scan display on the video screen, and said, "Let's cut this son of a bitch, shall we? See how he likes it on the other side of the knife."

CHAPTER FOUR

Detective McRay was already there in the staff cafeteria when Anna arrived. He was carrying a bag from a take-out deli.

"Corned beef," he said. "You want a sandwich?"

Anna smiled. "There's food right here, Detective. Very reasonably priced."

"I don't eat hospital food. Nothing personal, I just don't."

"Afraid you might catch something?"

"Exactly," he said. "That's the reason. Also this little place on Seventh Ave. has great corned beef. Melts in your mouth. I got plenty here, honest. Extra pickle, just for you."

Anna eyed the cafeteria line, caught a whiff of the steam table casserole, and said, "Sure, why not?"

The deli sandwich required two hands. It was, as promised, remarkably tasty and tender. Anna discovered that she was famished—she'd skipped breakfast—and she finished quickly and was about to lick the mustard from her fingertips when she noticed that Detective McRay, a neat, methodical eater, was cleaning his hands with a paper napkin. She did likewise.

"You're in Manhattan," McRay said, sitting back in his chair and patting a firm, flat belly. "You can eat great here, even on the run."

"I thought cops lived on donuts."

McRay gave her a look. "Not this cop. Except I know this wonderful bakery on Hudson Street, they do unbelievable donuts."

Anna found herself smiling. "I shouldn't say 'cop.' "

"Cop is not an insult. Not to me. Not to most cops I know. Unless you *say* it as an insult, that's different."

"I should say 'detective.' "

McRay looked her right in the eye. "You could try 'Kevin.' My mother likes it."

Anna glanced away. "Thanks for the sandwich, Kevin."

"Anytime, Dr. Kane."

She hesitated. " 'Anna' is fine."

McRay shook his head. "Not yet. I'll know when you're ready for that."

"Whatever," she said.

"So what's the deal, you're from upstate? New to the city?"

"I was born here."

"Oh," McRay said, sounding disappointed. "The way you talk, I figured upstate."

Anna hesitated. She was reluctant to discuss anything personal, but she didn't want to offend the detective by acting stuffy. Keep it brief, general, and then move on, that was the strategy. "We moved to Plattsburg when I was five. I went to college at Cornell, then medical school at McGill, in Montreal. So I'm not really a city kid."

"You're going back up there, to Dannemora?"

Anna shrugged. "I haven't decided. They've offered me a permanent position here at the Annex. I figure I'll see how I like it, make a decision later."

McRay nodded thoughtfully, filing the information away. "So what about my buddy Marlon? The surgery went okay?"

"He's already back in his cell. Pretty groggy, they tell me."

Now it was McRay who hesitated. "If you haven't already guessed, I'm here to ask you a favor."

"I thought you were here to feed me corned beef."

"That, too," he said. "You know I was planning to interview Marlon again?"

"You mentioned that, yes."

"I changed my mind. No way another interview is going to get results, not with me involved. So I had this brainstorm."

"I'm listening."

McRay looked around the cafeteria. "Maybe we should do this in your office."

In her office—she still hadn't found time to get all of her boxes unpacked—McRay opened his briefcase, extracted a thick file folder. The folder contained information on Marlon's victims, the three confirmed in the subway tunnel and another twelve suspected victims.

"Residents of the Doll House," he said. "I'd stake my life on it." McRay dealt out the photographs, arranging them in one long row on the work table.

Anna pushed her glasses up on her nose as she bent her head to check out the pictures. "They really all do have a similar look," she acknowledged.

McRay nodded. "There's relevant data on the back of each snapshot," he said. "Name, age, the time and place the victim went missing. I've tried showing these to Marlon but his beady little eyes glaze over as soon as I open my briefcase. No reaction at all, I just can't get through to him."

Anna picked up a photo of a young woman with shoulder-length auburn hair. It was a studio portrait, the kind that might have been taken for a professional journal or business report. She turned the photo over. *Lois Steiner, 29, corporate attorney, last seen vicinity 72nd Street station. Upper West Side.*

"The station was under repair," McRay explained. "Marlon inspected the site at 2:45 P.M., according to the City Engineer logs. At 3:20 P.M. Lois Steiner waved good-bye to a friend just prior to entering the detour area. She was never seen again."

Anna put down the photo. Lois Steiner had a confident, intelligent smile that made her uneasy. "Marlon was known to be in the vicinity for all of these?" she asked, indicating the row of photographs.

McRay nodded. "We have him documented either on work assignments, or signing off on site inspections."

Anna frowned. "If you know that, why wasn't he a suspect much earlier?"

The detective sighed. "The fact is, Marlon was never a suspect until he was caught. These were all just missing persons cases. Last seen going into a subway or boarding a train—nobody put it all together, came up with a probable victim profile and culled these cases from the thousands of other missing persons cases until *after* Marlon was caught red-handed."

"So these are just the possible victims you can put in locations where Marlon was actually documented to be present?"

"That's right."

"So there could be other cases where he *wasn't* documented?"

McRay nodded. "Oh yes. I've got more than twenty other missing persons who fit his physical type. Just no proof he was in the vicinity when they disappeared."

"And you're still looking for this 'Doll House'? Based on the word of a police snitch who later sold his story to the tabloids? What makes you think there really is such a place?"

McRay dropped into a chair. He leaned forward, bracing his elbows against the work table. "The maps," he said. "The missing maps."

Anna sat down opposite him and waited.

"Look," he said. "First you have to understand how this city was built. There was no master plan, it just evolved. Nobody thought to put a sewer system in until they had an epidemic, and then it only happened in fits and starts. They had to burrow under the city, cut up the streets, make it up as they went along. The same for the subways, the train stations, power and lights, high-pressure steam, telephone, TV, and so on. You name it, they buried it. You had nine or ten different utilities companies digging, three different subway companies, all jealously guarding their own systems. You had Tammany Hall corruption. Even today each department works separately. Chaos, right? A water main breaks, sometimes they have to go in there with teaspoons to dig around all the other conduits. So what happens, finally a light bulb goes on over some bureaucrat's head and he decides we need a comprehensive mapping program. The big picture. Make sense?"

"Yes," Anna says. "So what happened?"

"What happens is they reorganize, set up the Bureau of City Engineers. Staff it with experts from all the utility companies, and the idea is, these guys will be in charge of the maps. You want to dig, you go see the engineers, they'll tell you where and how deep."

"Marlon."

"Right. City engineer John C. Marlon. He was put in charge of the mapping project. You wanted to get something done below street level, you went to Marlon. He was the authority. Nobody else knew his way around all these underground systems like he did. Cut through an old electric trolley tunnel or upgrade a sewer line, he was the guy who told you what you'd run into, how your project might affect the other systems. Like I said before, he was the resident genius."

Anna said, "And he had access to the maps."

"Exactly. Old maps of old systems, new maps, *all* the maps. The island is a honeycomb, Dr. Kane. So many tunnels and conduits, so many levels, it's worse than a maze down there, because you figure one person designs a maze. This is like a hundred people designing a hundred different mazes. There's like three hundred miles of subway tunnels alone. Not to mention five thousand miles of sewer lines. Hundreds of pedestrian tunnels. Something like a hundred thousand manholes and vaults. So the biggest problem we had with search parties, looking for his Doll House, is they kept getting lost. Even with radio contact and directional finders they kept getting lost. And what we discovered, after Marlon was arrested, quite a few of the older maps were missing from the archives."

"And no copies exist?"

McRay shook his head. "There was a project underway to put the whole thing on computer, these huge display screens, but the funding got cut. Which is typical, you work for this city. We're in decline, the infrastructure is crumbling at every level—and that includes underground."

"And what does Marlon say about the missing maps?"

McRay snorted. "About what you'd expect. He didn't steal or destroy the maps, why should he do that? Somebody else must be responsible, probably the mysterious individual who actually did the killing, because of course poor misunderstood Marlon is the innocent victim of a terrible conspiracy."

Anna nodded. "Not many killers actually admit to the crime," she pointed out. "That's typical, even when they plead guilty. I cut a deal, they'll say, but really I didn't do it."

"Right," McRay said. "Except Marlon isn't typical. He had something going down there, some nightmare scenario, and that's why he made sure the maps went missing."

"And you never suspected him when you were a Transit cop."

McRay shook his head. "He was just another city supervisor. Always wore that gold hard hat. He had a miner's light on it, he liked to shine it in your eyes, made it hard to see him, I remember that part."

"What did you think when he shined that light in your eyes?"

"I thought he was a jerk," McRay said. "But what could I do?"

Anna indicated the collection of photographs. "Maybe you're doing it now."

McRay looked puzzled, then shook his head. "This is about a lot more than me getting even with some rude dude in a hard hat. For every picture on that table there's a family, a loved one, a whole world of suffering. Somebody disappears, Dr. Kane, it's almost worse than if they just plain get killed. You can't grieve or mourn; the survivors get put on hold until the body is recovered. The man responsible for all this hasn't just murdered the women he snatched in those tunnels, he's ruined hundreds of other lives."

Anna stared at the photographs. All these young women looking back at her, smiling confidently, certain their lives would unfold as planned.

"He won't respond to me," McRay was saying. "You talk to him. Show him the pictures. He wants to make an impression on you, maybe he'll say *something*, give us a place to start."

Anna stood up, turned away from all those smiling faces. Whether the detective knew it or not, he was asking a lot. The implant experiment had to be strictly controlled, the behavioral study with Cody and the other volunteers was intended to document trigger reactive situations. Playing mind games with Marlon wasn't part of the project, it might skew the results.

"I'll think about it," she said, finally. "There may be a way to work it into the program."

McRay expelled the breath he'd been holding. "Whew! Okay, great. I think it's worth a shot or I wouldn't ask."

"I'll do what I can."

McRay walked to the door, then turned back to face her. "There's one other thing," he said.

Anna waited.

"You're new to the city, sort of. I'd get a kick out of showing you around."

She frowned. "You're asking me for a date?"

McRay grimaced. "We don't have to call it that. Could be business, right? Conferring about a subject of mutual interest or whatever. You prefer, we could meet on neutral territory. I know a couple nice restaurants. Seven o'clock? I'll be a real gentleman."

That made Anna grin, the funny emphasis he put on the promise to be a gentleman. "I'm out of here this evening," she said. "Personal business upstate."

"But I thought—"

"I'll be back in the city tomorrow morning," she said.

"Is this a brushoff? Because I don't want to be pushy. For all I know you're engaged to be married or something. Are you? Engaged?"

Anna shook her head, smiling at his persistence. "Call me tomorrow."

"Deal," he said.

CHAPTER
FIVE

The child molester made a knot of his hands, clenching and unclenching his small, delicate fingers. Prior to incarceration Arthur Glidden had
been employed as an automotive mechanic, had at one time owned his
own garage. In addition to fine tuning BMWs for an upscale clientele, he
had imported child pornography—explicit videotapes—and made a lu-
crative business of copying cassettes and retailing them through the kid-
die-porn underground. The molestation charges had been brought by a
social worker, after interviewing the children of one of Glidden's business associates.

Anna said, "Arthur, please try to relax. I'm here to help you, if possible."

"What can you do?" he muttered. "What can you do?"

"Are you being threatened, Arthur?"

He shrugged, his eyes twitching, then wiped his nose on his overall
cuff.

"I'll release you from this program, if that's what you want," Anna
said.

He shook his head mournfully. "Doesn't matter where I am, it's always the same. It's so unfair, D-d-doctor, it's really *so* unf-f-fair."

Sensing that he wanted to continue, Anna made herself nod sympathetically.

"These m-m-men," Glidden stammered. "Some of them raped and killed, or killed and *then* raped, okay? They're v-v-vicious. D-d-do whatever they want, and they d-d-despise me because I like to look at movies. Big deal, just look."

Arthur Glidden had done more than look at movies, but Anna didn't bother to correct him, or confront his continuing denial. Later for that. Right now the problem was determining if he was in any immediate danger.

"This isn't like the yard at Attica," Anna said. "Everyone is under constant surveillance here. You sleep alone in your own room. No gang showers. I think you're probably safer here than almost anywhere in the state prison system."

Glidden nodded miserably. "P-p-probably," he said.

"I'm aware of your situation, Arthur. I'll do my best to make you feel comfortable here. And as you know, participation in this experiment may make it easier for you to get into a therapy program. Is that what you want?"

"Y-y-yes." He sighed deeply, stared at his knotted hands. "Anything is better than A-A-attica."

The second of her individual interviews was with Ned Cody. The former actor seemed to have recovered some of his composure—the circles under his eyes weren't quite so deep, and the trembling in his hands had diminished. His skin was pale, though, and had a translucent quality that made him seem vulnerable, dissipated.

"Everything okay?" Anna asked.

"Copacetic," Cody said. "Tip top. Couldn't be better."

"I had the impression you were uneasy about something, Ned."

Cody pushed the hair back from his forehead, flashed a stage grin. "Me? Uneasy? The master thespian? Come on."

Anna smiled. "That was my impression."

Cody eyed the loitering security guard and said, "Damn! Can't fool doctor, can we?"

Anna waited.

"Stage fright," Cody said. "I'll be okay, once I figure out how to play the role. First few months in prison I threw up every morning, just like it was an audition."

"Stage fright?" Anna said. "You?"

"For lack of a better term," Cody said. "Also, to tell you the truth, this place gives me the creeps. Don't get me wrong, compared to bad old Sing Sing, this is heaven. But it's still, I don't know, maybe something about the lights, or the TV cameras, it gives me the creeps."

"The TV cameras?" Anna said. She raised her eyebrows, indicating that this was significant, and that Cody knew it. He had, after all, been dropped from an afternoon soap a few months before he went crazy drunk and throttled his girlfriend, an actress who was still employed by the soap at the time of her death. Cody still claimed not to remember the murder, although he did not deny his responsibility.

"God," he said. "Am I that obvious?"

"Maybe the bright lights and the camera remind you of something you'd like to forget?"

Taking that as a cue, Cody raised his hands over his head and held the pose. "I'm cured!" he shouted. "It's a miracle, Doc! No more sleepless nights, no more cold sweats. 'The Two Faces of Ned Cody.' I'm *cured.*"

He slumped beatifically into his seat as the ever-present security guard shot a questioning look at Dr. Kane. Anna indicated that she was in no danger. "Very good," she said to Cody. "Was that something from your show?"

Cody grinned ruefully. "Hell, the writers never came up with anything that good. Tormented lady-killer goes to jail, gets cured by beautiful doctor? Great stuff."

Anna tapped a pencil against her bottom lip, gazing with amused eyes at the handsome actor. "So you're cured?"

"Getting there," he said. "Only one problem."

"And what, pray tell, is that?"

Cody let his face relax. It was as if he'd dropped a mask, wanted Anna to see the real person behind it. "Patient has a crush on doctor," he said. "A serious crush. What do you think of that?"

Anna paused. This was not exactly unexpected; it often happened with males who volunteered for her studies. Men who had very little contact with females, men who lived with unrealistic expectations that were often expressed as rage or violence. On the other hand, she'd used Cody in a previous study on passion killers, and hadn't picked up any romantic fixations, which would have discouraged his inclusion in this program. Too late now, she'd just have to deal with it. "I think it's inappropriate for a subject to fixate on the doctor," she said. "But you already know that."

"What if patient doesn't *care* if his feelings are inappropriate?"

Anna shrugged. "We'll deal with it. But you must know this can't go anywhere, Ned."

Cody seemed faintly amused. "Why do people always say that? As if love has to go somewhere to be real? As if love is a train on a track, a car on a highway? Love: the destination."

Anna waited until he was finished, concentrated on maintaining a professional reserve. The distance she needed, a distance she kept between all males and herself. Not just male convicts, all males. "Ned? If this gets to be a problem you'll have to leave the program."

Cody was taken aback. "Problem? Problem?" he paused, looked away from her, and then in a different voice said, "Hey, I was just kidding. Playing a part. You know me, always on."

Anna said, "Ned, if you're really having trouble sleeping I can prescribe a mild sedative."

He shook his head. "No thanks. I like this edgy feeling. It makes me feel alive."

CHAPTER
SIX

He was floating just above his bunk, or that is how it felt with his eyes closed. No pain, less discomfort than he expected, and this rather wonderful sensation of floating.

Float right out of the cell, out into the world again.

Marlon smiled with his eyes closed. He saw interesting images there in his mind. Certain compelling forms and postures. Pleasing rigidities. He was, he believed, an artist with more courage and imagination than the world could tolerate. Look at the things he made, that no one can ever see. Images recorded only here in his remarkable brain. A brain unaltered, he was relieved to discover, by the unfelt intrusion of a hair-like platinum wire. Or the small bandaged lump on the back of his neck.

Microcomputer Sedation Device. What a grand term for a bit of silicon. Meant to sound impressive, threatening. And yet what could it do? Control thoughts? Modify behavior? Change the will? No—all it could do was induce momentary unconsciousness. And then only if certain physical symptoms were present—elevated blood pressure, adrenaline, and so on.

Marlon had read the literature and he was not impressed. Let the pretty female calibrate and quantify and reprogram her little microchip.

The implant was an essentially dumb device—triggered by raw, uncontrolled anger, or a crude display of emotions.

The idea of anger made Marlon smile. He was still floating on a cushion of residual anesthesia, but inside his mind his thoughts were clear enough: Anger is the key. Anger is what triggers the implant.

This is good, this is joyous. This will make him free again.

Because what the pretty female didn't understand, what no one seemed to understand, was that John Chester Marlon had never been angry.

Not ever.

CHAPTER
SEVEN

The train was due to depart from Grand Central Station in a few minutes. Anna, who had been dreading the descent into the bowels of the station, had no trouble locating the correct track, and boarded the Metro North train with time to spare. There was ample seating, the car smelled clean, her fellow passengers looked friendly.

No problem. So what had she been worried about, in that long taxi ride up from Washington Square? Shapeless, nameless things. Memories so remote and forbidden they had been banished from her dreams.

Anna was a student of psychology, and a practitioner—she knew her own psyche well enough to recognize anxiety transference. It was not the underground station she feared, or the train itself, but the ugly reality that would have to be confronted when she reached her destination.

Don't think about it now, Anna. Try to relax. Time enough for tension when you get there.

There was an uneasy moment when the slowly moving train came to a stop deep under Manhattan. Was this to be another breakdown, another walk through a darkened tunnel? But this time the lights never flickered, and in less than a minute the train was rolling again, gradually picking up speed, and soon emerged into the brutal and reassuring daylight of East Harlem.

There was another brief delay when the train converted from electrical to diesel propulsion. Underway again, Anna opened her purse, checked her return ticket, and then tried to unwind by reading the *New York Times*. Mistake—the front page was devoted to the subject of urban violence. Shootings, knifings, rapes, a gang war whose territorial disputes lay right outside the train. She turned to the review section, glanced at the crossword, and thought of Detective McRay poring over the empty blocks with his indelible ink.

The ride itself was actually a pleasure. Anna had always enjoyed the lulling rhythm of trains, and once they cleared the sprawl of the city the landscape rapidly improved. North up the Hudson Valley by train, often in sight of the river. What could be prettier, more soothing?

By the time she stepped off the train at the small, upstate town she knew so well, the island of Manhattan had receded into some distant place in her mind. She knew the routine from here on out, and that at least was comforting. The village taxi-van was summoned from a pay phone to the little station. The driver recognized her from many previous excursions, knew her destination without having to ask. The drive along the narrow lake shoreline was pleasant enough, and Anna tried to distract herself by making small talk—the weather, the tourists—but her heart wasn't in it.

By the time the taxi-van turned through the iron gates and down the long curving drive, Anna was silent. Her mouth had gone dry. She had been making this trip every month or so, for as long as she could remember, but the same thing happened every time she approached the main entrance to the sanitarium: suddenly she was out of breath and for a few unbearable moments the blood was pounding in her ears and she had to fight the panic. Focusing all of her will on the big brass door handle, forcing herself to reach out and grab it.

Go on, Anna. Thumb the latch, open the door, and enter the rubber-tiled hush of the lobby. You can do it—you've been doing it for years.

The receptionist knew her, of course. "Dr. Kane! So nice to see you again. No trouble with the train, I take it?"

"No trouble," Anna said. She was inside now, there was no turning back, and the sense of panic melted away. The worst part was over, just making herself come here. Now nothing remained but going through the motions, letting the white-jacketed floor matron escort her to the residential wing, down corridors Anna knew as intimately as she knew the lines in the palms of her hand.

"How is she?" Anna asked the matron. It was the normal question, the expected question.

"Fine," said the matron over the squeak of her rubber-soled shoes on the floor tiles. "Same as last time. Always the same."

"Yes. Is she eating okay?"

The matron shrugged. "The usual. Like a bird. Hasn't lost any weight, though. Very steady."

The door to the room was open. There were no bars on the windows, no special locks. Just a neatly made bed, a bureau, and a rocking chair positioned in the corner, facing the window and the last tinge of the setting sun.

The matron said, "Enjoy your visit, Dr. Kane."

Anna entered the room. "Mother?" she said.

The woman shifted in the rocking chair, turning her face to the sound of Anna's voice. Hair pure white and shoulder-length. Pale, smooth areas of scar tissue surround the blind eyes. The mouth opened and closed, shaping words without making a sound.

Anna sat in the window seat and reached for her mother's hands. Hands that appeared strangely soft and youthful. "I've been busy, Mother," she said. The hands responded with a gentle squeeze, acknowledging her presence.

Anna's routine, established over the years, was to describe everything of importance that had occurred since her last visit. Now and then she was rewarded with a cogent response, but mostly her mother smiled and nodded and gently rocked in her chair. Anna was never certain how much she understood—that wasn't the point. The point was to share what she could, to come away with some sense of having communicated.

Looking into the ravaged face and the sightless eyes was difficult. Much easier to focus on the silver-framed photograph displayed on the bureau. The woman in the picture was young and beautiful and her eyes were alive with mischief.

"At first it was a little intimidating," said Anna, referring to the city. "All those tall buildings made me feel out of breath. Or maybe it was just the smog, hey? A small-town girl like me, I wasn't sure what to expect. But everybody has been very nice. The hotel is lovely—I can see Washington Square Park from the window. The staff at the Annex couldn't be more helpful. The work is interesting—it may even be important. Wouldn't that be good, Mother, if we found a way to control violence?"

Mother said nothing. After a while Anna ran out of things to say and just sat there as the minutes ticked by, holding the old woman's hand. When the time came—she couldn't help glancing at her watch—she patted the hand and said, "I better go now, Mother, it's been a nice visit, hasn't it?"

The old woman rocked in her chair. "Anna?" she said.

"Yes, Mother?"

The chair began to rock faster. "Hide," the old woman whispered. "Find a place to hide."

Anna, her heart clenching, got up and pressed the white button that summoned the matron.

"Coming," said the old woman.

"Mother, please relax," Anna said. *Where is the matron, damn it?*

"Coming back," the old woman said. Her reedy voice was a chant now. "Coming back, coming back, coming back."

"Ssssh. Hush now. You're dreaming. That was long, long ago."

The old woman rocked wildly in her chair. "Hide!" she screamed. "He's coming back! He's coming back!"

DAY
3

Trigger Reaction

CHAPTER
ONE

Marlon looked serene as he waited for the lights to be dimmed.

"A slide show," he said. "What a nice idea."

He was securely strapped to the observation chair with canvas restraints. His ankles were, as always, manacled. A small, neat bandage covered the implant area at the base of his skull. He was accompanied by two Taser-armed security guards who stood ready at opposite sides of the small screening room.

Anna sat at a table to one side, where she could see the computer monitor and cue the projector. The monitor, picking up signals from the implant, indicated that Marlon's blood pressure was quite low, his heartbeat strong and steady. The EEG sensor showed normal brain patterns, and the metabolic levels were well within normal limits.

You'd never know, looking at the monitor, that the implanted subject was capable of extreme violence. Which proved, as Anna was well aware, the limitations of brain activity data. Hook a relaxed Charles Manson or a calm Joel Rifkin up to the same machine, it would fail to detect psychopathic thought patterns. No way to read thoughts, not yet—the microchip was programmed to detect an episode of frenzied mental activity, spikes on the EEG that precede a violent psychotic episode.

"Some of these images may be disturbing," Anna said.

Marlon laughed easily. "That's the point, right? You want me foaming at the mouth, then your little device will knock me out."

"It's not as simple as that."

"No? We'll just have to see about that. Fire away, Dr. Kane. I'll try to be brave."

Anna activated the slide machine. The first series of images had been taken from high-gloss magazines. Beautiful young women who radiated intelligence, all of them long-haired and confident. Similar in physical type to those known to be victims of Marlon's wrath.

"A fashion show?" he said, affecting a tone of airy dismissal. "That's supposed to make my blood boil? Surely you can do better than this. I expected a much more . . . sensual approach."

Anna did not respond immediately. The subject, familiar as he was with psychiatric journals, had to be aware that a simple review of erotic imagery was a conservative approach in a study of criminal behavior. He'd apparently been expecting the gadgetry used in sexual offender programs.

"I'm not interested in measuring your erections," she finally said. "This isn't about normal sexual response, as I'm sure you're aware."

"Are you blushing, Dr. Kane? The lights are so dim I can't tell."

"Direct your attention to the screen, please."

The next series was soft porn. Abbreviated leather costumes, high heels, whips. S&M poses, of the type found in popular skin magazines. As each slide flashed up, Anna was aware that the men of the security detail were reacting. Clearing throats, shuffling feet, a normal male response to soft porn images.

Unlike the guards, Marlon was not impressed by the display of flesh. "You're insulting my intelligence," he said. "This is for pimply adolescents."

Anna noted that the subject's heart rate had actually slowed. No surprise, really; this was a preliminary warm-up, a way of establishing a base-line response.

"These may be of more interest," Anna said, cueing the next series of slides.

These images, much more graphic in nature, were culled from police files of victimized females. Evidentiary photographs intended to document abuse. Women bruised, beaten, shown partially or completely nude to reveal brutal injuries. Powerful, disturbing stuff. Although she had selected and reviewed the images for this specific purpose, Anna still felt a twinge of revulsion. Surely this repulsive material would evoke a response from the subject, if not a violent reaction.

Marlon stared at the screen, his face expressionless. The monitor levels remained static.

"What are you thinking?" Anna finally asked. The stark, brutal image on the screen was of a female torso: ugly bruises, fresh burn marks, worm trails of scar tissue.

Marlon sighed. "I'm thinking how horrible it is, that anyone could do *that* to such a pleasant body."

"Is that all you see, an injured body part?"

"You're only showing me body parts, doctor."

Anna decided to skip the rest of the domestic abuse file, go on to the next series. A face appeared on the screen. A young, dark-haired woman with large, intelligent eyes. She seemed alive, ready to speak.

According to the sensors, Marlon did not react.

"Friend of yours?" he finally said. "A sister perhaps? Looks a bit like you."

"Mary Louise Dwyer. One of your victims."

"No," Marlon said, slowly shaking his head. "I never saw this woman before, and I certainly never killed her. Or anyone else for that matter."

Anna said, "You were found unconscious next to her body, and the body of Debbie Arno. Flesh from her neck was found under your fingernails. You were convicted of murdering Dwyer and Arno, and attempting to murder Frances Crowell, who identified you as the perpetrator."

Marlon sounded bemused. "I remember Miss Crowell, of course. She testified at the pretrial hearing. The poor woman was confused, mistaken. She attacked me for no reason at all. I was trying to help her."

Although the subject seemed outwardly calm and self-assured, the sensor indicated that his blood pressure was rising. Anna decided to keep pushing. Another image flashed on the screen. A female body on a mortuary slab.

"Debbie Arno," she said. "Asphyxiated. Note the deep bruises and scratches around her neck."

Marlon's blood pressure seemed to be stabilizing.

"Old stuff," he said. "They showed this at the trial. One of the jurors fainted. A bus driver, I think he was. That's when I decided to follow my attorney's advice and take a plea. The jury didn't care who did these terrible crimes, they simply wanted someone to be punished."

"It doesn't bother you, apparently, seeing these pictures."

"Should it? If it bothers me, do I pass the test?"

Marlon's voice was deliberate, impassive. And yet he was taunting her. Anna did not respond. Keep focused, she reminded herself. Force the subject to react. "You know what I think?" she said.

"I'd be interested to know what you think." Marlon turned from the screen, searching for her eyes in the dark.

"You enjoy hurting women. It turns you on."

Marlon did not respond immediately. His fingers tapped the arms of the chair. "You're not wearing a ring," he said.

"What?" Anna instinctually touched her hands.

"Are you married?"

She leaned back in her chair. "That's not the topic under discussion."

"Never married," he said. "Anybody special in your life?"

Anna activated the projector, advanced to the next slide. "Please look at the screen."

"You're a loner, Anna. Like me. We have that much in common."

"All we have in common," Anna said, "is an interest in what makes you dangerous."

"Touché," he said approvingly. "Well put."

"The screen," she said.

Marlon remained focused in her direction. The shadows masked his expression. He was a primal shape, a presence in the darkness. "No offense," he said. "But you seem to be emotionally frigid. What was it, a childhood trauma?"

He's probing you, Anna told herself. Resist. Show no reaction. "Please look at the screen," she said, keeping her voice level.

"Father? Mother? Sibling?"

"Mr. Marlon, please. You agreed to cooperate."

"Something of a criminal nature," he went on, musing. "That's why you want to study criminals. Who was it that hurt you, Anna? Was it your father?"

"Focus on the images, please. This isn't about me."

"Your father. What exactly did he do, Anna? Did he beat you? Did he rape you? What?"

Anna shut off the slide projector and stood up. She turned on the overhead light. The security guards looked at her, waiting for instructions.

"That's the hot button," Marlon said, satisfied. "Dear old Dad."

"Take him back to his cell," she told the guards. "We'll try again later."

CHAPTER
TWO

The inmate volunteer Leander Jones, wearing his bright orange inmate overalls as if they were royal trappings, held court in the small, windowless recreation room. His time was spent jiving with the security guards, messing with the other volunteers.

"Mr. Whitebread, they cut open his loaf, ain't that right?" he asked a guard. The guard shrugged—fraternization with inmates was forbidden.

Rebuffed, Leander pretended to study his nails as he contemplated his next move. The other convicts, used to such ritual displays of prison machismo, waited to see what would happen next.

The child molester Arthur Glidden, obliged to leave his cell and socialize with his fellow inmates, crouched uneasily against the wall. He'd positioned himself near the door, in close proximity to the guards. He kept his eyes downcast, his posture frightened and submissive, the orange overalls so baggy that he looked like he was trying to disappear inside his clothing.

Ned Cody, affecting a look of boredom, leafed through a *National Geographic*. He ignored Arthur Glidden, ignored the guards, did not quite dare to ignore Leander, who had quickly established himself as the undisputed boss con, the alpha male of the group. Cody's instincts, honed over several years of cohabitation with angry men, told him to avoid antagonizing an obviously dominant, clearly dangerous male.

Sitting at Leander's right hand, sucking up to him, was the pudgy confidence man Joseph Garvey, who smiled uneasily with his small wet mouth. "Right," he said, agreeing eagerly. "Right on, brother. They sure did slice him, that's a fact."

Leander laughed, a sound as sharp and ugly as a knife thrust. Ned Cody winced, kept leafing through his magazine. Stay cool, avoid looking directly at the brother. Like staring into the sun, making eye contact.

"Oh, yeah, right on," said Leander, enunciating each syllable. " 'Cept you got no idea what I just said, 'bout slicing Mr. Whitebread's loaf."

Garvey shrugged meekly, admitting his ignorance.

"Talkin' about John Chester Marlon, the subway token. Shit, they open up his head, you comprehend what that means? What they did, put a little transistor in that ivory skull. He think pussy, they see it on a TV screen, big as life."

Carl Nussbaum, mildly retarded, was playing with his crayons. "Pussy?" he said, looking up. His small, mild eyes surveyed the room, as if he expected to see a cat.

Leander was amused by the reaction. "Here, pussy," he said, pitching his voice high. "Pussy pussy. Better have nine lives, you mess with the man."

"So what do we do?" Garvey asked. "What's the deal?"

"Now that's easy," said Leander, making eye contact with one of the security guards. "Deal is we cooperate. Oh yeah. Do what the lady tells us, be good little boys." He paused. "Ain't that right?" he said, pitching the question to Arthur Glidden.

The child molester did not respond.

"Mr. Toys-'R'-Us, I'm asking you polite. Be nice you answer me back. Spirit of cooperation here."

Ned Cody glanced warily up from his magazine, checked out the power play. Glidden had turned his face to the wall, his hands were trembling. Now Cody had something new to be ashamed of: he was thankful that Glidden was the target of animosity, rather than himself.

"What the matter, Toys-'R'-Us?" said Leander. "You jealous of the man? Want a transistor inside your head, too, is that it? So we all watch what you thinking. That be fun, watch the Toys-'R'-Us man in action."

Glidden muttered something.

"What you say? Speak up."

His voice was small. "Leave me alone. Just leave me alone."

Leander stood up from his molded plastic chair, his throne, and laughed at Glidden. "You already home alone," he said. "Don't you know that yet?"

Having exhausted whatever pleasure he had extracted from tormenting the child molester, he turned to Ned Cody with a fierce, dark gaze that would not be denied. "Now what we gone do about you, Mr. Hunk Lite?"

CHAPTER
THREE

"This is getting to be a habit," Anna said. She was in her ground-floor office cubicle with Detective McRay, who again had brought along deli sandwiches. The scent of mustard and pickle brine was pungent.

"You won't let me take you out to dinner, this is the best I can do."

"Please."

"You're right," McRay said. "I'm out of line. Forget I mentioned it. Sandwich okay? This is from another deli, maybe it's not so good."

"The sandwich is fine," Anna said. Despite herself, she laughed, amused by his banter. She was surprised at her mood, which was remarkably good, considering her difficulties with Marlon. Something about Kevin McRay's gap-toothed smile put her at ease. Odd, since she barely knew the man, and he obviously wanted to come on to her, which she would normally find offensive or intimidating. For some reason with him it was different, not threatening. In fact it was sort of pleasant, this mild flirting.

"So," he said. "How did it go?"

Anna thought about it for a few moments. How much did she want to share? Nothing in her job description compelled her to brief the police after each session with the prisoner—and yet it was in her interest to be cooperative. Also, and this is what decided her, she enjoyed McRay's attention. After swallowing the first small bite of an absolutely mouth-watering corned beef sandwich, she answered his question honestly. "Not so good," she said. "It didn't go well at all."

"He got to you, huh?"

Anna nodded solemnly. "I knew exactly what he was doing, but yes, he did get to me."

"Marlon gets to everybody," said McRay. "He loves mind games like some people like crossword puzzles."

"You like crossword puzzles," Anna pointed out, reaching for a dill pickle.

McRay was taken aback. "How'd you know that?"

Anna shrugged impishly. "I'm a mind reader."

"Wait," he said. "That first day we met. I had the *Times* with me, right?"

"You don't believe I'm a mind reader?"

McRay looked embarrassed. "I sure hope not."

The implications of that, McRay's potential embarrassment at having his thoughts read, produced an interval of silence. Anna broke it by chomping on the pickle. The tart, sour taste made her mouth feel alive.

"Let me guess," said McRay. "Marlon tried to psychoanalyze you."

"Close."

"It's like a carnival trick with him. He takes a quick reading, keeps probing until you react. Pulled the same trick on me."

"So you think it's a trick?"

McRay nodded. "Absolutely. There's a hundred fortune tellers in this city can do the same thing, you walk in the door. Good cops can do it, too."

"If you're thinking about telling my fortune, forget it."

Anna was joking, but McRay seemed quite serious. "That's not what I mean," he said. "Reading the person, is what I mean. Picking up signals. You develop a feel for people. After a while you know if they're telling the truth."

"You can do that with Marlon?"

McRay was suddenly uneasy. "No. Not him. He's different."

"Different?"

McRay stared at his hands, then finally looked up and met her gaze. "I can't explain it. Two minutes in the same room and my heart is racing, my knees are weak."

Anna nodded sympathetically, but the truth was that Marlon didn't frighten her, not yet at least. He was a cipher, a riddle, a problem to be solved. She was confident that, given time, she'd find a way to unlock his psyche. The morning session was no more than a setback, to be expected with an intelligent, highly manipulative psychopath.

Lunch included a paper carton of chicken soup, and Anna was careful not to slurp the broth. She'd noticed that McRay was a fastidious, near-silent eater, and she didn't want to offend him with indelicate noises. Which, come to think of it, was not like her at all—why should she be so eager to please a cop she knew only on a professional basis? And why was she—admit it—encouraging his interest?

"That's the best," he said, indicating the soup.

"Delicious," she agreed.

"No, I mean it. Best in the city."

"Like your mother makes?"

"Are you kidding?" he said. "My mother, she wants chicken soup, she reaches for the can opener. Strictly Campbell's."

If McRay was a client, this would be an opening. Discussion of maternal relationship, exploration of family bonds. But the cop was not a client and Anna was, for her own reasons, reluctant to probe what she thought of as "the mother thing." She decided to return to the subject at hand.

"So he really scares you?"

"He really does," McRay admitted. "What I wanted to ask, how much do you really know about this guy?"

"What's in his files. Arrest files, psychological evaluation files and so on."

McRay was uneasy. "There's more to Marlon than just his files," he said.

"Of course there is."

"I've been on this guy for three years, right? Must have, I swear, a thousand pages of notes. And I still have no idea why he did what he did. Why he is what he is. You figure a sexual predator who stalks and kills women, there'd be some clue among his personal belongings, right? Nothing. We searched his apartment, his work locker, his office, nada. No pictures, no porno, no trophies, nothing. Same with his record—the guy is forty years old, worked in the city most of his adult life, he never even got a traffic ticket."

"Any juvenile indicators?" Anna asked, aware that juvenile records were often purged. There had been no reference to juvenile behavior in the evaluations that had been forwarded to her at Dannemora.

McRay said, "I went back and interviewed the juvy officers, retired now, who covered his section of Brooklyn Heights, where he grew up. As far as they're concerned, the young John Chester Marlon was a model citizen. Dad was a well-respected dentist, office on Park Avenue. Mom was apparently a housewife, by all accounts devoted to her husband and son."

"My files indicate he was an only child," Anna said.

"Right. 'Leave It to Beaver' without the big brother. The Brooklyn Heights version, anyhow. Mom and Dad died when he was in his twenties. No indication of foul play—that was the first thing I checked. I had it in mind, researching the family, that maybe he did the parents, that's what kicked him off. Nothing like that. Father had a bad ticker, died of a coronary while the son was away at college. Mother passed away a year or so later, cancer of the colon. By that time Marlon had graduated from Rensselaer Polytech with a degree in civil engineering, he was already working for the city. I went over to the old neighborhood, schmoozed with the old ladies, they all remember Dr. Marlon's boy as polite and well-behaved. If he engaged in any of his 'activities' back then, nobody noticed. Amazing, huh?"

"Actually pretty typical," Anna said. "We know that sexual predators frequently establish a pattern of deviant behavior from an early age, and often manage to stay undetected. They tend to be functional, able to convince others that they're normal or have normal feelings. Quite a few serial killers seem to live more or less normal lives, until they get caught. We also know that not all of them *get* caught."

McRay nodded eagerly. "Exactly. That's one of the things that bothers me the most about this guy—that he never made a mistake until the day he got nailed. If the survivor, Frances Crowell, if she didn't manage to whack him with that brick, he'd still be down there doing whatever it was he did, and we'd have no idea. Here's a model citizen, quiet bachelor type, never even got a parking ticket, and he's got this secret life as a monster."

"The secret life aspect, that's a typical profile for a socially integrated psychopath."

"A what?"

Anna had the impression that McRay knew more than he let on

about criminal psychology, but that he didn't want to come across as challenging her expertise. In his own way a very delicate man. "Socially integrated psychopath," she said. "Defined as one who experiences psychopathic obsessions and desires, but holds down a job, or lives for a long period undetected. Not a drifter. Most of them seem to have very intense fantasy lives. They become obsessed with their fantasies, and seek gratification through acts of violence that normal human beings find monstrous: rape, sadism, ritualized murder, necrophilia, cannibalism, and so on. And yet somehow they find a way to blend in. They work at the post office or the insurance company, they live in an average house in an average neighborhood. When they finally get caught all people can think to say is, 'He was quiet, he kept his distance, we never really knew him.' "

"Because they don't understand."

"I'm not sure any of us understand," Anna said. "All we seem sure of is that the condition can't be reversed. These men—most, but not all, are male—these men seem to have crossed a line somewhere in childhood or adolescence, a line between normal fantasy and homicidal obsession, and once they cross that line, once they make the fantasy real, they can't go back. They can't be taught to feel guilt, or empathize with their victims, or understand the revulsion the rest of us feel. The smart ones can fake it, make you almost think they actually care, but they don't. They can't. And more importantly, they don't want to—they hate the idea of being 'normal,' because they despise us. Being different, being killers, is what makes them feel special."

McRay was nodding in agreement. "That's how Marlon makes me feel, like I'm a cockroach and he wants to step on me. Not because he hates me, but just because he likes stepping on roaches."

"You locate any adult friends?"

McRay slowly shook his head. "Not one. At work he was all business, earned the respect of his peers, but like you say, they all described him as 'distant.' "

Anna studied the detective, decided that she was not disturbed by his intensity about the case. It was something they shared. She said, "You're doing all this, sifting through his past, because you're trying to locate this alleged 'Doll House' where he stashed more of his victims, is that it?"

"It's not just alleged," McRay responded quickly. "I know it exists."

"You've found proof?"

"In my gut," he said, thumping his stomach. "Remember, he was in charge of the maps. You get a chance, ask him about those missing maps."

"You can ask him yourself," she said. "Try it again."

McRay winced. "I'm afraid that Marlon finds me . . . amusing."

"Is that what frightens you?"

"That and a strong feeling he'd like to kill me very, very slowly."

"Ah," Anna said.

"Yes, 'ah.' Maybe you think I'm being paranoid but please, you need to be very, very careful with Marlon."

"Security is more than adequate," said Anna. "Canvas restraints, manacles."

"You're in a room with him, he has an advantage."

"I can take care of myself," said Anna. "And if I can't, the implant will."

"So it's functioning?"

Anna hesitated. "We'll soon find out. He may not be an ideal candidate, but if we get the levels right he won't be able to fool the MSD."

"Don't take any chances with him," McRay said. "I've seen his work."

Anna glanced at her watch.

McRay smiled. "Okay, I can take a hint. Look, I've got something for you. It just might give you an edge, dealing with this creep."

In the bottom of the lunch bag was a videocassette box.

"It's not X-rated," he said, handing her the cassette. "It's much, much worse."

CHAPTER FOUR

The very first thing Marlon did, as the security detail brought him back into the screening room, was sniff the air and say, "Somebody has been to the deli."

"Good afternoon, Mr. Marlon," said Anna. "Was your lunch adequate?"

"Don't talk to me about lunch."

The guards placed him in the viewing chair, attached the straps to the canvas restraint jacket, clipped the ankle chains to the legs of the chair. "Wait a minute," he said. "That mick detective. Am I right? I remember his breath stinks of cheap mustard. So now he's feeding it to you, is that the deal?"

Anna was taken aback by his instant connection to the detective's presence, but decided to play dumb. "Excuse me?"

Marlon winked at her. "What, he's your type? That cute gap in his teeth? Come on, Anna, you could do better."

"I don't know what you're talking about."

"Fine," he said. "Be that way. But trust me on this, the cop is a loser."

"Can we get down to business, Mr. Marlon?" Anna gestured at a guard, who dimmed the light. "Still photographs don't seem to have much effect," she said, wheeling over a television monitor. "Shall we try something a little more realistic?"

Marlon was staring at her; his eyes seemed even smaller in the dark. Steel marbles pressed into hardened wax. The indicators were level, revealing that his calm, cool demeanor was not faked. "I hope you're not going to try a snuff film on me," he said in his mildest voice. "I might faint dead away."

"Nobody dies in this," she assured him, activating the tape deck. "Not quite."

The videotape was in wide-angle black and white, and silent: the camera, a prison security device, looked down on a stark containment cell. Location, Ossining Penitentiary. Sing Sing.

"Home sweet home," Marlon said. There was an edge to his voice. The sensors indicated that his heartbeat and blood pressure had begun to increase. Metabolic levels were edging up. "That loser McRay, he gave you this."

On the screen a steel-jacketed door slid open and an image of Marlon shuffled into the picture, dressed in prison overalls. His feet hobbled by a short length of chain, his hands similarly restricted. His blunt head and powerful shoulders were prominent, but the downward camera angle obscured his facial expression.

"What's this?" Anna said. "You've got company."

In the recording Marlon was accompanied by a female prison marshal. A woman of average build, made broad-hipped by her wide belt and holster. Her scalp was visible where she parted her hair precisely in the middle. When Marlon turned to her she seemed to be attentive. His back was to the camera, but it was clear by the way his head moved that he was engaging the guard in conversation.

"What were you saying to her?" Anna asked.

"Oh, the normal chitchat," Marlon said. "How's the weather." The sensors indicated that his metabolic levels were climbing steadily.

On the screen the recorded image of the prison marshal remained virtually motionless as Marlon talked to her. Anna was not inclined to anthropomorphic archetypes, but she couldn't help thinking that the on-screen Marlon had the posture of a coiled snake, his head weaving slightly, and the female was a small animal, frozen by his presence. The tapes revealed, in stark black and white images, a powerful predator mesmerizing its prey.

"You must have known about the camera," Anna said. "You knew this was being recorded."

Marlon did not reply. He remained focused on the glowing screen, where the female was beginning to move quite slowly, as if submerged in an invisible fluid. Slowly she reached down and unclipped the flap on her sidearm holster. Slowly she withdrew the snub-nosed revolver. The weapon was now in the palm of her hand, a dark gift. Marlon, back to the camera, shifted, and his body obscured what happened next.

Suddenly the woman was down on the cell floor, lying inert at his feet. Her eyes were closed and a trickle of blood leaked from the corner of her mouth.

"You hit her with the gun?" Anna asked. "Is that what happened? You knocked her unconscious?"

Marlon stirred in the viewing chair. His voice was thick, clotted. "She fell," he said. "You can see quite clearly that she fell."

"And you knew," Anna insisted. "You knew they were watching and you didn't care. You had to attack her. You couldn't stop yourself."

Marlon did not reply to her taunt. He was intently focused on the TV monitor. On the screen he had his back to the camera and he was using his hobbled feet to shove at the unconscious body of the female guard. He rolled her over, facedown, and stood over her. The small, dark shape of the gun was almost obscured by his pale, manacled hands. He was sighting, taking aim, firing.

"You wanted to paralyze her," said Anna. "You wanted to punish her."

The sensors indicated that his heart was pounding, that his metabolism had been drenched with adrenaline. When Marlon spoke he sounded as if his mouth was full of honey. "The camera lies," he said. "The gun went off accidentally. I never pulled the trigger."

"You shot her in the spine."

Marlon sighed, shook his head.

"You hated her. You're filled with rage."

"No," he said softly. "You're mistaken. I'm not a hateful person."

Anna decided to risk a confrontation while his metabolic rates were still peaking.

"Loosen his hands," she ordered a security guard.

"But Dr. Kane—"

"Just do it," she said.

When the guards refused to cooperate, she moved quickly to the prisoner's chair and unsnapped the canvas restraints, freeing his arms.

"You like hurting women," she said, taunting him, getting right in his face. "You love it. It makes you feel powerful. It makes you feel immortal. Nothing can stop you. You can do anything. *Anything.*"

The security guards, alarmed by the prospect of the prisoner with his hands free, unholstered their Taser guns.

Anna could feel Marlon's cool breath on her face.

"Now's your chance," she whispered. "No one can stop you."

His hands rose, the tips of his fingers reaching to touch her face. His hands closed gently on her neck.

"Do it," she urged him. "Do it!"

Suddenly his head jerked back, his eyes rolled up, and he slumped unconscious into the chair.

The implant had been activated for the first time, the levels set.

"Are you okay, Dr. Kane?" a guard asked. "Did we do it right?"

Anna found that she couldn't speak. She forced herself to take a deep, shuddering breath. Her neck was clammy with sweat where his hands had touched her. Not his sweat, hers.

CHAPTER
FIVE

McRay was plotting. A utility conduit map was unfurled on his desk, the curl of the linen paper held down by a pair of ceramic coffee mugs.

"Planning a trip?" said Len Jakowski as he passed by the desk. "What is that, Rand McNally?"

"Yeah," McRay said. "We're all going to Disney World. Want to come?"

The detective chuckled. "Down there in the sewers with those corpse-sniffing dogs? No thanks."

The map was no longer a puzzle to McRay; over the last few years he had been down into many of these tunnels and conduits, into the vast network of labyrinths under the island of Manhattan. Old steam pipe junctions, electrical and telephone conduits, natural gas facilities, the defunct network of pneumatic tubes that used to move mail through the city. Sewers, subways, trains, low-pressure water systems, high-pressure water systems. Everything buried, submerged, hidden.

The complexity was mind boggling. Water mains alone accounted for more than five thousand miles of tunnel and pipe. The sewers were of a similar length, with some of the older storm drain systems as yet unsurveyed. There were nearly four hundred pedestrian tunnels connecting hundreds of miles of subway and train tunnels, stations, underground workshops, and repair yards. As McRay was painfully aware, there was no accurate count of subterranean rooms, storage bays, vaults, access tunnels, or the abandoned endeavors of more than a century of industrious, antlike burrowings by dozens of independent utility and subway companies. No hope of knowing. Only a small portion of these thousands of miles of tunnels were actively patrolled or inspected by the Transit Authority. There were no routine patrols of unused areas like the abandoned Second Avenue subway system or the unfinished East River tunnel to Queens. Or the six-lane highway buried under the Bowery. Or old pedestrian tunnels sealed up decades ago. Or stations and storage areas long ago walled off and forgotten.

"Looks like a mess of spaghetti," said Jakowski, leaning over McRay's shoulder. "You can actually read that?"

"More or less."

Jakowski shook his head. "Good luck, pal," he said, slapping McRay on the shoulder.

"We're narrowing it down," McRay said.

"Sure you are," the detective said, sauntering away.

McRay sighed, went back to his examination of the utility map. Somewhere in this mazelike confusion was Marlon's lair. His Doll House. It could be anywhere. In three years of periodic searches McRay had managed to eliminate only a small number of possibilities. What haunted his efforts, what drove him to distraction, was the missing archival maps. No one even knew for sure how many maps had been taken or destroyed by Marlon, or what areas, precisely, the maps and blueprints detailed, because the documentation was also missing from the archives. Enter this netherworld and you had to do it blind, groping from tunnel to vault, relying on flashlight and compass. As McRay had done. As he would have to do again, if only he could find a way into the killer's mind.

Using the grids of a computer printout, likely areas had been identified, those parts of the system most frequented by John Chester Marlon in his official capacity as a city engineer. Areas within easy access to subway stations and public passageways where the killer might have stalked and then snatched his victims. And yet these "likely" areas covered thousands of acres, hundreds of tunnel miles. Something more was needed, a way to focus the search.

Doll House, McRay thought, puzzling over the term. Why call it a Doll House? Why not "the morgue," or "the boneyard"?

"Doll house," he said aloud. "Make believe. Play time. Let's pretend."

Behind him Len Jakowski grunted. "He's going off the deep end, folks," he announced to the bullpen. "Detective McRay needs a vacation."

"Dolls," McRay said, looking up from the map. "Tell me, Len, you ever play with dolls when you were a little girl?"

CHAPTER
SIX

The box on the table was big enough to hide a small arsenal and that made the guards nervous, despite Anna's reassurance that it was okay. Hardware for the inmates—this violated all the rules of standard procedure.

"What is it?" Carl Nussbaum wanted to know. "Like a Christmas present?"

When Anna entered, she found the inmates seated around the table in the rec room, surrounded by double the usual number of security guards. Joseph Garvey had placed himself sycophantically close to Leander Jones, who regally ignored him. The child molester Arthur Glidden was at the far end of the table, looked ready to bolt if anyone so much as raised a voice in anger. Ned Cody was leaning back in his chair, arms folded, a small, tight smile imprinted on his handsome face. Acting tough—and Anna suspected that it was, indeed, just an act.

"Don't be stupid," Leander Jones was saying. "You see Santa Claus in here? I sure don't."

"You're right, Carl," said Anna. "The box does contain a Christmas present. It was donated by F.A.O. Schwarz and the proceeds will go to a child trauma center in the South Bronx."

Leander Jones snorted. "What kind of crap is that? Supposed to make the honky rich feel better?"

"Yeah," Joe Garvey said, mimicking his protector's tone of voice. "What's in it for us?"

Anna surveyed the men around the table. "There's nothing in it for you. It is simply a task."

"What?" Garvey said belligerently. "You want us to wrap it up, put a nice red ribbon on it?"

"No," said Anna. "Your task is to assemble the toy. So it can be put on display and then auctioned off."

"Charity," said Leander. "I knew it."

"Those who don't want to participate can go back to their cells," Anna said firmly.

Ned Cody, staring at his fingernails, spoke up for the first time. "Let's do it. Let's just cut the bullshit and do it."

That brought a sharp reaction from Leander Jones. "Hey, Mr. TV Faggot. Bullshit on your bullshit."

Cody gazed at him levelly, and without apparent fear. "All I said was, let's do it. You have something against kids in the South Bronx?"

The security force was uneasy, hands on their batons.

"Gentlemen," said Anna, stepping in to make peace. "This will require a spirit of cooperation. The box contains a complex mechanism, and you will each have a specific task to accomplish." She opened her briefcase, handed around photocopied instruction pamphlets.

Nussbaum, who was illiterate, was given a series of silhouetted images. "These are the tools enclosed in the box," Anna explained. "Your job is to pass out the tools to those who need them, and then return all the tools to the box after the assembly is completed."

"Oh," Nussbaum said, smearing his fingers over the slick copy. "I can do that. I can, I can."

"I'm sure you can," said Anna. "And if you have any trouble, Leander will help you. That is if you'll agree to help him."

Jones grinned at her, a tiger smile. "Old Nussy need all the help he can get."

Ned Cody stood up, lifted the cover from the box. "You've got to be kidding," he said.

Inside the box, carefully arranged and packaged, were hundreds of small plastic parts, and a variety of plastic tools that matched the images on Nussbaum's instruction pamphlet.

Anna said, "What we have here is a scale model of the Empire State Building. F.A.O. Schwarz tells me that assembly time is estimated to be twelve man-hours. By expert toy assemblers. I assured them that you could do better than that. Which means that with a five-man team this model should be completed before you break for supper."

Jones was chuckling and shaking his head. "You figure to starve us, that it?"

Anna looked at the box of plastic girders and panels, at the men around the table. "Okay," she said. "Maybe a six-man team would be more efficient."

She signaled the guards, who opened the door. John Chester Marlon was escorted into the room. He smiled at the sudden silence, as if pleased with the impression he'd made.

"Don't worry," he said, holding up his manacled hands. "I'm as harmless as a pussycat."

Leander Jones glanced at him nervously. "Cat got claws," he said. "Cat can scratch out your eyes."

Marlon turned, revealing the small, neat bandage on the back of his neck. "It's like a sedative," he said. "A very clever computerized sedative. If I even *think* of violence it puts me fast asleep. Isn't that a fact, Dr. Kane?"

Anna looked at the inmates, finally managed to catch Cody's eye. "That's a fact," she said. "And just as a precaution, the guards will remain outside on full alert."

The rec room was, as always, under full video surveillance. Anna took up her position at the security station, made her observations via the monitors. A small, hand-held unit tracked Marlon's metabolic levels.

"What's this like?" asked Henry Portis, chief of the security detail. "An encounter group kind of thing?"

"That's one way of describing it," Anna said, staring intently at the screen. "What we want to do is observe a trigger-reactive psychopath interacting with less violent inmates. Assembly of a complex toy is analogous to, say, a prison workshop."

"I getcha," said Portis, blinking his moist blue eyes. His tone was polite but doubtful.

The monitors showed the bulky form of Carl Nussbaum, who was attempting to match the tools to his pamphlet illustrations. When he became flustered, the others shoved him aside and reached into the box.

"I thought every man had a specific assignment," said Portis.

"They have to work this out among themselves," said Anna. "Just as they would in an actual prison environment."

"And that bug-thing in his head, it'll zap him if he tries anything?"

"It's a microcomputer sedation device."

"Yeah, well the inmates call it a 'bug.' So do most of the guards."

Anna let it go. Portis wasn't being unfriendly, he was simply using the term the inmates had already invented to describe the implant.

On screen the confusion was apparent as all but two of the inmates jockeyed for position around the toy box. Arthur Glidden remained apart, as did Marlon. The child molester looked terrified—Anna could see the whites of his eyes, and she was considering an intervention when Marlon made his move.

"What's this?" said Portis.

"Let's see what happens," Anna said, noting implant levels indicating the serial killer was calm, unperturbed.

Marlon approached Glidden, holding up his hands. Glidden was frozen with fear, a creature caught in the headlights. Marlon muttered something—too faint for the audio pickup—and Glidden slowly raised his hand.

The two men shook hands. Marlon leaned closer, murmured a few words in the smaller man's ear. Glidden appeared to relax.

"Ain't that cute," said Portis. "They're making friends."

A few minute later the tableau had changed. The inmates had backed away from the toy box. Marlon was handing around the tools, his movements restricted by the wrist manacles. He was smiling, evidently at ease. Glidden remained by his side, eyes downcast.

Before long Ned Cody was dipping into the toy box, handing around packets of plastic parts. Leander Jones assumed a defiant posture and refused to accept his package.

Marlon looked at him. Leander Jones reluctantly took the package.

"I'll be damned," said Portis. "That didn't take long."

"Seven minutes," Anna said.

That was how long it had taken John Chester Marlon to become the new alpha male.

Under Marlon's leadership the model was assembled in record time. When Anna entered the room, clipboard in hand, the inmates were already posed in a semicircle around the five-foot-high, all plastic version of the Empire State Building.

"All it needs," said Leander, "a monkey crawling up the side. Kind of a King Kong thing."

"It's beautiful," said Anna. "But there's something else missing, besides the ape."

An uneasy silence ensued. Anna waited patiently, tapping her fingers against the clipboard. Finally Ned Cody spoke up. "You must be mistaken, Dr. Kane. It's perfect."

"Not quite. Look at the top of the building, Ned. That piece above the observation deck. Can't you see? You of all people should know."

Cody gave her a dirty look. "What is this, pick on Ned Cody day? I tell you it looks perfect."

Anna reached out, touched the top of the model. "The television antenna."

More silence. Marlon looked on with amusement, and then focused his mild gaze on Anna. She returned it, meeting his eyes, exerting her will. All deals with inmates involved tests of authority—back down once and you were lost, you could never regain the advantage.

"Garvey," Marlon said.

Joseph Garvey looked at Leander, seeking backup. The black man shook his head, dropped his eyes.

"Give it up," Marlon said. "Do what the nice lady wants."

Garvey opened his right hand. Even then it wasn't obvious until he picked up the piece from his palm. A thin, sharp plastic spine. Anna stepped forward and took it from him. She handed it to Cody, who placed it where it belonged on the top of the model building.

"What were you going to do with it?" Anna demanded, focusing on Garvey.

"Nothin'," he said evasively.

"Nothing?"

"Protection," he said at last. "A man has a right to protect himself."

"You will be confined to your cell for the next twenty-four hours."

Garvey was sullen, but he did not protest.

Anna looked around at the others. "We can do this by the rules, and maybe learn something useful, or we can stop right now. One more serious infraction and the program will be aborted and you'll all be returned to a normal prison environment. So it's up to each of you to see that no one spoils it for everybody else."

There was a sudden eruption of sound. Flesh on flesh. Startled, Anna stepped back and then saw that Marlon was applauding. Smacking his strong hands together in short strokes, restricted by the manacles.

"Bravo, Dr. Kane," he said. "Well done. Very well done indeed."

"You have something to add, Mr. Marlon?"

"Only this," he said. "I consider this a rare opportunity to get away from that fetid toilet bowl known as Sing Sing. And I would be very, very disappointed if any of my fellow inmates did anything that resulted in cutting my vacation short."

"I hope that's not a threat," Anna said.

Marlon's smile was gentle, reassuring. "No, no. Simply a statement of fact. I wouldn't dream of threatening my fellow inmates, would I, boys?"

That was when Joseph Garvey fainted. His eyelids fluttered and he fell to the floor. None of the others reacted, but Anna recognized the symptom that had caused the inmate to lose consciousness. It was pure, unadulterated fear.

CHAPTER SEVEN

The restaurant was on MacDougal Street, a few blocks from her Washington Square hotel. Anna had checked her charge cards before leaving because this was not, in her mind, a date, it was business. Okay, socializing with a colleague, but definitely not a date. That was her rationalization, and the only way she'd been willing to agree to meet him outside of work.

The detective was seated at the bar just inside the door of the Minetta Tavern, grinning around a pretzel when he saw her enter. "Hey, you made it." Reaching for her coat as though she shouldn't handle it herself, but he was so nice about it, so polite without being pushy, that Anna just let it happen. Let him take her coat, let him take charge of securing a table—in the back, under celebrity photos of mostly long-dead boxers—let him select a wine and order from the menu, if that's what made him feel comfortable.

"The Village has a lot of great Italian restaurants," he said, "and this is one of the best. Try not to eat the bread, I dare you."

"It's delicious," she agreed.

"Dip a piece in the olive oil," he suggested. "It's what they call extra virgin."

Anna smiled. She knew about extra-virgin olive oil, but McRay was so eager to share his intimate knowledge of the city and his love for the food it offered, that she let him rattle on about al dente pasta and red sauces and white sauces and quality of the primavera. The aproned waiter, who seemed to know the detective, was surly but efficient, as Anna remarked when he was out of range.

McRay was astonished. "You think Salvatore is surly? Anna, please, the man is a sweetheart. Better he should keep his integrity than swoon all over us. This way we tip him because the service was superb, not because he's coming on like a long-lost friend."

"Maybe surly is the wrong word," she conceded.

"It's a city thing," McRay explained. "Live in close proximity with seven million people, you have to find a way to keep your distance. Believe me, surly is when they spill the soup in your lap."

"Kevin," she said. "It's the best, really."

Her face was warm. Was she blushing? No, that was the wine, somehow they'd finished the bottle, and she was feeling warm and pretty, and it was nice to be out on the town with an attractive gentleman who seemed more interested in her than he was in himself. On a strictly social basis, of course, because this was not, repeat not, a date.

Over cappuccinos and cannoli they got down to business. "So," McRay said, "he was a good little boy today?"

"He didn't attempt to kill anyone, if that's what you mean," Anna said.

"For Marlon, that's being good," he said. "But he made an impression on the other inmates?"

"Most definitely," she said, nibbling at the rich, cheese-filled pastry. "Oddly enough, he seems to have made friends with the pedophile."

"Comparing notes," McRay suggested.

"There's no indication of pedophilia in Marlon's file," Anna said, feeling oddly defensive. "Do you know different?"

He shrugged. "All I meant, they're both outsiders. Considered monsters, even by prison standards. Where, for instance, raping a woman is pretty much okay, but raping a child is not."

"You've got a point."

"Beyond that, my guess is there's something in it for Marlon. He makes an alliance, there's a reason."

"You mean a group dynamics thing?"

"Possibly. You say that the other boss con, Jones, he backed down?"

"It was more subtle than that. I'm not sure what happened, exactly. It was like Marlon flexed his personality and suddenly Leander was no longer at the top of the pecking order, and he knew it."

"They exchanged words?"

The strong cappuccino seemed to counteract the wine, and her mind was feeling clear again. "Not threats, if that's what you mean," she said. "It's just the way Marlon carries himself. His confidence. He has a way of exuding, I don't know, call it intelligence, or power."

McRay looked at her. "I'd call it fear," he said.

"That, too."

"He doesn't scare you?"

Anna shook her head firmly. "No more than, say, the third rail."

McRay looked puzzled. "What?"

"In the subway. The third rail. Twenty thousand volts."

"More," he said.

"Okay, more. Whatever, it's enough to kill you if you touch it. So you keep a careful eye on the thing and you don't touch it."

McRay looked at her over his cup. "You don't even get close."

"Sometimes you have to get close," she said. "But you're very, very careful."

The detective was shaking his head vehemently. "Listen to me, Anna," he said. "I know him. I know who his victims are. And trust me on this, he wants you. He's not some force of nature you can avoid, like electricity—he's an extremely cunning human being who has chosen the dark side."

"You make it sound spooky," she said, trying to lighten his mood. He looked so intense, so concerned.

"Go down into those tunnels where he did his thing, spooky is not the word. He preyed on women just like you, Anna. I know he killed them and he hid them and even now I'm not sure I really want to know what else he did to them."

"Kevin, please. I know what I'm doing."

"Of course you do."

"Precautions are taken. Guards, manacles, and the bug."

"The bug?" he asked.

"That's what they're calling the MSD. It worked. It knocked him cold. He raises a hand to me, or anyone else, it knocks him out."

"You're sure? He didn't fake it?"

"You can't fake an EEG. He triggered the device, it rendered him unconscious. I must admit, I had my doubts, but you have to trust the data. We'll continue to keep a close eye on him, of course."

McRay leaned back in the booth and sighed. "What bothers me is the way he doesn't quite fit the profile."

"The serial killer profile?"

McRay nodded. "Look, you're the expert, but one thing I did get to do was attend the FBI's forensic psychiatry seminar. They hold it a few times each year, mostly for local investigators like me. All the data they've collected about various kinds of killers, the conclusions you can draw about what motivates a psychopath and so on. Anyhow, it was all very interesting—fascinating, in fact—but I came away feeling really uneasy."

"That's understandable," Anna said. "Some people have a more physical reaction. They feel sick."

"Not that," McRay said. He leaned forward, his hands so close to hers on the table that she could feel the warmth he radiated. "They told us, based on all the data, that virtually all serial killers have this in common: they are failures. Failures in living a normal life, I mean. Maybe they manage to hold down a job, but they're going nowhere. The one thing they succeed in, the career that makes them feel superior, is killing. No other serial killer I've been able to document had a high-ranking job like Marlon. The man was respected, Anna. He was successful by any standards—hell, he was more successful at his job than I am at mine, that's for sure."

"Come on."

"I'm serious. So the thing is, if he doesn't fit the typical serial killer profile, that leaves two possibilities."

Anna smiled, waited.

"One, he's innocent. We've got the wrong man."

"You don't believe that."

"No. What really bothers me is the second possibility. That he's something new. Okay, maybe not new, but what if he's a kind of killer that no one has diagnosed? Maybe none of them have been caught before, or they just get lumped in with serial killers because they have multiple victims."

"New in what way?" Anna said, interested.

McRay shrugged. "That's what *really* scares me. I've no idea what made this guy do what he did. That's another reason why we have to locate the Doll House. If we know what he did with his victims, maybe then we'll know what's going on in his head."

Now it was Anna's turn to lean forward, bringing her face within inches of McRay. He did not draw back. Anna could feel his breath touching her; an odor of fresh garlic that was not, she was surprised to discover, offensive. "Listen to me, Kevin. You don't want to know what's going on in his head. Nor do I. The important thing is to control him, to prevent him from taking more victims. That's the best we can do."

The detective blinked first. Leaning back, shaking his head as he acknowledged the truth of her conclusion. "You're right," he said. "I've still got a bad feeling about this."

"About what?" she said, kidding. "The bill?"

Before she could get her card out of her purse, McRay had snatched the bill. "No way," he said. "My treat."

"We'll split it."

"Nope. Consider it your welcome-back-to-Manhattan dinner. A great meal, with murder for dessert."

Anna surprised herself when they exited the restaurant. She agreed that he should walk her back to the hotel. Not because it was a date, but because you never knew, after dark, who might be lurking in Washington Square Park.

"If you're lucky it's only a purse snatcher," McRay said.

"And you'll save me?" Anna said.

"I'll save myself. But you're with me, so you get saved, too."

That seemed, on reflection, a compromise she could live with.

CHAPTER
EIGHT

Ned Cody paced his cell. It wasn't a bad little room. The toilet and sink were immaculate, the bed was firm. There were even framed, motel-style paintings bolted to the walls, but it was still a cell. No window. No inside latch on the door. Plus he'd spotted two of the video cameras, tiny fiber-optic lenses set into the ceiling panels. Probably another camera built into the television monitor, so there was no getting away from direct observation. Big Brother, prison style, courtesy of Dr. Anna Kane.

On one level the woman was, to his way of thinking, almost unbearably attractive. Sensual without being aware of it, and so intelligent that her eyes seemed to glow from within. On another level she was infuriating. That self-assured, professional attitude of hers, the way she kept him at arm's length. The prison grapevine functioned even here at the Isolation Unit, and Cody knew about her confrontation with Marlon—facing him down in the slide room, letting him make a move for her throat, confident that her little computer would protect her. Convinced she had outsmarted the infamous Subway Killer.

As if you could ever outsmart Evil.

Ned Cody wasn't sure if he believed in God—if the Big Guy existed He'd never gotten in touch—but he was convinced that Evil existed, because he'd felt the thing. He had, on that terrible night that changed his life, allowed a malignant force to overwhelm him. Result: death for someone he loved.

Anna Kane, for all her professional expertise, did not really understand that dark force, that terrible impulse. She thought she could quantify it, control it, read it in brain waves and blood pressure. She seemed convinced that Evil was a misfunction of the brain, not a corruption of the soul. And if she really believed that, she was in terrible danger.

What did Marlon have to lose? There was, currently, no death penalty in the state, he was already serving what amounted to a life sentence, so taking another trophy would not materially affect him. The possibility of another trial might even relieve the boredom of prison routine, from his point of view.

He meant to kill her. Cody knew this in his heart. Not a word had been spoken between them, other than a few murmured suggestions while assembling that silly toy building, but Cody had convinced himself that John Chester Marlon was focused on Anna in a way that could only end with an attempt on her life.

Okay, what to do about it? Warn her? She wouldn't listen, and he had no evidence beyond what instinct told him. Confront Marlon himself? The very idea made him cringe inwardly. He did not have the power, the fortitude, or the courage to take on John Chester Marlon. Maybe there was nothing he could do, except wait.

And so he paced. Five steps this way, five steps back.

Marlon sat on the edge of his flame-proof mattress and watched Candice Bergen dissing some pansy assistant on her television show. What wonderful bone structure, he thought, what physical confidence. A woman like that wouldn't be afraid of anything. Until it was too late.

He lay back on the cot, hands folded behind his shaved head, aware of the bandage that concealed his recent surgery. He could feel his own machinelike pulse, the steady fifty beats per minute of himself in repose. The sound was muted on the TV—he had no use for silly dialogue, he just liked watching the faces, the eyes, the brightly colored lips. So disconnected, so unreal, so attractive. Look at Candice with her hands on her hips, shaking her pretty head. All that taffy-colored hair, and those eyes. Eyes like cat's-eye marbles, the kind he used to carry in a chamois bag to the school yard.

Marlon smiled at the memory of carrying glass eyes in a soft bag. Behind him, barely audible, he was aware of the faint pitter-patter of feet.

Someone pacing in his cell. Mildly irritating, to be made aware of another man's frayed nerves. He reached behind him and thumped his fist on the wall.

The pacing ceased. Good.

Silence was required, and peace. He intended to lie in repose, allowing his body to store energy, letting his mind tick over. Looking at his idea from every conceivable angle, until the idea—a burst of creative energy, really—became so familiar that it assumed a reality all its own.

He was planning a little surprise. If it worked, the world would soon be a different place. More stimulating and much, much more interesting.

DAY
4

Underground

CHAPTER
ONE

The sniffer notified Homicide. That was the procedure. The Special Task Force then beeped McRay, who was informed that a sniffer had reported a possible floater at the Vestry Street tide hole. The sniffer being one Jefferson T. Roberge, an exterminator with the Department of Sanitation, who McRay knew from a previous recovery.

When the detective arrived at the access site along the West Side Highway in lower Manhattan, the sky was a lovely burnt orange and the Hudson River appeared to be hammered from dull, molten bronze. Normally the abandoned piers looked as if they'd been bomb damaged and then left to rot for a century, but the crepuscular glow of dawn softened the whole waterfront area. Times like this, special moments when the light was right, the city came alive again for McRay, dazzled him with its raw grandeur, made him feel fortunate to be alive in such a time, at such a place.

Then, of course, he stepped off the curb into a pile of something especially fetid, and he was a cop again, and the magical city of his childhood was crumbling all around him. "Ah, shit," he muttered, and he had to chuckle, because it was typical, here he was about to open the car trunk, take out his rubber waders for a sewer inspection, and he'd already soiled a perfectly good pair of shoes.

He'd eaten a good diner breakfast at a place on Eighth Avenue because in his case it wasn't true, that remains were best examined on an empty stomach. Not that he was a barfer; the only time he'd even come close was observing an autopsy, and it hadn't been the condition of the cadaver that got to him, it was the sick humor of the pathologist juggling a human brain for a gag and dropping it splat on the floor at McRay's feet. Oops, he'd said.

McRay reached into the trunk, lifted out a canvas bag. Inside was a powerful halogen flashlight, a charcoal-filter respirator, a Polaroid flash camera, a hand-held VHF police radio, a box of cotton balls, and a pair of thick rubber gloves. He stepped into the rubber waders, adjusted the straps, and walked away from his unmarked cruiser expecting never to see it again—that way if the vehicle wasn't stripped or stolen it would be like a present he could open on return.

The sniffer was waiting at an open manhole not far from the ruined wharf. Called a "tide hole" because the river rose and fell within the old sewer tunnel down below, and you didn't want to be down there on an incoming tide.

"Morning, Jeff," McRay said.

"Ain't it pretty?" said the sewer man, indicating the burnt-orange sky. He was sipping a cup of coffee and smiling beatifically, as if prepared to conduct a tour of some beautiful, fragrant garden. Jefferson Roberge had been born to Creole parents, but had himself never been further south than Atlantic City. Roberge was a "sniffer," in the noble olfactory tradition of the legendary Smelly Kelly, who'd been employed by the city to sniff out gas leaks, dead rodents trapped in electrical raceways, and once, in a famous case, the source of elephant stench in a water main. Nowadays the source of disturbing odors was likely to be more malevolent than mere dead rats or even elephants, and the Special Task Force (now reduced to McRay) had a standing request that it be notified whenever human remains were discovered in any of the tunnel systems. If there was no connection to the Subway Killer—and so far there hadn't been—the case was handed off to regular homicide detectives. Not every body discovered was the result of murder, but department regs required an investigation, even if death was later determined to be from natural causes.

"Lady in a basement called it in," Roberge explained, in no hurry to enter the open manhole. "Over there, this apartment building on Vestry. I uncapped the back-out drain and right away I knew."

"You got a visual, though."

Roberge nodded, studying McRay with his wet brown eyes. "Tide lifting pretty good, but I spotted a bundle near the outfall grille."

"Bundle?"

"Maybe wrapped up in plastic. Can't be sure. Wouldn't clear the grille, so it has to be in the vicinity." He smiled, finished his coffee. "Thought of you right away."

"I'm flattered, Jeff."

"Hey, you said to make sure you heard about it, I located any more floaters."

"You're right," McRay said. "I did. Okay, let's get this over with."

Roberge dropped agilely through the open manhole and was waiting there under the vault when McRay arrived at the bottom of the ladder, feeling clumsy and ponderous in the rubber waders. Norton in the old "Honeymooners," waving his plunger at Ralphie-boy. The smell was not terribly strong here, under the manhole vault, but it was a sewer, no doubt about that. McRay stopped to shove a cotton ball in each nostril. He didn't need the respirator yet.

"Any gators down here, Jeff?"

"Yeah, hundreds of 'em, watch they don't bite off your feet," Roberge quipped. After fifty years it was still a running joke, that old rumor about pet alligators flushed down toilets and growing huge in the sewers. Roberge had been just about everywhere in the system. He'd seen everything *but* alligators; it was amazing what got flushed under the city.

"Gators would be okay with me," McRay said. "They'd keep down the rats."

He was only partly kidding—the idea of rats bothered him. Rats dropping down from the overhead, getting down the back of his neck. Scratching and biting with their diseased, verminous teeth. So far, in all his forays underground, rodents had not been a problem. They were there by the millions, red eyes at the limits of darkness, but they kept their distance from humans who were as noisy as the detective. So he purposely stomped along behind Roberge as the sewerman led him down the slight incline of the tunnel, through a shallow stream of ankle-deep black water, McRay breathing through his clenched teeth.

This was a storm sewer tunnel, part of the overflow system, accessible to anyone who could pry up a street grate, and often used as a crude garbage disposal, despite numerous regulations against such activity. And unlike the main system, which flowed into various sewage treatment plants, this vented directly into the river.

The basic problem was that the island of Manhattan was densely populated before anyone thought to build a sewer system, and even then it was done in fits and starts, whenever pestilence threatened the population. The open drainage ditch that ran alongside the old canal on Canal Street was eventually covered over, not because it was unsightly, but to prevent apartment dwellers from dumping their chamber pots into it at every street corner. Wooden gutters were buried, draining cesspools into wells that had become contaminated. Wooden troughs became brick troughs, and later fired-clay pipes, and portions of this ancient system still functioned, patched into cast-iron pipes and stone vaults and tunnels. Human waste was often the least of it—chemicals were illegally dumped into the storm drains, paints, solvents, old motor oil, animal renderings—if it was putrid or toxic, down it went.

A hundred yards or so into the tunnel, McRay stopped to don his respirator. Roberge, used to the stench, didn't bother. "It ain't far," he said. "I can tell."

The beams of their halogen flashlights painted the vault directly ahead. It was here that two tunnels converged, and McRay knew from previous expeditions that it was a likely spot, a place where large objects tended to accumulate. When they got to the intersection, however, Roberge shook his head and directed his beam of light to the left.

"More toward the river," he said. "Might be caught up in the grate."

"Tide is out?" McRay asked, trying to sound casual and failing.

"Don't worry," Roberge assured him. "You won't hardly get your feet wet."

As it turned out, "not hardly getting your feet wet" meant wading through a pool of waist-high water where the tunnel had sagged. After that it did indeed get drier, and the tunnel sloped more sharply. A faint, ghostly daylight was reflected by the glistening walls, and McRay knew they were very near to the mouth of the tunnel, and the river beyond.

The respirator removed the worst of the stench, but McRay could feel his eyes smarting from the fumes. He was in the vicinity of death, no mistake about that.

"I hear he's on vacation," Roberge said. "Your guy, what's his name, the Subway Killer."

McRay had to lift away his respirator to make a reply. "John Chester Marlon and he's not my guy and he's not exactly on vacation."

Roberge chuckled as he trudged along, sure-footed in the slippery curve of the tunnel. "Back in the city, I mean," he said. "What is it, he's in the hospital?"

McRay grunted in the affirmative, unwilling to remove the respirator again.

"There!" Roberge said suddenly. "A bundle, like I said."

The bundle, as the sewerman insisted on calling it, was partially enclosed by a sheet of black poly secured with a tightly knotted extension cord. A bare, badly decomposed limb extended from one end of the bundle. Thick, dark hairlike substance bloomed from the other end. Not hair, he soon realized—a clump of seaweed caught up in the bundle. He got the Polaroid out of the canvas bag he'd been lugging and took shots from as many angles as he could think of, documenting the situation. Each time the flash went off he closed his eyes, not wanting the image imprinted on his brain as well as on the photo emulsion.

When he put the camera away, Roberge held out a jackknife. "Want to open it up?" he asked.

"Not here." McRay said. "You have a rope, by any chance?"

They dragged the "bundle" back through the tunnel to the manhole vault, where it could more easily be retrieved. Didn't weigh much, less than a hundred pounds, and McRay wanted the bundle closed because that way it was easier to forget that the contents had once been human, and alive. Think about that too much and you'd freak.

An hour later, when the Crime Scene detectives responded, and a bleary-eyed medical examiner finally arrived at the scene, McRay was breathing the nice fresh traffic fumes from the old West Side Highway area. He waited topside until the ME emerged from the manhole, huffing and groaning his way up the ladder.

"What I like," the ME said, "is street level crime. No ladders, no walkups."

"A little variety is good for you," McRay said. "What have we got?"

The ME made a face. "You got a dead body, but you knew that."

"I'm with the Special Task Force," McRay explained. "The Subway Killer."

"Oh right," the man said, nodding. "You're the guy looking for where he stashed all the victims. I hate to disappoint you, detective, but unless your guy is getting furloughed on weekends, he didn't do this one."

"Too recent?" McRay said.

"Two, three months tops. Putrefaction is pretty complete, but the remains are not skeletonized."

McRay nodded. He'd already guessed as much, and he didn't at all regret having to turn the case over to Homicide. "Any chance of an ID?" he asked.

The ME shrugged. "Anything is possible. Remains in this state, submerged in sewer flow, there's not a lot to go on."

"Dental records?"

That made the ME smile. "Slight problem," he said. "The head is missing."

"Oh."

"Keep looking," the ME suggested. "It may turn up."

CHAPTER TWO

Anna stood under the shower, head down and eyes closed, letting the warm water erode the last vestiges of sleep. She'd been dreaming again, a nightmare fog of childhood memories, a confusion of inexpressible anxiety. Someone chasing her. Someone large and powerful, an angry god. She was hiding and she couldn't breathe, she was suffocating, and He was getting closer and closer.

Who was it, Marlon? Had to be, she decided. Couldn't possibly be that other nightmare figure, the one that had haunted her childhood, made her the adult she had become. That was over now, that nightmare was ended long ago.

Had to be Marlon.

Anna adjusted the water, made it hotter. As hot as she could stand, making her skin tingle, her breasts ache with the heat of it.

Get a grip, she chided herself, it was only a dream.

Forcing her mind to think rationally, she decided the MSD trials were having an effect on the tester, as well as the subjects. This she knew: you couldn't be in contact with a psychopath and not experience a disturbing linkage, even a forbidden empathy. On some secret, inner level, serial killers were capable of the most heinous acts, but in most other respects they were entirely human, and therefore familiar, like a mirror reflection with a hidden flaw. That recognition was disturbing, even to experts in criminal behavior. No matter how you guarded yourself, what mental walls you erected, a feeling of uneasiness still permeated the relationship between killer and psychiatrist.

"Sympathetic transference," that's what the textbooks called it. Never mind the psychobabble, it came down to this: just knowing that she was in Marlon's thoughts gave her the creeps. To be trapped in that twisted psyche, to be an object of his morbid fantasies, it made her shudder with revulsion.

Anna grabbed a bar of soap and scrubbed herself clean under the hot needles of water. Knowing it was foolish, this delayed reaction, but unable to control it. Marlon's mind wrapping itself around her, it was like an invisible sewer slime. Kevin McRay was right—Marlon had gotten to her, he'd probed at her so deftly, identifying the weak points in her professional armor, that he had gained a kind of psychic leverage over her. The power of fear.

Stepping from the shower, Anna made a silent vow to turn the tables on the manipulative son of a bitch. Today, first thing, she'd have to show him who was in charge.

CHAPTER
THREE

B aboons at breakfast.

That's what the scene looked like to Ned Cody as he carried his tray into the small cafeteria. Five apes imitating human beings as they spooned up their cold cereal, munched at the toast and scrambled eggs or the optional generic pancakes. Six apes, counting himself. And he had to count himself because he was just as stupid and worthless as the rest of the primates.

Chickens had a pecking order; what was it called with baboons? Right, alpha male, he'd overheard Dr. Kane using that phrase. The new boss baboon was John Chester Marlon. Before that it had been Leander Jones, himself an exceedingly dangerous and cunning convict, a black prince among prisoners. Now poor old Leander was looking like someone had snatched his ice cream cone just as he was about to taste it. All Marlon had to do, smile that small, cool smile of his, and big bad Leander was demoted, just like that. Because the other baboons knew that Marlon had the power. They all sensed that John Chester Marlon might do anything, anything at all. Never mind about the electronic bug in his brain, they didn't trust science to save them from his legendary wrath.

And yet, sitting down to join the others at the only table provided in the little cafeteria, Cody was surprised to have the new boss baboon giving him the mildest of looks, greeting him warmly and saying, "Morning, Ned. You sleep well?"

Cody mumbled, unsure of his lines.

"What was that?" Marlon asked, as if genuinely curious.

"I hate sleeping," Cody found himself saying. "You can't trust it."

Marlon nodded, as if he, too, had a mistrust of sleep. "That's a fact," he said. "What you have to do, find a way to take control."

"What?" Cody asked, puzzled.

"Control of what you dream, Cody. Do that, and you won't *need* to sleep. Control your dreams, you control reality."

Leander, looking sullen, muttered a curse.

"What was that, Mr. Jones?" Marlon asked.

"Heavy duty bullshit," Leander said uneasily, not meeting his eyes. "You talkin' trash."

Marlon stared at the black man, made a smile with his lips. A smile that looked, to Cody, like a pucker in a surgical scar.

"Point taken," Marlon said, and the moment passed.

Cody noticed that there had been another new formulation within the pecking order. The pedophile Arthur Glidden now sat at the right hand of John Chester Marlon. Yesterday Glidden had been cowering alone, positioning himself near the security guards; today he no longer reeked of fear. The nervous emanations that made it almost painful to be in his proximity had diminished. The child molester now had the stunned, brain-numb expression of a religious convert.

Marlon is his new god, Cody thought in a flash of insight. In his small, egocentric mind, Arthur was strolling through the valley in the shadow of death and he no longer feared evil, because Evil protected him.

"You okay?" Marlon asked.

"Sure," Cody said uneasily. "Fine."

"I noticed you shivering there," Marlon said. "You have a fever or what?"

"Nothing," Cody said. "Just a chill."

"You don't want to let a fever build," Marlon said. "Fever can cook your brain."

"Listen to him," Arthur Glidden said urgently, his eyes glittering. "Marlon speaks the truth."

That was a stunner, the child molester expressing an opinion, and the convicts fell into silence, unsure how to react. Even Garvey, the mouthy con man, refrained from making a wise remark, scoring points off the pedophile. They were all waiting, Cody realized, waiting for Marlon to react.

The big man made eye contact with each of them before speaking. His eyes said: pay attention, this is important. "Arthur has made a new beginning," he began. "Let's welcome him into the world of men."

"Come on, is he for real?" Garvey asked in a tone of sneering skepticism. No one responded.

"Go ahead, Arthur," Marlon said. "Tell them what we discussed. Tell them what you learned about yourself."

"There is only one sin," Arthur Glidden said, "and that is the sin of weakness."

"What?" said Leander. "Where you get that?"

"Marlon says that if you leave shame behind, you leave fear behind." Arthur Glidden's explanation had the tonal quality of a mantra, a phrase repeated so often it had virtually lost meaning.

Leander Jones shifted in his plastic chair, made a noise of disgust.

"You disagree, Mr. Jones?" Marlon inquired. "You're of another opinion?"

Leander scowled. "Man, your boy sure got religion." He gestured rudely at Arthur Glidden. "Holy Church of White Baloney, that his new religion."

"Very clever," Marlon said, beaming. "It shows wit and intelligence. I like intelligence."

"Now you bullshittin' on me," Leander said heatedly. "Call me intelligent means you think I'm stupid, you think I don't see that? Huh?"

"You seem very agitated," Marlon said in his honey voice. "Now why is that?"

"Why? I tell you why: no matter how you slice the meat, your boy Arthur is a worm, he a short-eye faggot, a skinner, he wave his little white winky at baby children. You didn't have a bug in your brain, maybe you'd see the truth of that."

Marlon nodded. "I understand."

"Don't understand shit."

The serial killer's unexpected and inexplicable mildness was like an invisible mist that had been released into the enclosed atmosphere of the unit. The mist was a lie because the mildness was feigned. Cody sensed this; it was all an act meant to fool the security guards who watched and waited, hands on their Tasers. "I understand that you disapprove," Marlon said soothingly. "For now, that's all I need to understand."

"Understand shit," Leander repeated. "He what, your disciple? Like a Jesus freak, only he a Marlon freak, is that the scene?"

"Arthur?" Marlon said.

When the child molester spoke up, his voice had the serenity of a true believer. "He prepares a table in the presence of my enemies," Arthur Glidden said, "and I am not afraid."

Marlon reached out, patted him on the hand. "Your cup is running over," he said. "Be quiet now, we'll talk later."

Leander made a face, showing his teeth. "He your little altar boy," he said. "Wave his winky at all the children."

"Please refrain from insults," Marlon cautioned. He glanced at the guards, nodded pleasantly, assuring them that all was well. "We must nurture a spirit of cooperation," he said as his left hand gently patted the bandage at the back of his skull. "This is the brave new world," he continued, "and we must have the courage to change. I have changed. Arthur has changed. The rest of you can do it, too."

"You crazy," Leander said, shaking his head. "The both of you crazy as squirrels. Now who got extra maple syrup? Garvey, you want to share that syrup over here, or what?"

With that, the confrontation was over and the convicts began to attack the food with their plastic utensils. Ned Cody found that he had no interest in eating. The food wasn't bad, but his stomach was clenched, his guts were twisted, and just for a moment there, when Marlon's eyes beamed, he had been touched again by the cool breath of a dying woman.

Cody, she had said, as if his name was death.

He was still messing with his uneaten pancakes when the security guard approached and told him that Dr. Kane wanted to see him.

"Good morning, Ned. Take a pew, please, and make yourself comfortable."

Anna Kane was seated in a small consultation room situated behind the main security station. There was a clipboard and notebook on a laminated table, and a small lamp illuminating the notebook. A guard monitored them from behind a Plexiglas window.

Cody lowered himself gingerly into a molded plastic chair and forced himself to remain outwardly calm. It helped that dark-haired Anna Kane did not in any way resemble blond Tracy Vega, the woman he had strangled. Best to keep reminding himself of that: Anna Kane was not Tracy, not even close.

"I have a proposition for you," Dr. Kane was saying, using that distant, professional tone that got under his skin and made him itch deep inside his head, a maddening brain tickle. "It's a job offer, really."

"A job offer?"

She nodded, made a check mark with her felt-tip pen. "Can you still do it?" she asked. "Can you still act?"

"What?"

"I need an actor," she said. "I was hoping you were available."

"You're serious," he said.

"It's a difficult role," she said. "Possibly dangerous."

Cody grinned. "The Scottish Play," he said. "*Macbeth* is always dangerous. Actors believe the play is cursed—even the name means bad luck."

"Not Shakespeare," she said, sighing. "Not even close."

CHAPTER FOUR

The machine started to chirp before McRay got there, sounded like a rabid bat trying to escape from a hatbox. The security guard came right at him with a hand-held metal detector.

"You win," McRay said, lifting his service revolver out of the small belt-holster he wore at the small of his back. "NYPD, Detective McRay."

"No can do, Detective."

McRay shook his head. "Come on, you know the rules. I'm on duty."

"I do know the rules, sure, and the rule is there are no firearms allowed above the sixth floor."

"What?"

"You want to go up to the Isolation Unit, you'll have to leave the sidearm here." The guard held up a Ziploc bag and a receipt form. "And empty the cylinder, please."

"Let me ask you this," McRay said, clearing the cylinder. "What happens you get a problem up there?"

"We have a number of options. Tear gas is first. Need be, we send up a sharpshooter. But no weapons on the floor without special authorization. Safety precaution, okay? We got a guy up there, he already disarmed a prison guard. You know what he did to her?"

"Yeah," McRay said, surrendering his weapon. "Unfortunately, I do."

* * *

Ten minutes later McRay entered the Annex briefing room and sipped his cup of take-out coffee. Just a little worried that the stink of death was still clinging, although he'd taken a quick shower and changed his clothes before coming over. Probably it was his imagination, but the thought was enough to make him take a seat in the back, away from the olfactory range of Anna Kane. He'd never been a front row kind of guy, why change his habits now?

Anna had tendered an invitation to be an observer; he'd eagerly accepted. To be able to watch Marlon undetected, that was an offer he couldn't refuse. Also, and this was no small consideration, it gave him a chance to observe the lovely lady up close, watch how she handled herself in a professional situation. Not that he had any doubts about her ability, from what he'd seen and heard so far.

"Glad you could make it," she said, looking from her notes, a cooler welcome than he would have liked. "This should be interesting."

"Wouldn't miss it for the world," McRay said, flashing a smile. He wanted to add something about their dinner date the previous evening, some sort of compliment, but thought better of it. Dr. Kane was giving off those kinds of vibrations that said this was not the time nor the place for whatever personal business was developing between them. If in fact anything was happening—maybe it was all in his head, wishful thinking.

Sit back, be cool, he admonished himself, take this one step at a time.

Forcing himself to relax, McRay watched the Annex security detail file into the briefing room. Six uniformed guards, all with considerable experience handling pathologically violent offenders. Tough hombres, every one of them, even Hank Portis, who despite his boyish looks was in fact pushing forty and had years of experience. The guards took seats in a row of chairs behind the Annex medical staff. Portis coughed discreetly into his fist, signaling that his people were ready.

Anna smiled a welcome. "Thank you all for being so prompt," she began. "Before I go into the details of today's trial, I'd like to update you on what has been established thus far.

"As you all know, our main focus is the serial killer John Chester Marlon, who is voluntarily participating in this study. A microcomputer sedation device has been implanted in Mr. Marlon, and it appears to be functioning exactly as designed. The implant detects and interrupts episodic violence by rendering the subject unconscious. In this sense the device is quite primitive, you might even say Pavlovian."

McRay liked that, the way she assumed that everyone in the room was familiar with Pavlovian response. Ring a bell prior to feeding a dog for long enough, it would salivate whenever the bell was rung, anticipating food—he knew that much, but what exactly was the connection to controlling human violence?

"My assumption—perhaps I should say my hope—is that this primitive device will, by interrupting violent episodes, help us find a way to make the prison environment safer, both for staff and inmates. Of course psychopathic offenders are not as easily controlled as Pavlov's dogs—the MSD can't actually alter the thought process. But there is a chance that the experience of being rendered unconscious whenever violence is contemplated will imprint itself on the psyche."

Several of the medical staff were nodding along, having read, apparently, Dr. Kane's articles on that very subject.

"The results from the first trial at Dannemora suggest that implanted inmates are themselves vulnerable to acts of violence, which raises a whole other set of issues we must address before we can conduct evaluations in an actual maximum-security prison environment."

Portis politely raised his hand. "That's easy, Doc. Implant 'em all. The yard'll look like nap time at the nursery school." He looked around, pleased with his joke.

Anna smiled. She didn't attempt to dissuade interruptions; the whole idea was to get a dialogue going with the staff.

"We don't know yet that the MSD will ever be utilized in a real situation," she admitted. "This type of behavioral modification is, as you all know, highly controversial. There are political and legal factors over which we have no control. All we're attempting here is a scientific evaluation of how effective the device may be in controlling levels of violence among dangerous prison populations. If the Marlon experiment is successful, we'll apply for a long-term trial at one of our maximum-security facilities."

Reasonable, McRay thought, the lady is a realist, she knows who she's dealing with. He'd known this from their first encounter, but it was nice to have the impression reinforced.

One of the staff psychologists was raising her hand, a young, delicate woman with large eyes magnified by her thick glasses. "Dr. Kane? We were wondering—I mean I was wondering—is it possible for a convict to fake a reaction? I mean, could he fool the device? Some of these characters are awfully good liars."

Anna shook her head. "The MSD is not a lie detector. It monitors physical data, and as far as we know elevations in metabolism can't be faked. Also, a record of each incident is recorded on telemetry. In other words, we can go back and check out the brain wave patterns, hormonal levels, adrenaline surge, blood pressure, and so on, and determine if a rage situation actually took place. Does that answer your question?"

The staff psychologist smiled uncertainly, her big eyes blinking like goldfish up against aquarium glass. McRay felt sympathy for her concern, intimate as he was with the details of Marlon's behavior. Good liar didn't cover it—that man could bend truth into pretzel logic and make it sound reasonable.

"Let me be more specific," Anna said. "It is quite possible that the subject could fake a fainting spell, but we'd know he was faking as soon as we checked the telemetry. The point is, a clever, intelligent subject can fool the guards or the other inmates, but he can't fool the computer. According to our telemetry, Marlon was definitely experiencing psychotic rage when the implant was activated. He really was rendered unconscious. Most important, if the device continues to function he really will be rendered unconscious, and therefore harmless, if and when he has another psychotic episode."

The young staff psychologist was obviously not yet convinced. "Excuse me, Dr. Kane," she piped up. "But that was just a snuff film, right? He's reacting to images on a screen."

"That was the stimulus employed, yes," Anna conceded.

McRay picked up a flicker, a barely detectable hesitation that made him uneasy. Was Anna concealing something about how the psychotic reaction had been induced? Had she taken some personal risk, put herself in peril to test her own device?

The thought left a chill in his guts.

"Okay," the young psychologist was saying. "He gets it off on a TV screen. But what happens when he's with real people?"

Anna smiled reassuringly. "That's what we're about to find out."

The experimental encounter was scheduled to take place in the holding cell area. Anna toured the area with Hank Portis and his security detail shortly before the test was about to begin. McRay, clutching his now empty coffee cup, kept to the rear, doing his best not to intrude, as Anna gave what amounted to a mini-lecture on the problems of controlling violent offenders.

"Statistics gathered from a variety of maximum security penitentiaries indicate that the majority of violent acts take place either in the yard, where gang rivalries can develop, or in a work environment, where observation by security staff is often difficult. Shop, kitchen, laundry and so on. In consultation with the Annex staff, we chose a 'laundry' situation as being the safest environment in which to conduct the first working trial." Anna smiled primly. "In other words, we want to avoid power tools, welding equipment, and so on."

Portis chuckled. "Right. Marlon with a chain saw, I don't think so." The other guards laughed dutifully, obviously made nervous at the thought of the serial killer with any weapon, however unusual.

McRay noted that industrial laundering equipment, borrowed from the adjacent hospital, had been installed in the holding cell area. Push carts containing bed linen and staff uniforms ranged against one wall, full to overflowing, and a half-dozen industrial steam irons were set up, two in each of the three cells.

Anna pointed out the surveillance cameras. "This area is covered from every conceivable angle," she said. "The security staff will be assigned to monitors."

"How many of us in the room?" one of the guards wanted to know.

Anna shook her head. "None. That's the whole point of this exercise. We want to observe what happens when a dominant, MSD-implanted offender has to interact with a typical inmate population. Without guards physically present."

"Yeah, but you're going to be in the room, right?"

"No," Anna said. "I have already agreed to abide by the house rules. No staff present without security guards."

Damn right, McRay said silently. Never, ever be alone with John Chester Marlon. Bug or no bug, the man could not be trusted.

CHAPTER
FIVE

"**W**ho put you in charge?"

The challenge came from Joseph Garvey, who had taken exception to Cody's elevation to laundry foreman.

"Not important," Cody said. "All you have to do, follow orders."

"She wants you to fuck her, is that the deal?" A smirk twisted Garvey's small, spittle-wet lips. "Sexy shrink wants to play hide the sausage with the pretty actor boy?"

Cody shook his head. "They can hear every word," he cautioned.

"Good," Garvey said, raising his voice. "You hear that, Doc? We know you got the hots for the fag actor! Okay, fine, he can be the honcho, we'll iron your dirty sheets."

As it happened the linen was already freshly laundered, and smelled of industrial-strength bleach. Close your eyes, it was like breathing in the atmosphere of a big California hot tub, all that chlorine flashing off the chemical-blue water. Made Ned Cody think, for just a moment, of better days, or rather nights. Hot tub nights on his first trip to Los Angeles. A bust, career-wise, but oh the women, the fine, long-legged women in their thong bikinis, skin so soft and resilient it was like making love in a weightless condition. He hadn't had a clue then, that his life was already slip-sliding away, like the song said.

"Cody!"

Back to business. He hadn't wanted to be foreman—leadership didn't come naturally to Cody, he knew that—but it was all part of Dr. Kane's plan, so he had to think of it as acting. A role to play, boss of the prison laundry. Edward G. Robinson or Paul Muni, he could go either way. Maybe just a hint of Cagney, an in-your-face, top-of-the-world-ma attitude.

"What's the problem?" he said to Leander Jones, who was holding his hand up like a school kid begging the teacher's attention.

"No problem," the black inmate said. "Got a question is all. What procedure we suppose to follow, handle all this shit? Got enough white sheets here to outfit the entire Ku Klux Klan, have plenty left over for every towel-head cabdriver in the city."

"What do you suggest?" Cody asked.

Leander grinned. "My suggestion, we tie all these sheets together, skinny on down from the window."

"What?"

"Bad joke, man. They hearin' every word we say, right? Hey you! Mr. White Guard, that a joke about escaping! No windows, right? So it *have* to be a joke."

He was correct. There were no exterior windows in the Isolation Unit. And when no security guards stormed in to take Leander away for mentioning a means of escape, Cody understood that they were being left to sort it out among themselves, exactly as Dr. Kane had promised.

"Okay, guys," Cody said. "I guess we better get to it. Nussy, you bring a cart full of sheets over to each ironing station."

"You mean it?" Carl Nussbaum said, eyeing the laundry carts as if they were forbidden toys. "I can do that?"

"Sure," Cody said. "Just take it slow, you'll be fine."

"I'll be fine," Nussbaum muttered. "I'll be fine, fine fine."

"Marlon?" Cody said, deliberately not making eye contact with the big man.

"Yes?"

"You help Nussy with those carts."

Marlon smiled sweetly and nodded. As he turned away Cody was acutely aware of the fresh bandage on his thick, muscular neck, looked like a small white exclamation mark just below his close-shaved skull. A warning sign: Do Not Touch.

Cody wanted to shiver, but that was just nerves. A touch of the old familiar stage fright. Ice water sloshing in the gut. He almost welcomed the sensation, the way it made him feel alive. Working and alive.

Something touched his shoulder. Cody whirled, found Arthur Glidden staring up at him. His eyes were not properly focused, and his small, unpleasant face looked as if it had been molded from rubber. "What do you want?" Cody managed to say, made uneasy by the pedophile's proximity.

"I go with Marlon," Glidden said in his weirdly flat voice. No inflection there, despite the underlying intensity, and Cody was thinking the little man could work airports with this new routine, do the Hare Krishna thing, or pass out pamphlets for Lyndon LaRouche.

"No way," Cody said. "You'll be folding at station two. Right over there," he said, pointing.

"With Marlon," Glidden insisted. "I must stay with Marlon."

Cody assumed a pose, hands on his hips, jaw jutting forward—Cagney in *White Heat*, yes, that was the role model. "Listen to me, you little dirt bag—I said station two. Now move it."

Glidden did not budge. To Cody the smaller man seemed frozen, or not so much frozen as trapped in some sort of stop-time situation, waiting for the next second to tick over. Waiting, obviously, for Marlon to intervene. Cody sensed all the attention of the cell block being refocused on the confrontation. No spotlights heating up the scene, but that's what it felt like. The curtain goes up and the sun comes out, right on cue.

Let it build, savor the moment, they'd be eating out of his hand.

"Forget your big bad buddy," Cody said, carefully enunciating the alliterative syllables, making each word lash out and sting. "He's just another lifer, a loser. I'm the boss now."

There was a sudden and distinct tingling sensation at the back of Cody's neck. It made him feel short of breath. Marlon was staring at him, no doubt about it. Cody forced himself to relax, or to appear to relax, which was the same thing. You did it on stage, in front of the cameras or whatever, appearance was reality. Appearance *became* reality, if you rehearsed it enough.

No rehearsal here, this was method acting, flying by the seat of his pants. Take a deep breath and jump right in. As the actor turned to face the killer, he assumed an aggressive posture and made his voice drip with contempt, "You have any objection, your altar boy does what I tell him?"

Marlon let go of the laundry cart and ambled forward, heading for Ned Cody.

* * *

"He's making his move," said Portis, eyeing the monitor.

In the surveillance room Anna was watching the video screen that showed Ned Cody standing his ground. Marlon was coming into picture now, looming as he moved closer, taking his time.

"Not yet," Anna said. "He's too smart, too controlled to respond at the first provocation."

"But the other inmate is challenging him." Portis sounded worried.

"Check the levels," Anna suggested. "The situation is stable, for the moment."

The MSD telemetry clearly indicated that Marlon was not being physically affected by Cody's challenge to his authority. Pulse was steady, blood pressure had not elevated, there was no trace of adrenal gland activity. No indication of impending violence.

"Look at his face," McRay suggested. The detective had been staying in the background; this was his first comment since entering the surveillance room. He touched the monitor screen, indicating the image of Marlon. "Check out that smart-aleck expression. He knows something is up."

"I'm sure he does," Anna acknowledged. "They're all aware that this is an experiment. They know they're being monitored."

"I don't get it," McRay said. "How is this supposed to work if they know it's fake?"

"Because it isn't fake," Anna explained. "Awareness of the situation does not necessarily negate the experiment. You have to factor it in, of course, when you sum up the results." She paused, favored McRay with a soft, inquisitive look. "You must have observed, detective, that certain habitual offenders go ahead and break the law even when they're certain to be arrested and prosecuted."

McRay grinned. "That's true," he said. "That live-for-the-moment attitude, they don't care what happens ten minutes later."

Anna nodded. "And keep in mind that all correctional facilities are, in a sense, controlled experiments," she said. "The guards are the observers and the enforcers, while the inmates act out, or cope, or adjust, or fail to adjust."

"Or kill," McRay said.

"Sometimes," Anna conceded. "It happens."

* * *

Marlon had this look, Cody couldn't read it. Like the man was inside a dream, pretending to be awake.

"My oh my," he said, ambling closer. "What have we here?"

"Beat it, pal," Cody said. "Go help the retard."

"Such an unkind thing to say. Poor Carl is, what do they call it, learning impaired."

"Whatever," Cody said. "You give him a hand with that cart, like I told you."

Marlon seemed vastly amused by everything Cody said. "You must have had your Wheaties this morning, hey champ?"

"That's it."

"You get put in charge, you feel obliged to mouth off."

Cody stood his ground as the larger man advanced ever so slowly, walking on the balls of his feet, filling the actor's field of vision. "Hey Marlon?" he said softly. "Fuck you."

"I think not," Marlon said. "Celibacy is a way of life. Control the sexual urge, you control the world."

"Come on, that's crap. You get off on the ladies. You rape them and you kill them."

"Not true," Marlon said. "Not even close."

"Then you're a phony, a fake. What it is, you're just another loser," Cody said, trying a new tack. "No different than all the rest."

"No different than you?" Marlon asked. "Is that what you mean? You killed a woman, didn't you? Throttled her with your bare hands? I'm curious, what was that like? Did you enjoy it? Did it get you off, Ned, is that what happened?"

Cody took a deep breath. Ignore him, keep focused on the scene, on his own lines. "You're never getting out," he insisted. "You'll die in a cage. Like a big, bald rat. And anytime they want to make you twitch, all they have to do is push a button."

"So that's it," Marlon said. "The implant. You want to see if it really works."

"I don't care about that."

"No, wait," Marlon said, his eyes lifting to scan the cell block area. "This is my friend Dr. Kane. Of course it is. Anna? You're watching us, Anna. What is it you want? You want me to have a temper fit, is that it?"

"I'm talking to you here," Cody said.

Marlon ignored him. "Sorry, Dr. Kane, but I'm not in the mood. I find your little collaborator quite amusing, actually. He's rather good."

All Cody could think was that he was losing the audience. They were rustling the programs, squirming in the seats, consulting their watches. Push through to the next level, he told himself, make an effort.

What he did was shove Marlon. Pushed him with both hands, hard.

"Ned?" Marlon said. "Please restrain yourself."

Cody balled up his fist and threw a punch. On stage or in front of the camera it was all in the angle, the other actor ducked away and the fist never connected, the illusion was supplied by sound effect, a wet slap of leather. But Marlon didn't duck and Cody's fist connected with the side of his chin, hard.

"Oops," was all Cody could think to say.

"Amazing," Anna said, tapping the telemetry monitor. "We're seeing amazing self-control."

"It's a bluff," McRay said. "Look at the son of a bitch, he thinks it's funny."

"Something's wrong," Anna said, sounding worried.

"Are you sure he's really a trigger-reactive psychopath?" asked the young, big-eyed staff psychologist. "If he was prone to fits of uncontrollable temper, wouldn't he be reacting by now? I mean he just got punched in the face and he's just standing there, smiling."

"That's what bothers me," Anna said. "The trigger diagnosis was made on the basis of the guard he attacked in full view of the cameras."

"So?" McRay said. "He did it, didn't he? What difference does it make what he was thinking?"

"It makes a difference to the implant," Anna said. "The levels are set to go off when it registers a psychotic episode. If he was a real trigger, the implant would have kicked in by now."

"You lost me," McRay said.

"What if he *wanted* to be misdiagnosed, so he'd be eligible for this study?" Anna said.

"You mean that's why he shot the guard? To make it look like he couldn't control himself?"

"I'm starting to think that's a distinct possibility," Anna said. "I think we should pull the plug on this and reevaluate. We'll have to find a more suitable candidate."

"Dr. Kane?" said Portis. "This is all very interesting, but aren't you forgetting something?"

Anna looked at him expectantly.

"Marlon may be as peaceful as a saint," said the security chief, pointing at the monitor. "But if I'm not mistaken, Arthur Glidden wants to kill Ned Cody."

CHAPTER
SIX

Cody wasn't sure what made him duck. Instinct, maybe, or the glimpse of a reflection in Marlon's deceptively mild eyes. Whatever, there was a flare of movement from behind, and as Cody suddenly dropped into a crouch, something cut the air above his head.

He rolled to the left, clutching his skull with both hands, aware of how vulnerable he was, how exposed.

"Die," Arthur Glidden croaked. "Now you must die."

Glidden, who weighed one-forty tops, had somehow torn lose a support from one of the industrial ironing machines. He was gripping it two-handed, swinging ten pounds of steel rod like it was a thirty-ounce bat and Cody's head was a potential home run.

"Somebody stop him!"

Is that me shrieking like a girl? Cody thought. Matter of fact, it was. Hadn't heard his voice so high-pitched in years. Since he was a panicked kid running from a bully on the playground, some huge lummox with fists like hams.

Come on, Cody, don't be a sissy. Arthur Glidden is a little guy, what harm can he do?

"Die!"

The steel rod crashed down, missing Cody's skull by inches.

"Help! Somebody help!"

Cody was rolling, trying to protect his head and at the same time kicking out with his feet, attempting to connect with Arthur Glidden, knock him off balance or at least spoil his aim.

Out of the corner of his eye he could see Marlon just standing there, rubbing his jaw where Cody had punched him. The big guy wasn't going to interfere with his protégé's insane attack, that much was obvious.

"You son of a bitch!" Cody managed to shout as he ducked and rolled. The steel rod slammed so close his ears were ringing. Shouting his fear and anger at both Glidden and Marlon, they were in it together, and he was also shouting at the goddamn security guards, where were they? Was this part of the experiment, let Ned Cody get his head crushed?

And then, what a relief, the room was flooding with uniformed guards and he heard the sizzle-snap of Tasers going off. A man screaming in rage. That was Arthur, wired up to thirty thousand volts, still managing somehow to swing that steel bar even as his frail little body convulsed.

Cody got to his knees, crawled away from Marlon, who was smirking at him. "Fuck you, man," Cody said, and then he was shaking, the aftereffects of an adrenaline surge, the fear and anger making him shiver and convulse as if he, too, had been zapped by electronic pulses.

After a few deep, shuddering breaths he was able to get to his feet— knees weirdly soft and jointless—and see what the hell was going on here, this theater of the absurd.

"Hold him, goddamnit!"

Four of the six guards were straddling Arthur Glidden. Big men, trained in physical confrontation, and they could barely hold him down. Glidden's eyes were rolled up, there was foam on his lips, he was having a fit of some kind, no doubt about it.

"Get the doctor, we need to sedate this crazy son of a bitch!"

Little Arthur twitched and two of the guards went flying. One cracked the back of his head on the floor, groaned, and passed out. The other was merely stunned.

"Quick, we can't hold him!"

This was quite true. The pedophile was shaking them off, one by one, and Cody backed away, getting out of range. The little guy was fighting like Superman and nobody had the Kryptonite.

Then a door opened and in came Dr. Kane, holding a mean-looking syringe. Trailing her was a civilian, a good-looking guy in an off-the-rack sport jacket and scuffed wingtips. A cop, Cody decided, and competition, from the way his eyes followed the pretty psychiatrist.

"Make room," said Anna with the kind of no-nonsense authority that caused several dangerous inmates to instantly obey, clearing a path for her.

If Cody hadn't been backing up himself, he might have missed it. Marlon gliding through the confusion, moving like Willie Mays used to float after a fly ball, making the catch look so easy, so inevitable. The guards, in contrast, seemed to be standing still, unable to react.

It was all done in a heartbeat.

Marlon's left arm went around Anna Kane's waist and he lifted her up into the air as if she was weightless.

At the same time his right hand engulfed hers, turning the syringe around, and before Cody could quite comprehend what had happened, the syringe plunged into her neck.

"Gahh," she said, as if her tongue were a fat slice of beef, and then she went rag-doll limp. The empty syringe dropped to the floor. Plink.

And then silence.

Arthur Glidden had curled up in a fetal position, his struggle over. The guards who had been attempting to restrain him crouched over his inert body, mouths open, looked like a row of stunned fish gasping for air.

"Calm," Marlon said quietly, breaking the silence. "Everybody be very, very, calm."

His massive right hand and forearm had coiled around Dr. Kane's throat. Her legs were loosely splayed, feet dangling. Her black hospital pumps had come off and Cody could see where her pantyhose bunched at the toes.

For some reason that made him want to cry. At the same time, of course, he couldn't help but look up her skirt.

"Calm," Marlon was saying. "Take a deep breath. There, wasn't that nice? Let's all just be extremely calm, shall we? Or this lovely lady will have her spinal vertebrae snapped like a dry pretzel."

"Put her down," the cop said. He had pushed through the crowd and Cody saw his hand go inside the jacket.

"Tut, tut," Marlon said, and his arm coiled tighter. Anna's left foot jerked, as if in spasm.

"You bastard," the cop said. His hand came out of the jacket, fingers twitching. No gun.

"Detective McRay, isn't it?" Marlon said. "You know I'll do it."

"The implant," the cop said helplessly.

Marlon smiled. "I haven't lost my temper," he said. "It won't go off unless I lose my temper, and I never lose my temper, not unless I want to."

"What do you want?" said the cop, his voice going thin at the edges.

"Nothing much," Marlon said. "A ride on the elevator, that's all."

CHAPTER
SEVEN

They were at the elevator before Portis managed to get McRay's attention.

"Delay," he whispered in a voice so small McRay had to strain to hear it. *"Sharpshooter."*

That was all it took for McRay to understand: a sharpshooter had been alerted when the alarm went off for Arthur Glidden. If they could hold Marlon up, the shooter would be there in the car when the elevator doors opened. The single elevator was the only access in or out of the Isolation Unit, a precaution that McRay was beginning to appreciate.

"Open the door or she snaps," Marlon said, focusing his attention on McRay. "I've got nothing to lose, Kev. Not a thing. You know I'll do it. Count of three," he said, entwining his fingers in Anna Kane's long hair. "One, two—"

"Don't!" McRay almost shouted. Came out more of a yelp, but it seemed to reassure Marlon. "Open it for him, Hank," McRay said to the security chief. "Now."

Portis sighed and then hit the button under the guard desk. The elevator doors opened and McRay was looking at an empty car. No sharpshooter.

Maybe just as well, the way Marlon had flexed that powerful arm.

Anna looked so lifeless, a bundle of thin clothing and loose limbs, as limp and unmoving as death itself. Could an injection in the neck be fatal? Just the thought of it made him feel lightheaded—don't even think it, shove it from your mind.

Marlon pivoted into the open car, carrying Anna.

"Wait!"

Somebody shoved McRay aside. It was the actor, the damn fool who had messed up the test. His eyes were bugging out and McRay could smell the pong of flop sweat coming off him, the stink of fear itself. "Wait up," he was saying. "Take me with you."

Marlon placed one foot against the elevator door, which continued to bump against him like an impatient child. "Why would I want to do that, pray tell?" the big man asked.

"You're bluffing," Cody blurted. "You can't kill her."

"Shut up," McRay said. "Keep out of this."

"Let him talk," said Marlon, who seemed vastly amused.

"You can't kill her," said Cody. "Not with that bug in your head. But I can."

Marlon laughed, a chortle that sounded to McRay like the rattle of wet bones. "You're jumping in front of a train, little man. Don't expect it to stop."

"You need me," Cody insisted.

Marlon shrugged. "I can always use another hostage," he said, indicating that Cody enter the elevator.

At the last moment the actor turned and his eyes connected with McRay's. The detective had never seen such an expression: a mask of fear, anguish, and belligerent courage. And somewhere in there a plea for trust.

The crazy bastard either loves her, McRay decided, or he really does want to kill her. Maybe both.

A moment later the doors slid shut.

The car dropped through the shaft, cables humming.

"I know what you want," Marlon said to Cody. "You can't fool me."

"Is she alive?"

Marlon shifted the limp body, flopping it lightly over his shoulder. Hefting her, as if weight was a clue to her condition. "For the moment," he said. "More or less."

"I can help you," said Cody, trying to position himself in the small elevator car. Maybe he could get a look at Dr. Kane's face, see if he could detect signs of life.

Suddenly his body was moving backward and upward. Marlon pressed him against the side of the car, hard enough so he could feel the sheet metal buckling against his back.

"Never, ever touch what belongs to me," he said. "Not without permission."

Cody desperately wanted to agree, but he couldn't speak because Marlon had cut off his air.

"Got him!" Portis shouted when the elevator doors shut. "By God, I didn't think he'd do it. Like a rabbit into the trap."

McRay was frantically trying to find the right intercom button, alert the ground floor security detachment. "What the hell are you talking about, Hank?" he said.

The security chief was jubilant. "There's no way out. We can control the elevator from here."

"He's got Anna," McRay reminded him. "He's can do what he wants."

Portis ignored him, hurried behind the control desk. "There they are," he said, pointing at a video monitor. "We're getting this on tape, we can use it as evidence."

McRay caught just one glimpse before the screen went blank. Marlon with a limp body slung over his shoulder, reaching for the surveillance camera. Hand moving like a shadow, blocking the picture.

A moment later Portis checked the floor indicator and said, "Aw nuts."

"What?"

"He must be screwing around with the emergency mechanism. Got the car stopped between floors."

"I know what he's doing," said McRay. Thinking, of course, nothing he does is accidental. Son of a bitch, he had it planned.

"Yeah?" Portis sounded dubious.

"He's rewiring the controls. Cutting you out."

Portis started to respond but the retort died on his lips as he watched his panels go blank. "I'll be damned," he said. "You're right."

"The basement," said McRay. "He's headed underground."

CHAPTER
EIGHT

Cody didn't remember blacking out, but it must have happened, because here he was waking up on the floor of the elevator. Breathing was an effort, as if that powerful fist had done some damage, crushed his throat. No, not crushed, he decided after a tentative exploration with his fingertips, just badly swollen and bruised.

The next thing he noticed was that he could barely see—had he been blinded, too? Cody forced himself to check it out, touch his eyes. Relief. No damage there. It was dim because the elevator light was out—a tangle of wires extruded from the control panel—and the only source of illumination was from outside the car, a low-watt bulb suspended in a metal cage.

The elevator had gone all the way to the bottom, that was now obvious. The basement? What the hell was he doing here? Why not the lobby, for instance, with the prospect of street-level freedom? And where was Marlon and his hostage, had they left Cody behind?

"I see you're back among the living," said a voice from above.

He looked up to see Marlon silhouetted against the light, looked like a shadow blocking a pale sun. He had something in his right hand, was it a gun?

"Where's Dr. Kane?" Cody panted. He got to his feet, stumbled woozily.

Marlon grabbed him, fingers bunching up the prison jumpsuit. "You're going to come in handy," the big man said, jerking Cody along with him. "I can feel it in my bones."

Not a gun, Cody realized, a wrench. Marlon was hefting a sizable pipe wrench. What the hell was *that* all about? He was carried along, feet shuffling to keep up, his sense of balance out of whack, and then flung up against a damp concrete wall, hard enough to knock the wind out of him.

"Take this."

Another, smaller wrench was thrust into Cody's hands. A weapon, he thought, he handed me a weapon. Was this a test of some kind?

And where was Dr. Kane, what had he done with her?

"Do exactly what I say or I'll crush your skull. Put the wrench right there. Careful now, no sudden movements."

Cody had to squint as his eyes gradually became used to the dimness. A threaded steel bolt protruded from a cast-iron panel embedded in the wall. Marlon had the big wrench around the outside of the bolt, and he wanted Cody to hold a rusted lock-nut with his smaller wrench.

"Now," Marlon said. He heaved and Cody sank involuntarily to his knees. "Hold tight, damn it, you can't be as weak as you look."

"I'm holding," Cody protested.

Marlon heaved again and this time the locknut shifted.

"Stand where you are and don't move."

"Sure," Cody said. "Anything you say."

He'd caught sight of a foot under a pile of cardboard that littered a nearby corner. A woman's foot, no shoe. The sight was curdling, it twisted him up inside, knotted his guts. So the big wacko had killed her after all, tossing her body aside like so much debris.

The wrench was suddenly hot and slick in Cody's hands. Marlon wasn't a superman—hit him hard enough on the thick, hairless skull, he'd go down.

"You're thinking again," Marlon said in a warning tone. "Thinking will kill you."

"Like it killed her?" Cody said, his fist clenching on the wrench.

Marlon moved swiftly, showing an agility that seemed unreal in a man so large. The sheets of cardboard flew away and Cody saw that Dr. Kane was not dead, but semiconscious, her head lolling.

"I know what you're thinking," Marlon said. "Always remember that." He was using his wrench to pry at the cast iron panel, coaxing it free of the threaded rod. The panel came loose with a dull thud as it dropped a few inches to the floor, narrowly missing Cody's feet.

A gust of warm air flowed from the opening in the wall. In the darkness Cody could barely make out a maze of pipes. Were those steam pipes? Jesus. No time to be sure before Marlon was shoving him into the opening and Cody was trying to shield his head and at the same time keep his hands off the scalding hot pipes.

"Move along," Marlon said, coming up behind him, hefting his bundle. "I've got your girlfriend. Be quick," he added, "or you'll see what live steam does to human flesh."

CHAPTER
NINE

Ninety feet above, in the elevator shaft, McRay clung to the access ladder with sweaty hands. Struggling for balance, he kicked at the sealed shaft doors to the level beneath the Isolation Unit. The doors were thin, sheet-metal things, but all he could do was make dents and a lot of noise, a deafening boom each time his foot hit the target.

You're a damn fool, he chided himself, never get it open this way.

Above him, Hank Portis the security chief was leaning out into the shaft, trying to keep him in sight. "I got one of the elevator maintainence guys on the phone. He said something about a hand crank."

"Crank?" McRay grabbed the rung with both hands as his foot slipped. Shit, the way he'd been flailing at the goddamn doors he'd be limping for sure. Assuming he didn't fall.

"There's a crank handle, he says," Portis said. "You know, a mechanical thingamajig?"

"Great," McRay said, "wonderful," but he searched the unfamiliar mechanical contraptions above and around the sealed door. There, on the side, was a device that resembled a collapsed scissors jack. Suspended from a short length of chain alongside the jack was an L-shaped thing that might be construed as a crank handle.

"I think I got it." He could just barely reach the scissors jack with the handle. Sure enough, it fit in the slot. "I bet I screwed it up, all those dents in the door," he said, but when he turned the handle clockwise the doors actually made a creaking noise and unsealed.

"We're rolling here!" he shouted, elated. Each full turn of the handle was good for about a half inch. It took all the strength he could muster, with his leverage pretty much nonexistent, to keep cranking. "What about the sharpshooter?" he shouted upwards. "They get him down to the basement?"

Above him, Portis cleared his throat. "Had a little problem, there," he said. "Time they got there the door was sealed from the inside. They're busting it down as we speak."

"Beautiful," said McRay. "Perfect."

"Don't you worry," said Portis. "We got him cornered, that basement. New York's finest'll have a hostage negotiation team here before you know it."

McRay grunted, twisting at the damn handle with all of his strength. "Forget it," he said. "Too late for that."

"What?"

The doors were open a foot or so, enough for him to slip through if he could swing over from the ladder without killing himself. "You don't have him cornered," McRay shouted as he poised for the jump. "The son of a bitch is getting away."

"Impossible!"

McRay jumped. His sweaty palms made a grab at the door jamb and missed. It didn't matter; with the momentum of sheer panic he slammed through the narrow opening and sprawled full length on the floor. Linoleum never tasted so good.

"Hey McRay! Hey, Detective!"

But the detective was already sprinting for the stairwell.

They'd had to drill through the steel-jacketed door to the basement. Soft metal, but still it took several minutes, and even then it was a job, having to pry out the pin that had been shoved into the pushbar and broken off. The security detail, lugging SWAT gear and bullet-proof shields, had no choice but to wait as the building super fiddled with the lock.

"Pain in the ass," said the super, a heavyset guy with a sour expression embedded on his bulldog face. "Ruin a perfectly good lock set. You know what these go for?"

McRay, panting from his run down the stairwell, shoved the larger man aside.

"The fuck you think you're doing, pal?"

"I'm a cop."

"So? That means you can assault me?"

McRay took a deep breath. "Give me a hand here," he said, facing the super. "He's got a woman down there, God knows what he'll do to her."

"Whyn't you say so?"

"Count of three."

McRay and the super hit the door together. Maybe three hundred fifty pounds of mass and momentum, the detective figured. The hinges popped, the door creaked away from the casing. "Hey," said the super, a big grin creasing his jowls. "Whattaya know, it worked!"

Not knowing what to expect made it all the more difficult, forcing himself down that last flight of stairs. The incident at Riker's, he couldn't get that out of his mind, the image of a woman paralyzed for life in the time it took Marlon to snap off a shot. What made it worse, what made it so alien and terrifying, was how casual he had been about it, sending a bullet into a human spine with all the emotional intensity of a man picking his teeth.

First problem, the power was out and all they had to go by was the super's flashlight. "The SOB musta yanked the circuit breakers."

"What's down here?" McRay wanted to know as they descended the iron steps, booming dully beneath their feet.

"Electrical, mostly. Sewer pipes. Also you got your steam exchange for the first three floors."

"Steam exchange?"

"Converts the steam heat to hot water. There's another unit on the fifth." The flashlight flitted, painting the darkness with a pale circle of light.

"You smell that?" McRay asked.

"I got allergies, I don't smell nothin'."

"It smells hot," McRay said.

"Come on, 'hot' is a smell?"

"Hot metal," McRay said. "Look."

The flashlight had found a waft of steam, motes of moisture catching the light.

"I'll be damned, there's a hole in the wall."

They were quickly able to determine that the "hole in the wall" was a previously sealed access to the city steam pipes that delivered heat to the building. A heavy, cast-iron coverplate had been removed, and the hot smell came from a leaky pipe vent.

A moment later the super gave a triumphant yell and the lights came on.

The sniper detail fanned out, searching through the scattered debris. "Nobody here, Detective."

All McRay could do was shake his head. Too much to hope for, that Marlon and his accomplice might leave Anna behind. The bastard had her, and he'd keep her so long as it was to his advantage.

"What do we do now, sir?"

"We follow him," McRay said, staring into the darkness of the underground access.

CHAPTER
TEN

She was at sea. Bobbing up and down in the dark, buffeted by waves. Night and the sea, that was her first impression. The next thing that floated into her mind was an awareness that she could not move. Her limbs were asleep, prickly and numb, and nothing worked. Gradually the dream of the sea melted away and Anna knew she was being carried.

Words fluttered, independent of meaning.

". . . blast the far fathometer . . . casing causes deeper carnivals . . ."

Nonsense phrases, bandersnatches, like something out of *Alice in Wonderland*. And then, gradually, her ears cleared and she could distinguish two men talking.

"Just do exactly what I tell you."

"But this is crazy. I can't see a damn thing."

"I know where we're going, that's all that matters."

Cody, that was one voice. The other was John Chester Marlon. Impossible, of course. Both men were in the Isolation Unit, participating in a controlled encounter. The laundry scenario. Cody was going to challenge Marlon, demonstrate the efficacy of the implant in a typical prison work environment. So this had to be a nightmare, she must be in her bed dreaming, which explained the numbness in her limbs and the weird hollow voices and the smell—

The smell?

The smell was distinct, and so strong it made her eyes water. The fetid, ammoniated stench of human waste. Splashing. She was being carried through a sewer.

She was underground.

Scream and you'll wake up, she told herself. Go on and do it. But when she tried to open her mouth the pain in her throat made it impossible to do anything more than whimper. The pain in her throat. Yes. The needle.

Now she really wanted to scream.

"What's that?" Cody said.

"Nothing. Keep moving."

"I heard her," Cody said. "She's choking."

There was a thudding noise, the grunt of a man losing his wind, and then Cody's voice, ragged and diminished, pleading: "Okay, okay, you don't have to hit me, I'm on your side."

Marlon laughed, and that's when Anna knew for sure it wasn't a dream. Not even the worst nightmare could summon laughter so hollow, so empty. So like the dead.

"Another hundred yards," Marlon said. "Keep moving."

Not a dream, no. She could feel the shape of him, the strength of him, as her body draped over his massive shoulders. Her legs were being gripped so hard that circulation had been cut off, it was needles and pins below her thighs. Her arms, though, her arms were free. If only she could make them work.

Concentrate.

She willed herself to focus on making her hands function. Count your fingers, Anna. You can feel them if you think about it. Ignore everything else, the numbness of your legs, the blood pounding in your head, the awful stink of the sewer, and concentrate on counting your fingers. One, two three. Yes, they twitched because you made them twitch. Keep going. Four, five. Okay, maybe not five, but who cares about your little finger? Go ahead, try making a fist. Harder, Anna, squeeze harder. Make a fist. A fist is a weapon.

Why hadn't the implant kicked in? Why was he not rendered unconscious? And how did Marlon know it wouldn't work? What was it they had noticed while monitoring the telemetry? Something. An important something. A misdiagnosis? Yes, that was it. But the thought skittered away, she couldn't hold it.

Never mind the "why" part now, let's stay focused on your hands. Your fingers, which can blind a man. Gouge out his eyes. Don't hesitate if you get the chance, you know what this man does to women. What he'll do to you. So go for his eyes—and you're going to have to do more than blind him. You'll have to kill him.

Kill him or he kills you.

Can you do it, Anna? Can you kill?

After a few minutes of unrelenting effort she was able to form both hands into fists, but there was no strength, no power. No matter how hard she tried she couldn't squeeze hard enough to feel her fingernails marking her skin.

Try harder.

Something changed. Now she was floating, head down in the dark. Cool breath on her face. Was it him, was it Marlon? Make your hands work, go for his eyes.

She fell. And falling, prayed that she would wake up.

Anna landed hard, a *womp!* of colliding flesh that knocked the air from her lungs, a sensation accompanied by a blaze of light. Blinding light.

"Home sweet home," said Marlon, his voice seeming to come from the source of light. "All the comforts."

Anna still could not breathe. Her mouth was working, trying to bite at the air, but her lungs no longer functioned. Somebody was making the most awful fish-out-of-water noises. Shut up, she wanted to say, shut up and let me die. Then air shot into her chest like a knife thrust and she was breathing again.

"There's something wrong with her."

That was Ned Cody's voice, coming out of the light. Light so bright it was a form of pain saturating her mind. She reached out, trying to touch the light, and something strong grabbed her by the wrists.

"That'll hold her."

Marlon's voice. She squinted, willing her eyes to focus, and gradually was able to discern shapes, and then human forms. She was lying on her back in a small area, not much more than a crawl space. An incandescent tube ran the length of a curved ceiling or roof. A vault. Marlon was standing over her, holding some sort of implement or tool, and she could make out Ned Cody's lean face, looking at her anxiously.

"Should I do her ankles?" Marlon was saying. "That is the question. Carry the creature or make her walk. You decide, Cody."

"Make her walk," said Cody.

Anna realized that her wrists had been bound with a strip of plastic. That was the tool Marlon had in his hands. She recalled that his last victims had been bound in just this way, with a plastic fastening device.

"Whahhh," she said, amazed at the voice that came out of her throat. A sound unrelated to what she had intended. Focusing on her throat, she became aware of a sharp pain just under her chin, in the softest part of her flesh. A needle, yes, he'd shoved the hypodermic into her throat, that explained the pain and also the surrounding numbness, her inability to speak.

"Imagine her surprise," Marlon said. "This must be quite a shock for Dr. Kane, waking up underground."

"They'll be after us," Cody said, glancing fearfully behind him.

"I sincerely hope so," Marlon said.

Anna, lying more or less immobile, unable to communicate, suddenly realized why she was so weak. It was fear. She was paralyzed by fear.

CHAPTER
ELEVEN

A stink that made the eyes water, the throat itch, the belly tighten.

"We need gas masks," remarked a Kevlar-armored sniper, wedging himself into the partially obstructed tunnel opening occupied by McRay. The detective, struggling to find access around closely fitted steam pipes, agreed with the assessment: the air was putrid, possibly dangerous.

"No time," he said, and found himself coughing. When he'd recovered, McRay gestured for the sniper and his men to get on with it. "Let's go. He's getting away."

"Hey, excuse me, Detective, but I gotta think about the well-being of my men, here. They're not equipped for this."

McRay turned back, aimed the borrowed flashlight at the young man. "What's your name?" he said.

"Crowell, sir."

"Mr. Crowell, you're a security guard, do your duty. Get into that tunnel."

Crowell squinted, his nose scrunched up against the stench, and shook his head. "We could get sued," he said. "Injury sustained without proper equipment."

"Goddamnit," McRay said.

"Plus I heard of guys getting asphyxiated by sewer gas."

"You're refusing to pursue a convict who has taken a hostage?" the detective asked, incredulous.

"All I'm saying, we need the proper equipment. Bottom line, we're not police. We're a civilian detail. This is a city cop kind of deal developing here."

McRay tried to reason with the squad leader, but it quickly became obvious that he could not prevail, and there was no time to waste arguing with the young blockhead. "Look," said McRay. "At least wait here for the cops. Can you do that?"

"Sure."

"I'll need a gun. You idiots took mine at the checkpoint."

"No way. You know the kind of paperwork we'll have to file?"

"Get me a fucking gun, damn it!"

In the end he had to wait until someone fetched his service revolver and holster.

"Make sure they know I'm going on ahead," he said, clipping on the holster on his belt. "I don't want to get shot from behind, okay?"

"Gas gets bad, you won't feel a thing."

"Thanks," said McRay. "I feel much better."

He sucked in his gut, managed to get around the pipes, into a slightly less obstructed area. The tunnel access was some sort of conduit, he realized, maybe five feet in diameter, with steam pipes running in on either side. He ducked down, tried to jog along the center track, and instantly banged his head against a wire light fixture. Damn it, there was illumination available, but he didn't know how or where to activate it. No time to look for switches or fuse boxes. Best he could do: hunch over, keep his head down, and scuttle along as fast as possible.

I'm a cockroach, McRay thought, what was that story about the guy who turns into a cockroach? Another thought: how fast can Marlon move, carrying a hostage, accompanied by another convict? He had, at most, a ten-minute head start. Couldn't be far along.

McRay picked up his pace, adapting to the constriction. Kind of a skittering, hippety-hop way of moving, he could almost anticipate where each wire-caged light fixture protruded from the low ceiling.

Move it, duck, move it, duck, move it.

In another part of his mind, a long and silent scream: *He has Anna. The crazy, sick bastard has Anna.*

He was just getting up to speed when the conduit came to an abrupt end.

"Ah, shit!"

Pipes intersected into the main steam pipe, a mother lode of heat that seemed to glow under the flashlight beam. Had he taken a wrong turn somewhere? But there had been no turns or intersections, the conduit ran in a long straight shot.

The smell. What was it about the smell?

Right, the sewer. Why would a steam heat conduit stink of the sewer?

McRay turned himself around, headed back. He'd missed something. A connection. There had to be a connection.

He had retraced his path about two-thirds of the way along the steam conduit when he was alerted by a waft of hot air, stirring the hair plastered to the back of his neck.

Hot air rising.

He aimed the flashlight beam, found the overhead tunnel where it intersected with the roof of the conduit. Damn, how had he missed it? And yes, despite the outflow of heated air, the sewer stench was particularly strong. McRay reached up into the round opening, found a handhold. After jamming the precious flashlight under his belt he grunted, oofed himself up, heaving and kicking until he was on the next level, gasping for breath in the bad air.

A quick reconnoiter told the story. Lying under the flashlight beam was an iron ladder, pulled up and cast aside as Marlon fled. This was a chamber, a connection between two separate underground systems. Was it on the maps, McRay wondered, or was this one of the city engineer's secret pathways?

Before preceding he had the presence of mind to set the ladder down into the steam conduit, in hopes that whoever followed would get the message.

The light caught the metallic edge of an open door. A chamber door unsealed, left conveniently open.

As McRay approached the opening he couldn't help but cringe. What if Marlon was waiting on the other side, setting a trap?

The detective unholstered his service revolver, regretting that he hadn't traded in the old model .38 for the newer, faster 9-mil semi-auto the street cops favored. Empty the magazine in a few seconds, if necessary.

Except for Anna. Marlon was counting on that, using his hostage as a human shield, and he was right. McRay wasn't much of a marksman, he couldn't risk a quick shot, and so he lowered the revolver as he edged through the chamber opening, swinging the flashlight beam. Found another, narrower chamber massed with iron pipes passing overhead.

One of the larger pipes was leaking at the joint, a steady, noxious drip. Sewer pipes, he surmised, carrying waste from the highrises into the sealed effluent pipes, which in turn flowed, eventually, into the sewage treatment system What was it, more than a billion gallons of "black water" per day? And how many uncounted gallons leaking into the infamous Manhattan schist, saturating the porous bedrock of the island?

That leaky pipe, was it the source of all this bad air? Didn't seem possible. Had to be an open vent or pipe, or a leak into the storm drain system.

Storm drain. The idea passed through him like an electrical current. *Marlon was fleeing via the storm drain system, just under the city streets.* McRay had been in that very system earlier in the day, and knew that even with the water flow underfoot, it was still easier to make headway than in these enclosed passageways, crammed with pipes and conduits. Marlon would want to cover ground; he would take the fastest route possible. He had found an opening. That would explain the stench, the wafts of rising air. But how did he get from this chamber to the storm drains? Where was the connection?

Hold your breath, McRay told himself, listen. He forced himself to stop, really concentrate on what he could hear and feel. The steady drip of the leaky pipe, ignore that. A low, constant vibration that seemed to have no point of origin. Electrical transformers, perhaps, or maybe it was the vibration of the city itself, of life burrowing down into the island. Block it out. Listen to the air, feel it move.

This way. McRay glided into the darkness, not using the flashlight because the instinct was to follow the path of illumination. Moving easily, almost languidly—was this how Marlon moved through his underground kingdom? Alive in the darkness, sensitive to every current, in his blood the pulse of subway lines, rumbling trains, surface traffic? Yes, this was how he did it, how he became invisible, a force of nature spiriting away his human trophies.

Anna.

McRay felt it then. A change in the current. Without breathing he switched on the flashlight, allowed the beam to play through the bundle of iron pipes. The piece of torn clothing jumped out, vibrant. Her blouse, wasn't that the color of her blouse? Kind of a muted green, the shade of weathered bronze?

He ducked under the pipes, duckwalked to where the scrap of material had caught against a bolt head. Now he wasn't so sure, maybe it was the artificial light, tricking his eye. Just a piece of cloth, it didn't mean anything.

McRay coughed into his fist, and that's when he heard it. An echo. He stood up on the other side of the pipes, a few yards from where he'd spotted the piece of cloth, and realized that he was at the bottom of an overhead passageway. Welded to the cylindrical wall were ladder rungs, a way up.

Looking up, he saw a faint light. Daylight.

He began to climb.

CHAPTER
TWELVE

Anna's head was starting to clear as the powerful tranquilizer wore off. Which made the situation worse—there was no pretending this was a nightmare. This was as real as the stench of sewer gases, and it was all her fault. Everything she thought she knew about John Chester Marlon was wrong. How was that possible? Was there an inherent flaw in the implant, or, as Kevin McRay had suspected, was Marlon a new kind of killer, a form never before identified?

"Don't fall down," Marlon said, his mouth only inches from her ear. "Fall down and we'll have to drag you."

Although he'd left her ankles unfettered, her wrists were wired together by a plastic binding strap. Given time and the opportunity, she might fray it against a rough surface, but there was no time, no opportunity to work herself loose. Not now, not yet.

Ned Cody was in front of her, aiming a flashlight along the narrow, fetid tunnel. Marlon, who'd donned a miner's-style hard hat, with lantern affixed, was right behind her. That light blazed like a centaur's eye, making it difficult to look at him—maybe that was the idea.

If she paused for so much as a heartbeat he shoved her along, not roughly, but firmly.

At first she'd hardly been able to walk, having lost one of her shoes.

Then Marlon had reached into a dark corner, withdrawing a pair of black rubber boots. His eyes glinting with amusement as she struggled to put them on, not having free use of her hands. Finally Cody had been ordered to help her, and as he knelt and slipped the boots on her, the actor made eye contact. Some message there, as if he wanted her to know he was on her side. But if that was true, what was he doing here, helping Marlon escape into these stinking tunnels?

Anna sloshed along, hardly able to focus because of the bobbing flashlight, trying to concentrate on keeping her balance because she did not want to fall into the ankle-deep water. Not with Marlon looming behind her, willing her to fail.

The aftereffects of the tranquilizer gave her thoughts a fuzzy quality, but the serial killer remained in sharp focus, even when she couldn't see him.

"Another hundred yards," he said, his tone almost conversational, as if they were out for a friendly stroll. "Then we'll take a little break, see if we can flush out your boyfriend."

Her throat hurt, the deep swelling left by the syringe felt like a wound, but it seemed important to make him understand that she and Kevin McRay were not romantically involved, and she was able to form a couple of words: "Not boyfriend."

Marlon laughed. "Not consummated, you mean?" The laughter sounded genuine, as if he really was amused by her denial. "You hear that, Ned? There's hope for you yet."

"Rats," said Ned Cody.

"Don't be rude, Ned, I'm just trying to help," said Marlon. "Playing Cupid."

"Rats," Cody insisted. "Small red eyes. I can see the little bastards. They're waiting for us up ahead."

"Keep going," said Marlon.

"But the rats!"

"A rodent will keep its distance from a human being, if you give it the chance. Keep moving."

Cody kept moving. Anna purposely did not look at the red eyes of the retreating rats. Think too much about the small terror of sewer-dwelling rodents, there wasn't room to think. And she had to think. What was it she knew about Marlon? What had they been discussing, there in the observation room, when he made his move? Was there something, anything she could use against him, a way to trigger the implant?

Behind her, his voice pitched to a lover's croon, Marlon said, "I know what you're thinking, Dr. Kane. That magnificent brain of yours is attempting to suss me out. A waste of energy, my dear. I am unique. Your implant failed because I willed it so."

A bone-cold tremor passed through her. How had he known? Was her thought process really so transparent to this man? Then irrational, instinctive fear bumped up against her fundamental understanding of the scientific process, and she recovered some of her composure. Marlon was not telepathic. Whatever elements of information might or might not be transmitted by what the kooks called ESP, no one could actually read thoughts. Marlon was playing a mind game, a confidence trick not unlike fortune telling. Of *course* she was trying to figure him out, she was a psychiatrist trained in the modification of criminal behavior, anybody who knew that could "read" her thought process, given the circumstance, as Marlon had done.

But what about willing the implant to fail? Was that possible? Did he really have such remarkable control over his involuntary nervous system? Or was there some other, simpler explanation for why the implant had not kicked in when he seized her? The answer was there, floating just beyond where she could grasp it. Her mind lunged, the answer skittered away.

It wasn't just the tranquilizer that made it hard to think clearly. It was impossible to concentrate with his physical presence so claustrophobically close, as overpowering as a bad smell.

"You're in denial," Marlon said, using his intimate, lover's voice. "You've convinced there's a rational explanation because that's what you've been trained to believe. But the answer is this: there is no answer."

There was a splash and then the flashlight went out. The snaky beam of Marlon's helmet lantern settled on the form of Cody, where he'd fallen in the tunnel. Struggling to keep his face out of the noxious water, he was soaked from head to toe. Cursing bitterly as he tried to wipe his eyes on his sleeve, making matters worse.

"This stuff'll blind me," he complained, splashing around. "Oh god, I hate this. I really, really hate it."

"Stand up."

"I keep slipping."

"There's a dry tunnel ahead, once we clear the system."

"Clear the system?"

"You'll see," Marlon said.

* * *

Storm drains. It made sense, McRay decided. The system of storm drains went everywhere in Manhattan and it was just below street level, so Marlon could escape upward, out of the underground, anytime he chose. And you could move relatively quickly through the drains; there were no pipes or raceways clogging up the tunnels.

No doubt Marlon knew this system like the back of his hand. All the points where storm drains intersected with other conduits and tunnels. The good news was that existing maps to this particular area were fairly complete and accurate. The bad news was that McRay didn't have the maps with him, of course, and he was just blindly following a trail. A trail that was starting to seem almost deliberately marked. Ladders handily left in place, scraps of cloth, indications of recent passage. As if Marlon were taunting him, daring him to follow. *Come and get me, copper.*

But he was too smart, too cunning for that kind of macho daring, wasn't he?

Maybe not.

Despite his much vaunted intelligence, Marlon had shot a guard knowing he was on camera, with no hope of escape. That was indisputable, whatever his motivation. Was he acting on impulse again? Did he want to confront McRay, a man-to-man kind of thing? Or was it—and this made the detective very, very cautious—a trap?

Getting ambushed by John Chester Marlon on his own territory, that was the ultimate nightmare. No, not quite. Getting shot in the spine with your own gun by a grinning psychopath, *that* would be worse. And that, McRay feared, would be the inevitable consequence of an ambush.

The detective stopped to catch his breath, used the pause to check his sidearm. Wishing once more that he'd opted for the magazine-loaded 9-mil semi-automatic instead of the manual .38 revolver. He'd never bothered to carry a speed-loader, like the TV cops always had conveniently along, nor did he have any extra bullets. He figured his accurate range to be twenty feet or less. Be honest, more like fifteen. Beyond that it was iffy—no way could he take the chance if Anna was in the line of fire. For that you needed a sniper, and even snipers sometimes missed, or hit the wrong target. Officers wounding each other, or innocent civilians, it happened all the time. Not to mention the danger of ricochet, in an environment like this.

You're getting spooked, McRay told himself. Keep moving or you'll find a reason to quit. He waded through the ankle-deep sewer water, wishing in vain for the rubber boots he'd left in the trunk of his car. Or, for that matter, the respirator; it would help filter out the heady, suffocating stench of sewer gases.

Sewer gases.

Wait a minute, this was the storm drain system, not the sewer tunnels. Why, then, the unmistakable smell of sewer gases? In torrential rainstorms the treatment plants overflowed into the storm drain system, but there had been no torrential rains lately.

Something was wrong. Raw sewage was leaking into these drains. Think about it, Kev. Concentrate. What do you know about the intersections of these two systems? You've studied the maps, waded though miles of tunnels much like this one. Was the leakage between the systems a coincidence, or did it have a bearing on Marlon's escape plans?

Think.

Damn. Hard to concentrate when the gases made your eyes water, your throat itch. Never mind the constant fear that a genius-level psychopath was leading him on, setting him up.

Think. Lower Manhattan, the Battery. Sewer systems, storm drains. Repair projects? New construction? What was going on underground in this particular district, something that Marlon could use to his advantage?

Or was he going completely nuts here, trying to read sewer water like tea leaves, as if it had to have some particular meaning? Get on with it, man, keep moving, they can't be too far ahead. You've got a gun, he doesn't. A tunnel is just another form of enclosed wall. Would your nerves be this raw if you were pursuing an unarmed man through an ordinary building? What does it really matter if this happens to be a few yards below street level?

He's not even in sight and he's psyching you out, making your spine tingle with the fear of a bullet when he doesn't even have a firearm. Amazing how that son of a bitch gets in your head, messes you up.

Don't think about it, just keep moving. He's running away, he can't hurt you. Hell, he's probably more scared of you than you are of him.

McRay tried to believe that, but it was difficult, very difficult.

Obey the light.

The beam of Marlon's miner's light painted the rungs of a ladder.

Anna knew without being told that she was being ordered to climb the ladder. But how could she climb the damn thing if she couldn't grasp the rungs?

The answer was simple, and terrifying. Marlon gripped her firmly by the hips and lifted her as her feet kicked, blindly seeking the rungs. Surprising, the touch of his strong hands was not sexual. He was not copping a feel, it was an impersonal grip, as if she were an object that need to be moved. And that, come to think of it, was as frightening as the idea of sexual intrusion. What did it mean to be an object in Marlon's world, a thing to be transported?

"Rest here a minute," he said. "And, Dr. Kane? If you want to live, don't even think about dropping back down the ladder into the tunnel. In about thirty seconds it'll be flooded."

Anna felt ashamed. She hadn't even been thinking about attempting escape from this particular spot. How could she get back down the ladder when her hands weren't functioning?

Marlon moved away, became a shape against the light. "Cody, dry your hands on this rag."

"What rag?"

"The one I'm handing you," he said, as if instructing a small boy. "Stop asking questions, Ned, just do as I say. Grip this wheel."

"I'm too weak," the actor complained, making a face. "I can't get a grip."

Anna had the distinct impression that he was putting on an act, assuming a pose. Playing weaker than he really was. Could that work to his advantage?

Not with Marlon pushing, pushing.

"How long can you hold your breath underwater, Cody?"

"Okay," said Cody. "Anything you say."

Anna heard the actor groaning with effort. A valve squeaked and Marlon shifted against the light, grunting with satisfaction. There was a rush of air, followed by a loud gurgle of liquid. The gurgle rapidly changed into a roar and suddenly the sewer gases became not merely an irritant, but overpowering.

She was choking, trying not to take a breath, when Marlon grabbed her bound wrists and pulled her through a small passageway.

"Seal it!" he screamed, making himself heard above the torrent of rushing water.

Anna tripped and fell to her knees. It was dry here and the air, although dense, was not poisonous. Behind her, Marlon and Cody struggled to swing shut a heavy steel door. The effort seemed endless, but at last the door clanged into place and the noise was much diminished.

Marlon directed his miner's light into Anna's eyes, blinding her. "That'll take care of any rats in the tunnels," he said pleasantly. "Human and otherwise."

McRay felt it before he heard it. A distinct vibration underfoot. He aimed the flashlight at the flow of ankle-deep water and saw that the surface was roiled; the vibration had been imparted to the liquid, breaking the surface tension.

What the hell was going on? Something was happening. Was it a train going through somewhere below? Shock waves from a distant explosion?

And then the air began to move. At first it felt like a mild breeze, and then his hair lifted and his damp clothing began to flap and he was leaning into a gale, thinking: what happens now?

McRay never heard the onrush of liquid that filled the storm drain, but he saw it a heartbeat before it engulfed him. A dark, shimmering wave racing his way so fast he could not even turn and run, not that running would have done any good.

He lost the flashlight in the first torrent, surrendering it to a black tidal rip that was instantly up to his neck, lifting him away like a piece of flotsam, like the bundle of bones and flesh he'd recovered that very morning.

He had time for one gulp of air, and then his forehead slammed into the top of the tunnel and he was turning, rolling head over heels, his hands reaching out. Trying to get a grip on something, anything. Trying to live without air or light.

No thoughts now, nothing in his mind but the lack of air, and the terrible wanting.

CHAPTER THIRTEEN

They crawled for a mile. Ned Cody ahead, muttering to himself, Anna close behind, shoving along on raw knees and the palms of her bound hands, and Marlon with his miner's light bringing up the rear, filling the small conduit with his overwhelming presence.

"The discomfort will pass," he said when Cody lodged a complaint. "The beauty of the human mind is how quickly it forgets pain."

"I'm not feeling this in my mind," Cody responded.

"Consider the alternative," Marlon pointed out, and the actor fell silent.

About halfway into the long crawl Anna was doing just that, considering the alternative. It now seemed clear that Marlon was successfully eluding any pursuit, and that he had some use in mind for her, other than as a mere hostage. What that use might be she did not allow herself to imagine, other to conclude that death would be a preferable alternative.

Better to die here, on her hands and knees, than as a toy in Marlon's Doll House. And yet, her mind having arrived at that conclusion, her heart continued to beat, her lungs kept drawing air, and her hands and knees kept crawling.

"You're thinking bad thoughts," said Marlon in a conversational tone. "Contemplating self-destruction."

Anna did not respond. Why give him the satisfaction? If you didn't respond he couldn't play his nasty little mind game.

"Someone you know committed suicide, Anna. I feel that in my bones. I see it in your eyes. The painful memory. That's why you became a psychiatrist, because you want to understand. That's the classic motivation for a career in psychology, by the way. Curing the neurotic parent. Except in your case the parent wasn't merely neurotic, was he? Was he, Anna?"

From up ahead Cody said, "Leave her alone."

Marlon chuckled. "Another country heard from," he said, "and another career motivation. Except you're not just another neurotic actor, you're an actual woman killer. What was she, Ned, a critic? I don't suppose you can really blame an actor for throttling a critic. I'm surprised, frankly, that it doesn't happen more often. 'Ned Cody fails utterly in the supportive role of lover and friend.' And so you strangled the bitch."

Now it was Anna's turn to say, "Leave him alone."

Marlon was delighted. "Hear that, Ned? The doctor cares, she really cares. Maybe she loves you, Ned. That would be fun. She loves you, she loves you not. You kill her, you kill her not."

He made murder sound as easy as reciting a child's nursery rhyme, a whimsical thing. That's when Anna decided that an easy death was no longer an alternative. She would fight the son of a bitch. She would not go willingly, she would bite, scratch, claw out his eyes, fight him as long as she could draw breath.

Whatever happened, she would not end up in a wheelchair, blind to the world, trapped inside her own mind.

The Good Samaritan paused at the corner of Wall Street and Broadway. He was thinking about sushi, the simply divine California roll they served at the Kabuki. All those stressed-out brokers looking for quick protein, getting high on the rice wine and fingering their platinum Rolex watches. Oh, yes, a working boy could eat his sushi and play the market, too.

"Help."

The Good Samaritan tried to shake it off. Ghostly voice calling for help, it was some kind of auditory hallucination. A departed friend—he had lots of those now, and he wasn't in the mood for beseeching, otherworldly visits. So ignore the poor soul and walk on.

"Please help."

The ghost-voice was so faint it seemed to be emanating from the sidewalk under his feet. The Good Samaritan executed a slow three-sixty, maintaining a casual attitude, just to see if anybody was checking him out. Allen Funt with his candid camera, Geraldo working the street, that sort of thing.

The voice called again, this time more distinctly. "Down," it said. "Look down."

The Good Samaritan looked down. He saw nothing. Just sidewalk, street, gutter. A storm drain grate.

Something crawling along the grate. Ugh! A small pale thing, a worm. No, it wasn't a worm, it was a finger.

"Help."

The Good Samaritan knelt by the grate. The finger was alive and it was connected, under the grate, to a hand. Another hand, so black and grimy it blended into the filth of the gutter, clutched at the bars of the grate. A powerful, noxious odor emanated from the storm drain.

"I'm a cop," the ghost said, panting with effort. "I need help."

That's when the Good Samaritan saw the eyes. Brown eyes blinking between the grates. Eyes imploring him to help. Handsome eyes.

"Oh you poor baby," said the Good Samaritan, reaching out to take the trembling hand that reached up through the bars. "Did someone throw you away?"

DAY
5

Limbo

CHAPTER
ONE

The patient would not remain in bed. He kept throwing back the covers and pacing around the room with a telephone receiver clamped to his ear. Oblivious to the fact that his bare buttocks were flashing under his thin green hospital night gown. A female nurse watched him from the doorway, her expression somewhere between bemusement and concern.

"Goddamnit, the lines are still jammed," he said, banging on the receiver. "What the hell kind of hospital is this, you can't make a simple phone call?"

"This is St. Vincent's, Mr. McRay, in the Village. Would you please return to the bed, or at least sit down? You're gonna get 'scoped in about a half hour, the pulmonologist ever gets here."

"Scoped?" McRay demanded. "What the hell is 'scoped'?"

"Endoscopy. To check out your lungs. See if there's any fluid retention or inflammation."

"My lungs are fine. What I want right now is for somebody to connect me with Midtown South, 239–9811, is that so hard? Call a cop, goddamnit! I don't care what precinct. You got a cop in this hospital, right? Well, get him up here!"

A figure came into the room, coughed into his fist. "Hey," he said. "You're kinda cute like that, with your butt hanging out."

"Len! Jesus!"

Detective Leonard Jakowski jerked his thumb at the nurse. "Police business, could we have a little privacy? Thank you, dear."

"I'm not a 'dear,' " said the nurse, backing out of the room.

Jakowski plopped down on the empty bed and lay back, hands behind his head. "Not bad," he said. "I could do with a couple days kicking back. Getting my weenie washed by Nurse Ratchet there."

"Come on, Len, I'm dying here. What's going on? Who's in charge?"

Jakowski cranked himself up on one elbow and feigned a yawn. "Our intrepid captain of detectives, Michael Francis Harnett himself, has organized a search party. Several search parties. They got uniforms in every subway station on the island. Also the connecting stations, Brooklyn and Queens, make sure he doesn't leak into the boroughs."

McRay sat down, tried to cover himself with the wispy hospital gown. "Nuts," he said. "He won't be in the subway tunnels. Too many people, too much activity."

Jakowski nodded. "I believe the idea is to protect civilians. Or look like we're protecting civilians. In other words, it's ass cover time. Which is more than you can manage at the moment."

"Please, Len."

Jakowski sighed, kicked himself up from the bed. "I know, I know. You've had quite a time. Drowned like a rat in the sewer."

"I grabbed hold of a grate and held on. This guy pulled me out."

Jakowski snorted. " 'This guy'? A well-known fruit, trolls Wall Street for gay brokers. Been busted for soliciting like ten times."

"Yeah? Well, he saved my life, maybe I'll give him a kiss."

"Bet he'd love to see you now."

"They won't give me back my pants."

"Can you blame them?"

"Len, please. He's got her down there, okay?"

"Ah," said Jakowski. "You're worried about the girl."

"Dr. Kane."

"The girl doctor. The lady shrink. Pardon me for saying so, but isn't this all her fault?"

Jakowski saw McRay's face draining white and knew he'd said the wrong thing.

"Get me a pair of pants, Len. Right now."

"Sure, Kev, anything you want."

* * *

By the time McRay got to the precinct house on West 35th Street, he figured almost twenty hours had passed since Marlon had staged his escape. McRay had been in St. Vincent's overnight, so doped up he thought he was dreaming, and hadn't really come out of it until dawn.

Twenty hours was a lifetime. Marlon could be anywhere. Anna might be alive, she might be dead, and the uncertainty gnawed at him, made him crazy. The Doll House. The psycho son of a bitch was heading for his own personal mortuary. Somewhere down there in ten thousand miles of conduits and sewers and storm drains, and that didn't even count the hundreds of miles of subway and pedestrian tunnels. It was a needle in the haystack situation, except that if you found it, the needle might kill you.

He never made it past Lois Curley, the day-shift desk sergeant who ran the precinct house like a personal fiefdom, maintaining strict order and access.

"Good morning, Detective," she said, holding up her hand to stop him as he headed for Harnett's office. "What can I do you for?"

"I need to see the captain."

"Would you care to make an appointment? Captain Harnett has a full schedule."

"Damn it, Lois, this is my guy got loose. I have to be in on it. Plus I've got all the maps. Most of the maps."

"I wouldn't know about that. But tell you what, Detective, the captain is setting up a command and control facility at Penn Station, coordinating with the Transit Police. You happen to bump into him over there, maybe he'll want to know about those maps."

"Thanks, Lois, you're a doll."

"I'm not a 'doll,'" said Lois primly. "'Specially not today."

Penn Station was not McRay's favorite location in the city. Not since they tore down the grand old original, with its spiderwebs of iron elevating acres of airy glass and light. For what? A bland monstrosity that had about as much charm as a midwestern bus station, all of its dirty drabness propping up the cheesy cakebox of the new Madison Square Garden. They'd tried to blow up the World Trade Center and the UN, how come nobody ever tried to blow up Penn Station? Weren't there any terrorists out there who wanted to target the banal evil of urban renewal?

By the time he located Captain Michael Harnett and his staff of snuffling sycophants, McRay had worked himself up into an ugly mood. As usual the captain was surrounded by a protective corps of detectives who'd made careers of ass-smooching and yes-sirring, in McRay's opinion, and he was feeling very opinionated at the moment.

"Well, well, if it isn't the Special Task Force," said Detective Slury, one of the biggest ass-kissers. "How you doin', Kevin, laddy?"

"I've been better," said McRay. "Tell the captain I gotta see him."

"The Cap ain't available."

"I can see him right over there, big as life."

"Thing of it is, Kev, he's real, real busy."

McRay shrugged and started to back away. When Detective Slury's attention shifted elsewhere, he feinted through the crowd of blue uniforms and elbowed his way to where Captain Harnett stood, conferring with his opposite number on the Transit Police.

"Captain! Sir! I'm Detective McRay, sir!"

The captain glanced at McRay. His cool gray eyes flicked elsewhere, dismissing him.

"Captain Harnett, sir, he's not in the subway tunnels. He's in the unmapped region, I'm sure of it."

"Detective Whoever-you-are, I'm talking here. Go tell it to your lieutenant."

"I can't do that, sir," McRay said.

Michael Harnett, a big, broad-shouldered man in a custom-tailored uniform, had himself a hundred-dollar haircut and the jaw of a Tammany ward boss. It was Harnett who'd first assigned McRay to the Special Task Force. Undoubtedly he'd forgotten all about it, McRay decided, determined to hold his ground. On that score he was wrong, the captain did remember him, sort of.

"You're the guy," Harnett said, his voice losing some of its boom. "McCarty, right? Used to work the subway, that's why we put you on the STF, that bastard Marlon."

"That's me," he said. "Except it's McRay, Detective Kevin McRay. I was there when he escaped, sir, when he grabbed his hostage. I followed him into the storm drains and walked into a booby trap."

Harnett was focusing on him now, and he nodded thoughtfully. "I heard about that. You almost drowned."

"I'm okay, sir. And I've got the maps."

Harnett's big jaw dropped, exposing teeth the color of old ivory. "What? The maps he stole? Where the hell'd you find 'em, Detective?"

"Uhm, no, sir, not the maps he stole. The maps he didn't steal. But that gives us a pretty good idea of his area of interest. I'd like to suggest, sir, that you focus the search parties in those areas where we *don't* have maps. That's where he's gone, sir, I'm sure of it."

"You're sure of it."

"My best guess, sir."

"There's a difference, being sure and your best guess. Which is it?"

McRay took a deep breath. "I just don't think he'd go into the subway system. Too dangerous for him, too many people, too many police. He's smart enough to anticipate that most of the officers would be deployed where civilians are in danger."

"I see," said Harnett. His eyes had the warmth and texture of stones unearthed in the Arctic permafrost, and McRay knew right then he wasn't persuaded. "You think this nut is smarter than we are," said Harnett.

"I didn't say that."

The captain's blunt forefinger found the soft spot in McRay's chest. He prodded. "Your assignment, as I recall, was to find where he hid the bodies, is that correct?"

"That's correct."

"And you haven't found it yet, correct?"

"Correct."

"Detective, I have a small piece of advice, and you'd do well to follow it. Here it is. You do your job and I'll do mine. Is that clear?"

"Very clear, sir."

McRay backed away before Harnett could add anything more, or reassign him to the South Bronx.

As it was, he'd been ordered to do his job. And the last time he checked his job description, the primary objective was to locate the Doll House. Where, presumably, Marlon would eventually be heading.

Find the Doll House.

That was exactly what he intended to do, with or without the assistance of Captain Michael Francis Harnett, or the Bureau of Detectives, or the Transit Police.

If anybody asked, he'd say he was following orders.

CHAPTER TWO

They were eating airline food, and considering that she was starved to the point of shivering, it wasn't bad, not bad at all.

"Fly the friendly skies," Marlon had said, handing round the sealed food trays. "Fell off a truck, as the saying goes."

The weird thing was, he had a small freezer down here, a microwave, a cache of canned goods, bottled spring water, all the comforts of a well-stocked bomb shelter. It was not, of course, a bomb shelter, but an area that had been sealed off and forgotten after a water project was abandoned in the 1940s. The concrete room was about fifteen feet square, and located directly over a pumping station, what Marlon insisted on calling a "regulator."

As they had crawled through the conduit, passing through and around other conduits and tunnels, Marlon had kept up a running commentary, describing the various systems: high-pressure steam lines, city gas, telephone and cable raceways, even the remains of an old system of pneumatic mail tubes, long since defunct.

He was especially proud of the water system.

"The high-pressure line is deep, carved right out of the bedrock. You . have two major tunnels bringing water from the aqueducts—more than a billion gallons per day, and that's barely enough to keep up with demand, so they're working on Tunnel Three. That'll be good through the next century, maybe longer. Greatest water system in the world, and that's no exaggeration."

"Yeah?" Cody said, feigning interest. The actor looked terrible, as if he'd aged ten years after that long crawl through the access conduit. His hair was filthy and his blue, matinee-idol eyes stared out of deep sockets.

Anna, exhausted to the point of passing out, had actually slept a little over the past few hours. Something about the low vibration of the regulator, the deep hum as high-pressure water was reduced to a level adequate for street mains. There was a sense of time standing still, as if they were lost between moments. Marlon seemed to be waiting for something—an event or a particular hour, it was impossible to say what motivated the man—and her mind had become almost numb to the idea of what he might do to her. Impossible to think about for long, her fear became a fist she kept clenched in the back of her mind.

"You want to see a crazy bunch of boys, go watch Local 147 getting ready for work in Tunnel Three," Marlon said, chatting brightly as he sipped from a paper cup of microwaved instant coffee. "Compressed Air and Free Air Tunnel Workers. Better known as the sandhogs. Down there a thousand feet, under so much pressure they have to decompress like deep sea divers. You heard about the guy got blown up through the river, Cody, you ever hear about that?"

"No," said Cody wearily. "I never heard about that."

"Years ago. They're drilling deep under the East River, suddenly there's a leak, air pressure escaping. This one guy grabs a sandbag, he's trying to plug up the leak, save the tunnel before the water rushes in. So he's standing there when it blows. He's driven up through the river bottom, through all that mud, and he's blasted up through the river itself."

"Poor bastard," said Cody.

"The point is, he survived."

"Impossible."

"It happened," Marlon said happily. "Miracles happen, children. Let us all keep that in mind."

After a while their captor seemed to become bored with shop talk, and the bantering and anecdotes ceased. His mood shifted, his face became impassive, his small eyes went still. When Ned Cody tried to engage him in conversation, Marlon shook his head and said, "Shut up. I'll only tell you once."

Cody shut up. Something about that voice, it made you want to curl up and be silent. In Marlon's proximity you were a rabbit sharing a cage with a python.

"Put your hands out."

"There's no need for that," Cody said, but he complied, and Marlon adroitly bound his wrists with the plastic binding device. Snap, snap, and it was done. Ned Cody seemed to shrink inside himself, lost in thought, waiting to see what Marlon would do next.

Anna, lulled by her exhaustion, and by the steady, low-impedance vibration of the water regulator, began to drift into a place that was almost, but not quite, sleep. The concrete under her back and buttocks softened, the air became viscous, and she was floating. The bunker dissolved and she was in a place so familiar that it could only be home. Shadows moved, the darkness shifted, and her young and beautiful mother seemed to be speaking directly into her mind with a silent urgency.

Hide, Anna, hide. He's coming back. He's coming back.

The insane man with the black gun. Poppa. Coming back. The nightmare she'd been having for years.

Little four-year-old Anna hiding in the cupboard. Her father raging through the house, threatening to kill them both. Her mother pleading with him. Daddy crying with his mad eyes. *We're all going to heaven. Annie, come on out, Annie.*

Anna startled herself awake, fought back the urge to scream. She would not—she would absolutely *not* allow that old dream to haunt her now, when she had a living, breathing nightmare to contend with.

What had brought her back, she realized, was Marlon moving around the chamber. He was pacing. Eyes focused in the middle distance, face expressionless. He walked back and forth, his long, muscular limbs functioning on automatic. Under the single overhead light his close-shaved skull looked as if it had been machined from blue steel.

He was, she realized with a start, lost in thought.

The idea—Marlon concentrating so hard he was unaware of his surroundings—made her feel as if she were about to fall from a high place. A vertigo that threatened to spiral into blind panic. She held her breath, closed her eyes, fought it. Do not surrender to panic. Keep it fisted, clenched away. The walls are not closing in, that's just fear taking your breath away.

Finally the flutter in her chest slowed and she was able to breathe again, slowly expelling air, and she felt strong enough to open her eyes.

Marlon was looking directly at her. Looking but not seeing. He stood there, aimed in her direction, for what seemed like several minutes. She dared not speak or move, for to do so might make him strike out of instinct. Then he suddenly came to life and he was, indeed, focused on her.

"Ah," he said, and raised both hands to caress his skull, and touch the bandage covering the implant on the back of his neck. "Did I tell you how thick the walls are? No? Thirty inches. Two and a half feet of reinforced concrete. So don't waste your energy screaming for help."

Cody, roused from depression, or the lethargy of constant anxiety (it was hard to know which), lifted his head and spoke. "Why would I try to escape?" he said. "I'm on your side."

"Are you indeed," Marlon said. "We'll see about that, but not right now."

"I'm on your side," Cody insisted. "I'm a killer, just like you. Please remove the cuffs," he said, raising his bound wrists.

Marlon unbolted the steel access door. "Patience," he said. "I'll come back for you," and stepped through the door, closing it behind him.

The both heard a bolt slip into place.

"God almighty," Cody whispered. "Gone at last. The answer to my prayers. I can't believe it."

"Sssh," Anna said.

They listened. Heard a furtive noise on the other side of the door. A kind of metallic rustling. Vaguely familiar, but maddening—what was it?

"What's he doing?"

The noise changed, became louder.

"Ah shit," Cody said.

"What?" Anna said. "What?"

"He's welding the door shut."

CHAPTER
THREE

"Listen up. Command just came down, nobody talks to the press regarding the Subway Killer manhunt. All inquiries referred to Captain Harnett."

Those were the first words McRay heard when he returned to the precinct house. The media was in full cry now, alerted to the escape by leaks from the Annex staff and the security guards. It was inevitable, of course. There was no way to contain a story like this, he'd seen the tabloids screaming from newsstands all over the city:

> MAD MARLON RUNS AMUCK!
> SUBWAY KILLER TAKES DOC HOSTAGE!
> PSYCHO ON THE LOOSE!

Surprisingly, there had been no discernible decline in subway riders. If anything the commuters seemed to feel safer with more officers present, and every available Transit policeman assigned to the trains. A spokesperson for the Guardian Angels had vowed that citizens' groups would "take back the tunnels," and Howard Stern had challenged the escaped serial killer to a game of "nude cereal wrestling," whatever that meant. Local news anchors reported live from a variety of subway stations, and in one instance from aboard an Eighth Avenue train, surrounded by curious riders.

It was not panic that gripped the city, but a keen desire to horn in on the publicity.

McRay, who had no desire to commune with the press, returned to his desk and immediately placed a call to sanitation worker Jefferson T. Roberge, via his pager. Ten minutes later the call was returned.

"Jeff, how'd you like to join the Special Task Force for a few days? I already cleared it with your super, so the option is up to you."

The exterminator's deep, throaty laughter tickled the ear. "Man, you got to be kidding. You asking do I want to help locate this crazy dude snatched your girlfriend, right? I saw it in the paper."

"She's not my girlfriend. But yes, that's about the size of it."

"Figure I know my way around the down under."

"Better than most, I'd say."

"You got that right," said Roberge. "Hell, a man'd be a fool to pass up a chance like this."

"And you're no fool."

"Now that's where you're wrong," said Roberge. "But this fool can use a vacation from rat catching. Catching a real human being, that might be an interesting change of pace."

"I'm starting to think he's not human," said McRay.

"Oh, he's human," said Roberge. "That's what makes him so scary."

McRay was taking a chance, interpreting the captain's order as permission to add a few men to the depleted ranks of the task force. His idea was to let the search parties continue to comb the more easily accessible subway tunnels while he and a few trusted associates concentrated on detective work, attempting to anticipate where Marlon might go.

A tall order, as Len Jakowski was quick to point out. He planted himself on the corner of McRay's desk, ran his hands through his thinning hair. "Okay, it makes sense to concentrate on the unmapped areas. But that still leaves, what, hundreds of miles of old tunnels and vaults?"

McRay shrugged. "At least. A lot of that is impassable, though. Too small, or caved in, or flooded."

"But we don't know which parts."

"That's what we have to determine, Len. The areas most likely. Remember he was snatching his victims from subway and pedestrian tunnels. So wherever the Doll House is, you can get there from the subway."

Jakowski was peering intently at an unfurled surveyor's map of Manhattan. "Maybe one of the abandoned stations," he suggested.

McRay shook his head. "We covered all of those," he said. "I went back to the original documents. Any project as big or politically important as a subway stop made it into the newspapers—he couldn't hide those by stealing the maps. All we found in the old stations were vagrant camps. What the Transit boys call 'mole people.'"

"No bodies?" Jakowski was skeptical.

"I didn't say that. But no remains of any of the suspected victims. And nothing like the kind of secret hideaway Marlon alluded to."

"The Doll House. You think he'll go back there. If it exists."

"I think he will. And I'm sure it exists."

Jakowski smiled, tapping the survey map. "What if you're wrong?"

"If I'm wrong we'll never find him. Or Dr. Kane."

"Or the other guy went along for the ride. The actor strangled his wife."

"Not his wife," said McRay. "His girlfriend."

"Yeah?" Jakowski got a kick out of that. "You seem real sensitive, this girlfriend issue. I heard you and the doctor had a date."

"Strictly business," McRay said, poking at the detective with his pencil. "Move over, Len, you're sitting on the Upper West Side."

Transit patrolman Michael Ditmar checked his flashlight. It was a regulation police-issue flashlight, capable of cracking heads as well as illuminating the dark, and felt reassuringly heavy. As if the beam of light itself afforded some protection.

In addition to his regular uniform, Ditmar had put on a pair of high leather work boots. The idea, rats nipping at his ankles. Not that a rat had ever nipped at his ankles. You made enough noise, the nasty rodents—some as big as cats—would mostly keep their distance. Still, you never knew. Some overgrown rat with a bad attitude might go nuts, try to gnaw a human.

The patrolman did not have a particular fear of rats, per se, he just hated the idea of getting bitten. Getting chomped by a vagrant or a drunk, that was even worse. Ask any doctor, the human bite was dangerous, and it wasn't only AIDS, there were all kinds of weird microbes, things you couldn't be inoculated against. So you kept your hands close to your body and you wore hard boots and you stayed alert.

Staying alert, that was the most important part.

Ditmar had been dispatched to the transfer station at Sixth Avenue and 14th Street. One of the busier stops in Lower Manhattan because you could connect to the IRT, the L to Canarsie, the IND, hell, even the PATH trains to Hoboken cut through here.

If some wacko with a bug in his brain wanted to go nuts, he could do worse than target the Six-Fourteen. Which was exactly why Patrolman Ditmar and fifteen more Transit cops of the same rank were checking out the connecting tunnels, making a show of force where it really counted. They all had pass keys and radios and they were fully armed and it was like, come on you crazy bastard, show yourself. Nail the Subway Killer, that was good for an instant promotion, maybe a guest spot on a network TV show, New York's finest.

Hey, Dave, love the new haircut, oh, and Jay says hello.

Fantasies to sustain an otherwise tedious shift. Because absolutely nothing was going on at the Six-Fourteen. No jumpers, no token suckers, no flashers, no feelers—it was like they'd passed out anti-crime pills. So far, he hadn't spotted so much as a panhandler. Some of it was visibility—all the uniforms flooding the system—and some of it was just luck. There were shifts when every dirtbag in New York wanted to pound on your head, and there were times when the city seemed to have been temporarily disinfected of crime.

Patrolman Ditmar lifted the radio from his belt, reported his position to the supervisor, who was situated near the token booths. "Anything out there?" he asked.

"Nothing doing," was the terse reply.

Ditmar switched off, left the radio on low volume, just in case there was action somewhere else.

"Excuse me, officer."

He turned, saw a big guy in transit worker overalls, scarf around his neck and a knitted skullcap like the brothers wore, except this was no brother. Oh well, to each his own. Guy must be a jazz lover.

"Yeah?" said Ditmar.

"Might be a situation, I dunno."

The patrolman came a little closer, looked the guy over. Vaguely familiar, but then you saw about a million mugs a day on the job, everybody was vaguely familiar. "What kinda situation?" Ditmar said loftily.

"I dunno, exactly. Maybe I'm wrong. It's just, you know, they said report anything out of the ordinary."

"Go on," said Ditmar.

"Busted door," said the big guy. "Musta happened the last hour."

Ditmar got on the radio and reported a broken door in the pedestrian tunnel between the Six-Fourteen and the stop at Seventh Avenue.

Get a visual, he was told.

"I gotta see it," he said.

The big guy shrugged. "Hey, it's probably nothin'."

"Yeah, well I still gotta see it."

"Follow me," the big guy said, turning his back.

Transit Patrolman Ditmar followed him into the tunnel.

CHAPTER
FOUR

"**T**hey took all that money and they threw it in the ground," said the exterminator.

"I get it," said Jakowski. "This is a treasure hunt."

"Millions and millions. The tunnel's still there. They built it out of the water, then sunk it into the East River. Supposed to connect up to the Second Avenue subway, that was the whole point, but they never found the money."

"Politics," McRay said. "The usual corruption."

"Oh, you got that right. Imagine, they go ahead and build the new tunnel, a billion dollars, and you know where it goes?"

"Nowhere," McRay said emphatically.

"It goes to Queens."

McRay shrugged, as if that proved his point. Nothing against the borough of Queens, but the tunnel, assembled and sunk in place in the 1970s, never got beyond the shore, never hooked up to the proposed expansion because the money was frittered away, gobbled up by corruption and general incompetence. A billion-dollar boondoggle, with portions of the never-completed system buried along Second Avenue, from the Battery all the way to the Bronx. Money thrown into the ground. Every now and then a politician made points by promising to finish the project, but so far it had never happened.

"Thieves," Jakowski said. "Gypsies got nothin' on the pols who run this city. They oughta change the Statue of Liberty, show the lady with her hand out for the envelope."

The three men were stuck in traffic, crawling up Third Avenue at about the pace set by a geriatric in a broken walker. Their destination was 48th Street, to check out an anomaly on the maps, an electrical sub-station that might or might not have been built for a crosstown subway line that never got beyond the planning stages. Ghosts on the blueprint.

"Show 'em your light," Jakowski suggested.

McRay sighed, placed the flashing light on the roof. A few more horns blared in response. The traffic, if anything, slowed. "Don't say it," said McRay.

"What? We shoulda took the subway? Hey, I wasn't gonna say it."

Twenty minutes later, after an excruciating interval of gridlock, they finally arrived. Roberge directed them to an airshaft vent on the corner of Second Avenue, where he opened up an equipment satchel, handing out hard hats and flashlights.

"You gotta be kidding," Jakowski said, stretching his pudgy legs, which had fallen asleep in the car, "an air vent?"

"It's the most direct access."

"I dunno, I'm starting to think I made a big mistake, signing up for this detail."

The descent was easy enough. A steel-runged ladder had been left behind, welded in place by the construction crew, and the shaft itself was quite large, designed to move huge volumes of air from the crosstown tunnel. Why the vent should have been finished before the tunnel was completed, nobody seemed to know. Ask about the famous subway expansion screw-up, all the money wasted, eyes tended to glaze over. I wouldn't know about that, the city bureaucrats kept saying, or: before my time, or: that was another department. It was simply too huge, too symptomatic of bad local government, to be acknowledged. And the evidence was buried all over the city.

"Smells like a fart," said Jakowski as he let himself gingerly down.

Roberge laughed. "Are you kidding? This is nothing. You oughta take a walk in the storm sewer, you think this is bad."

"No thanks. I'll leave that to Kevin, he's in training."

McRay ignored the banter. He crouched on the floor of the shaft, some thirty feet below street level, and spread out the survey map. "Most of this was never built," he said. "Marlon's office was supposed to update the construction survey, indicate any actual structures, and then make recommendations for maintenance."

"But he never did."

"Either that, or he destroyed the evidence. All we've got to go on is the log book, shows where city engineers were assigned on a given shift. So we know he made at least four trips to this area, supposedly to investigate leaks in the air shaft."

"What kind of leaks?" Roberge wanted to know. His deep voice boomed down the shaft, disturbing the pigeons that fluttered down through gaps in the grate, heading for white-stained perches.

"It didn't say," said McRay. "Just leaks."

"Could be air, could be water. Might be gas or steam."

"Terrific," said Jakowski. "We get boiled or blown up."

"There's no follow-up report," said McRay. "Standard procedure is, if there's a leak the appropriate utility is notified, and a report to that effect is written."

"So there weren't any leaks?"

"That's my theory," said McRay. "Marlon was just visiting, for purposes of his own."

"What about this electrical thing?"

"The substation," McRay corrected. "If it was actually built, it should be within fifty feet of where we're standing."

Locating the substation proved to be more difficult than any of them had anticipated. Because the construction had been abandoned before completion, the shaft and the adjacent structures did not comply with the blueprints, and none of the three men were expert enough to discern exactly what had been done, or what changes had been made, if any.

"I'm going nuts here," Jakowski complained. He had paused to light a cigarette and the flame kept going out because of gusts passing through the shaft. "What if it never got built at all? That's my vote—the fucking substation does not exist."

McRay didn't bother to respond. No point in arguing, but he wasn't quite ready to concede defeat. Roberge, for his part, had crawled along a raceway, reconnoitering behind the shaft. McRay could hear the exterminator whistling to himself, a habit he'd formed to ward off small four-legged creatures. The detective was on his knees, aiming a flashlight at the blueprints, trying to make some sense out of the construction details, when he noticed that the cheerful whistling had stopped.

"Jeff? Hey, Jeff!"

Jakowski sucked on his cigarette and shrugged, but his hand went to the 9-millimeter semiautomatic he kept in a holster at the small of his back. "Maybe he's catching his breath," he said.

McRay crouched by the raceway, a dark opening barely wide enough to accommodate a man. "Jeff! Can you hear me?" He heard nothing but the faint echo of his own voice.

"Ah shit," said Jakowski, stubbing out his cigarette. "We better call for backup. The captain is going to fry your ass, Kevin."

"Wait," said McRay.

He lay down, shoved head and shoulders through the opening. The air seemed thick and cloying, but that was probably his imagination, his own personal form of claustrophobia. Hard to breathe, though, the way the small opening constricted his chest. How the hell did Roberge do it, skinnying into places like this? He took a deep breath, called out, waited for a reply. Nothing. Silence.

Then something yanked at his ankle and in a moment of heart-tripping panic he kicked out.

"Hey!" Jakowski roared. "Take it easy! Come on out of there. He's here."

"Who?" McRay managed to say.

"Look for yourself."

He inched backward, turned his head to get himself clear, and emerged blinking into the dim shaft. A dirt-smudged Jeff Roberge was standing there grinning at him. "I found something," he said. "Way around on the other side."

"How'd you get out?" McRay wanted to know. "I thought the raceway had only the one exit."

"That's what it shows on the blues, man, but the situation is different, you get up inside. Somebody been fucking around in there."

Roberge led them to his discovery, a laddered shaft that was not indicated on the construction diagrams. "Only way you'd find this is by accident, crawling around," he said, his long, sinewy frame gliding easily down the rungs. Above him Jakowski panted, tried to keep his light focused. "It's behind a phony baffle. I missed it the first time I went by."

"Baffle?" McRay said. "What baffle?"

Below them Roberge chuckled. "Just follow me, guys, you gotta see it to believe it."

The shaft came to a dead end at the base of the air shaft. Barely room enough for the three of them to stand shoulder to shoulder at the bottom of the ladder. "What is this?" said Jakowski. "A rat catcher's idea of a joke?"

"Hey, Len," McRay said in a warning tone, but Roberge seemed to be amused.

"Suck up that gut, Jakowski," he said. "Squeeze on through."

Then Roberge disappeared.

"What the fuck?" said Jakowski. "Where'd he go?"

McRay leaned against the wall of the air shaft, patted it with his hands until he found an edge. "This way," he said, and then slipped into the narrow opening.

The passage was just wide enough to accommodate him, moving sideways. Beside him the more heavily built Jakowski cursed and grunted and threatened to back out. At that moment McRay popped through and was able to take a deep breath. A light shined in his face. Roberge.

"Pretty clever, huh?" he said. "That was covered by a baffle. Except there was no air moving through it, so I pulled the cover to check it out."

"You what?" Jakowski said, catching his breath.

"The man is a natural born detective," McRay explained.

"I just know there's a baffle, air should be moving," Roberge responded.

"What's that smell?" Jakowski said, sniffing noisily. "I know that smell."

"Cosmoline," McRay said.

He'd begun sweeping his light around the compartment. Stacked in the concrete enclosure were enough weapons to outfit a small militia. Among the booty was a crate of Tech-9's unopened, more than a dozen AK-47's still shrink-wrapped in plastic.

"Holy shit," said Jakowski, reaching for what looked like a shoulder-launch rocket tube.

"Hands off," McRay warned. "We're gonna call in a Crime Scene van, dust this place for prints."

"We did it," Jakowski said, his voice rising. "Son of a bitch!"

McRay was checking out the small arms, slick with Cosmoline, and the neatly stacked crates of ammunition, all of the common calibers and grains. There were boxes of .38 revolvers, the old police standard issue model, Uzis, Glock machine pistols, high-powered rifles, sniper scopes, and spare magazines for semi- and fully automatic models.

"This isn't the Doll House," he said.

"Then what is it?"

"A weapons cache. And my guess is he has others, scattered around the city."

"Yeah?" said Jakowski. "What did he have in mind, a war?"

"Something like that," McRay said. "John Chester Marlon against the world."

CHAPTER
FIVE

The uniform was a snug fit, tight in the thighs and across the shoulders, but he didn't mind. It was a hoot just to be masquerading as one of New York's finest. The uniform cap covered his shaved head and the collar did a pretty fair job of hiding the surgical implant. Not that anybody looked too close—no eye contact at all, he'd noticed that right away. Disguised as a patrolman he was free to stare at every passing citizen—they seemed to expect it—but so far no one had eyeballed him back. Glances just kept skittering away.

The one thing to avoid, another cop. Which was why he'd decided not to ride the trains. Trains were crawling with uniforms, he would be expected to respond, join in the cop talk, and while he was confident of his ability to parrot a policeman, it simply wasn't worth the risk of exposure. Better to stroll along at street level, free and at ease, as if he were walking a beat.

"Excuse me, officer, can you direct us to the Empire State Building?"

Marlon stared at the two obvious tourists. A small Chinese male and his even smaller Chinese wife. The wife standing a pace or two behind, clutching her purse, eyes downcast. Listening attentively as her noble husband proudly utilized his virtually accentless English.

"The what?" Marlon asked, just to hear it again.

"The Empire State Building." This time the man was slightly less confident, and his eyes flicked nervously to the guidebook he had in his hand.

"Oh," Marlon said, coughing into his fist. "Right. Empire State Building. Let me see, that would be the corner of Thirty-third and Fifth Avenue. Takes up the whole block. We're on Park, so you go that way two blocks—long blocks, okay?—and then you turn right and go five more blocks. Five more *short* blocks, got it?"

"Oh, yes, officer. Thank you. Thank you so very, very much."

Very, very much. Showing off his r's. And off they went like a couple of startled jackrabbits, tittering to themselves in a language that sounded like small church bells in collision with a flock of birds. Wouldn't it be a kick when they got back to Taiwan or wherever, told all their friends about the nice, ever-so-polite New York cop?

Marlon had thousands of such small, somehow significant memories stored for easy retrieval. He thought of them as flavors. Messing with the Chinese tourists was kind of a lemony tang. Welding the door shut on the shrink and her faithful sidekick, that had the sweet afterburn of a mouthful of raw honey.

Let them ripen for a while. He had places to go, promises to keep.

As a long-time Park Avenue super, Hector Rivera never opened the service door to strangers. You had to be careful, this city, where a guy looked like a well-dressed salesman might be casing a break-in or a rape. Let 'em state their business over the speaker, leave the bolt on. Cops were an exception. Cop at the door, you were obliged to at least open up—leaving the chain on, of course—and speak to the officer directly. Anything less, you risked aggravating a man who had the power to make your life miserable.

"Yes, officer, what can I do you for?" said Hector, wearing his deferential, cop-pleasing grin.

"You got a lady, Mrs. Westerbeek, up onna third floor?"

"Sure, Gladys. Something wrong with Gladys?" Hector asked, betraying no particular concern. Old Mrs. Westerbeek was, if the truth be known, a pain-in-the-ass tenant, always complaining.

The big cop sighed, consulted a notebook. "Yeah, well, she's got a complaint, I gotta see her what about."

Hector relaxed, but he didn't unclip the chain. "The best thing, officer, buzz her from the lobby."

"No response," the cop said with a grimace. "Maybe the intercom is out, I dunno, but she's up there 'cause we got the call."

Hector hesitated. "She say what the problem is?"

The cop shrugged. "That's privileged. She wants to tell you about it, fine, but I can't say."

"Right," said Hector.

"How about you escort me up there and stand by?"

"I'll call her," Hector said. "Make sure."

He started to close the door, looked down and saw the cop's massive hand blocking the jamb. The next thing he knew he was falling down as the door blew open, and the big cop was standing over him, shaking his head.

"You shoulda been nice," said the cop as he loomed closer.

Then those massive hands were squeezing the light from his eyes and his carotid artery was crushed and Hector was almost relieved when he lost consciousness a moment before his heart stopped beating.

Four minutes later Marlon was in the sub-basement of the old landmark apartment building. He had no interest in Mrs. Westerbeek, whoever she was, no interest at all.

CHAPTER
SIX

Five blocks south, and three blocks east, Len Jakowski was carefully examining an egg roll.

"Whataya think's inside this thing?" he asked.

"The usual," said Roberge.

"Yeah," McRay chimed in. "The usual unidentifiable items. Chop it up small enough, anything fits in an egg roll."

"Thanks," Jakowski said, taking a tentative bite. "You're a big help."

They were standing around on the corner of Second Avenue and 48th Street, waiting for the crime scene van. Jakowski, who never let an hour go by without eating if he could help it, had emerged from a Korean grocery with a couple of egg rolls and a big shiny apple. He'd tossed the apple to Roberge, with instructions to give it to his favorite teacher.

"Nothing for me?" McRay had asked, feigning innocence.

"I gave up buying for you, Kev. You're a food snob, and that's a terrible affliction for a cop."

"I just want things a certain way."

"Exactly my point."

The crime scene van arrived with the news that a uniformed Transit officer had been found murdered at a Sixth Avenue subway stop. "Guy named Mike Ditmar, ever heard of him?" said the forensic detective who'd accompanied the van. "Assailant unknown, but the weird thing is, the body was naked."

"What?" said McRay.

"His uniform was missing. Also his sidearm, badge, ID, and radio."

"Ah shit," said Jakowski.

McRay was immediately attentive. "How big was Ditmar, anybody know?"

The forensic detective shrugged. "Not as big as the guy who killed him, apparently. The poor bastard was strangled. That's a new one on me. Gunshot, stabbed, beaten, motor vehicle assault, but I never once heard an on-duty get strangled."

"Where on Sixth?" McRay wanted to know.

"Sixth and Fourteenth, I think it was."

"A transfer station," McRay said. "He could go anywhere from there."

"Mmmm," said Jakowski, polishing off the egg roll. "Somebody was just saying, searching the subway tunnels is a waste of time. Now who was it, told the captain that?"

"He's gone," McRay said. "If it was Marlon, he's gone by now. Long gone. He's a woman killer, we know that much, so if he killed a male cop it must be because he wanted the uniform. Now why would he want a uniform?"

"I dunno," Jakowski said. "Maybe he always wanted to be a cop."

McRay was distracted by the news of the subway murder, and he had to struggle to focus on the business at hand. On any other day this would have been a big breakthrough. Although the existence of such caches had been a matter of speculation ever since Marlon's original arrest, this was the first one to be located. If indeed it was the serial killer's hoard—Roberge had made the disturbing observation that with all the psychos loose in the city, the stash of weapons could belong to anyone.

What McRay was hoping for, with the forensic team in place, was to establish beyond a doubt that the hidden cache was Marlon's. That would give him something solid at last, make the captain sit up and take notice that the one-man special task force was actually getting results.

"You're thinking, what?" Jakowski said. "Stake the place out, wait for him to show up?"

"Are you volunteering?" McRay asked.

"No way. Besides, if this guy is smart as you think he is, he'd never fall for it."

"He has other places to go," McRay said. "I'm sure of it."

"You mean where he stashed the bodies."

They moved aside, let the squad of forensic detectives by with their print kits and cameras. "He's got a plan," McRay said. "I just wish I knew what the hell it was."

"Yeah," said Jakowski, "and Nixon had a plan to end the war."

"I'm serious," McRay said. "Right from the beginning he had a plan."

"You mean he planned to get caught?"

"Not that, but everything before and after."

"You know what?" Jakowski said. "He got to you, Kev. He made you think he's some kind of crazy genius. But if he was that smart, he wouldn't have got busted in the first place. Down deep he's just another dirtbag, Kev. And we'll catch him when he does something stupid."

McRay nodded. "I hope you're right. I pray you're right."

CHAPTER
SEVEN

"**R**eality sucks," said Cody.

In the darkness his voice sounded disembodied, and close. Very close.

"I'm serious," he said. "In the movies, they find an air vent, that's how they escape."

"Right," said Anna.

"In reality, you locate the air vent, it's barely big enough for a goddamn rat."

"Right," Anna said.

"Sorry," Cody said. "I forgot, we're not going to talk about rats."

Not talking about rats was his idea. Anna didn't care one way or another. Her anxiety was focused on John Chester Marlon, not on any rodents that might or might not be in the small air vent.

The lights had gone out moments after the door was welded shut. All power to the small room had been cut off. Ned Cody was convinced that they had been left here in the dark to die. Which would take a while, what with the stores of food and water, and the air vent the actor had finally located.

Anna discovered that she wasn't afraid of dying in this small dark place. She was afraid of what might happen when Marlon returned, as she knew he would.

"He doesn't need us now," Cody had argued. "Why would he bother?"

"It's not need," Anna said. "It's desire."

"But he never touched you. Not that way."

"Not that kind of desire," Anna said. "Not while I'm alive."

"Jesus!" Cody said, his voice going up an octave. "You mean he's like a necrophiliac?"

"I don't know what he is," Anna said. "I used to think I did, now I know I don't."

"I don't get it," Cody said. "You're the expert."

"Experts can be fooled. He fooled me. He fooled everybody."

"You mean that thing you put in his head," Cody said. "It didn't work. Maybe it's like a bad circuit or something."

"There's nothing wrong with the microchip," Anna said. "It just won't work on Marlon, because he's not trigger-reactive."

This was her latest theory, and so far it fit all the parameters of his behavior. It was clear to her now that John Chester Marlon had faked being a trigger-reactive psychotic. That incident with the prison guard had been planned. He wasn't reacting to an overwhelming impulse, he was seeing to it that his diagnosis was wrong.

Which brought her to the next question. Why would a lifer like Marlon want to be diagnosed as a trigger-reactive? What was in it for him, other than more or less perpetual solitary confinement?

There was only one possible answer. Marlon had read Anna's articles in the *Journal of Forensic Psychiatry*. He'd admitted as much, but she hadn't understood the full implication. *He'd been setting himself up for an implant, and for the opportunity to escape.* There was no other explanation that fit the facts. The son of a bitch had been planning this for two years, ever since he'd read about Anna's theory of behavior modification. By shooting the female prison guard in full view of a camera he made himself look like a man possessed by an irresistible impulse. In all of his subsequent interviews and evaluations he'd been careful to reinforce that impression.

That display of rage in the screening room, when he'd attacked her, had been real enough, but it was not involuntary anger that caused the indicators to spike, or the implant to kick in. No, that was Marlon indulging himself, letting go of his rigid self-control. And Anna had believed him because she'd *wanted* to believe him. Wanted to believe it was possible to end the nightmare and render him harmless.

What did it mean, exactly, that he wasn't a trigger-reactive? Did it mean he wasn't capable of murder? Not at all—in fact, not being trigger-reactive made him much more dangerous. A killer in control of his impulses could plot, scheme, manipulate, exactly as Marlon had done. And he was no less homicidally inclined, of that she was certain. He wanted Anna not as a hostage, but as a victim. And he would be back to claim her, exactly as he'd promised.

What were the options? They could sit here like lumps, afraid of the dark, or they could prepare themselves for the inevitable return.

"I want you to help me," Anna said, turning to face Cody in the dark.

"Anything," he said.

"These plastic straps. We can fray them lose."

Cody helped, eagerly. Although his own hands were numb from lack of circulation, he was able to press the plastic against the rough concrete wall. "This may hurt," he warned, but Anna welcomed the pain; it meant she was alive and full of feeling: victims were numb, unresponsive.

Together they worked her wrists back and forth against the abrasive surface of the concrete. There was no way to avoid scraping skin, and soon the plastic was slick with her blood, which made it more difficult.

"Sorry," Cody kept saying as he worked. She was aware of his male odor, his body heat, and was surprised by his strength. "I hate doing this, really," he insisted. "Hurting you even a little bit, it makes me feel sick to my stomach."

"You ever read the *Reader's Digest*, Ned?"

"Not lately. Years ago."

"I remember this one story," Anna said. "It was about a lumberjack who got his leg caught under a fallen tree. If he waited for help, he'd die of exposure."

"Oh, please," Cody said. "He cut it off, right? Chainsawed his own leg?"

"He used a knife, I think," Anna said. "The point is, I know exactly how he felt. If cutting off my own hands meant escape, I'd do it."

Cody made a funny sound, she wasn't sure if it was a cough or a laugh. "You're as crazy as he is," he said.

"When I die," she said, "I don't want it to be him that kills me."

"There," he said, and she realized that her wrists were no longer bound together. Her arms were light and floaty and her fingertips alive with the tingle of regained sensation.

"My turn," he said.

"Wait, I've got an idea."

Anna scuttled on her hands and knees, reaching out until she located the food storage area. Boxes of canned goods, cases of freeze-dried suppers, even, as Marlon had cheerfully pointed out, a box of chocolate bars. "There must be one here," she said, aware of how the small, thick-walled room deadened her voice.

When Cody's reply came, he sounded very distant, despite their necessary proximity. "I don't know what you're doing," he said uneasily. "Tell me what you're doing, maybe I can help."

"I'm looking for a can opener."

"You're hungry?" he said incredulously.

"A can opener might cut the straps."

"Of course!"

They pawed blindly through the food cache. It was Cody who finally located the can opener, and when he did his laughter was so bleak that Anna's heart tightened. "How convenient," he said. "An electric can opener."

"You're kidding."

"Makes sense," he said. "He's stealing power from Con Ed, why not take advantage?"

Anna had an idea. "How much do you weigh?" she asked.

"Huh? I don't know, probably a hundred and sixty pounds. I've lost weight lately."

"Take this," Anna said.

"A can," Cody said. "What do I do with it?"

"Step on it," Anna said. "Crush it."

"But that's— Wait, I get it. You're a genius, Doc. Kind of crazy, but a real genius."

By standing on the side of the can, Cody was eventually able to crush it. He and Anna worked the crushed can until the seal finally broke, flooding their hands with a sticky, sweet smelling liquid.

"Pears," Anna said. "Smells like pears."

Gritting her teeth in concentration, she twisted the metal until it fatigued. The can finally separated in two halves, leaving a sharp edge.

Anna dried her hands on her blouse, used the jagged edge to saw through the plastic straps binding Cody's wrists.

Now they were both free to move about the darkness of the little room and use their hands—and they had a weapon. Primitive, but sharp enough to cut a throat.

CHAPTER
EIGHT

The dentist's chair swiveled easily on well-lubricated ball joints. Marlon eased his large frame into the sweet-smelling leather and released the hydraulic lever. The back of the chair slowly reclined until he was horizontal, blood rushing to his head, feeding his brain.

The old chair had a kind of dreamy magic purpose, for in a few delicious moments he was a boy of seven again, spending Saturday morning at his father's office. An intelligent boy of seven watching silently from unobservable corners as his white-jacketed father used his deep, melodious voice to soothe the fears of his patients. *Now, now, Mrs. Ibrovitz, you won't feel the needle, you won't feel a thing,* as he lifted the blue plastic nitrous oxide mask from the holder and placed it gently over the old woman's face. *Just breathe easily, dear, we're both humming a song, what song do you like, oh yes, we're singing in the rain, just singing in the rain, what a marvelous feeling, we're hap-happy again . . .*

Dr. Marlon was a large, imposing gentleman of the old school, stern without being overbearing, always prim and proper and polite—his small gray beard was exactly right, not an affectation—and little John Chester Marlon had loved him as much as he could love any living creature.

But what he had loved more than his doting, sometimes absent-minded father was the office where he made a living inside the mouths of his Park Avenue patients. That scrubbed-clean office with all the gleaming instruments and the autoclaves and the X-ray machinery, little Johnny got to know every inch of it.

The two large rooms where Dr. Marlon practiced dentistry had once been part a much larger suite of offices that had taken up the whole first floor of the building. A prestigious nineteenth-century law firm, long since moved on to a larger building. At some point the suite had been partitioned and subdivided, but traces of the old design scheme were there to be discovered by a curious boy. Wainscoting that ended crazily, as if indicative of a previous opening. Old speaking tubes that seemed to go nowhere. A dumbwaiter that no longer functioned. And his most exciting discovery, a deep closet with a back wall that boomed hollow when struck by a small fist.

The building had secrets, and over the years little Johnny found all of those secrets and made them his own. The blank space in the wainscoting, for instance, was where a private elevator had been sealed up behind a plaster wall. The speaking tubes were part of a servant communication system that had once run through the whole building, and which originated in the sub-basement. The closet with the hollow wall concealed an old, cast-iron service stairway that terminated in the same sub-basement, which was itself sealed off from the main floor.

Discovery of the sub-basement and other long-forgotten mysteries about the building convinced John Chester Marlon that he alone had the power, the cunning, and the intelligence to see behind the more obvious reality, to a secret reality hidden away behind the superficial banality of everyday existence.

Even his sweet-tempered father was blind to the possibilities. For instance, although Dr. Marlon was frequently alone with his narcoticized patients, he never took advantage of their immobility. Little Johnny, observing from the closet, or through a crack in the door, waited patiently for his father to do something, anything, that demonstrated his control over a prostrate human rendered defenseless by nitrous oxide. And never once did Dr. Marlon take advantage of his great power. He continued to work dutifully over their mouths, crooning his silly songs. He never lifted Mrs. Ibrovitz's skirt, he never checked plump Mr. Bartlett's fat brown wallet, or caressed Miss Alice Malloy's fine slim ankles—it was as if he was unaware of the infinite possibilities presented by the chair, the office, the helpless patients, the secret sub-basement that waited below like a sleek, feral creature hungry for unspeakable, unnameable pleasures. Watching him, Johnnie became convinced that his father was, when it came right down to it, as stupid as all the others. What was the point of making people immobile if you didn't take advantage?

By the time he was twelve, John Chester Marlon realized that his father had no imagination, and worse, no sense of adventure. He was a kindly old duffer plodding methodically through life, blind to the possibilities. And by his fourteenth birthday, Dr. Marlon's son had passed through the hidden sub-basement into another world.

Not an imaginary, adolescent world, but a real world. A subterranean world as immense, and complex, and dark, as the city of light overhead. A world that would become his secret office, his place of business, his work of art.

And yet, no matter how far he strayed from the building on Park Avenue, that relatively small receptacle of memories remained connected to him in a visceral way. For years he had returned here, using the subbasement access, with but one thing in mind: to recline in his father's chair and smell the sweet-scented leather. It was enough, in times of almost unbearable stress and excitement, to sustain him.

In the chair Marlon lay with his eyes closed, breathing deeply, easily, thinking thoughts that glittered like teeth in the dark. First thing, once he was situated, he would deal with the implant. It was like a decayed tooth, nagging at his mind, and it needed pulling. When that was done, and he was free to take pleasure, enter into the spirit of things, it was back to work. More than anything, in these years of confinement, he'd missed the work. Like any great artist, he need his materials.

After a while he began to hum. He had decided what his final display would be, and it was beautiful, beautiful.

CHAPTER
NINE

Back in the precinct bullpen, Kevin McRay was already famous. Detectives high-fiving him until his hands hurt. This was all before forensics reported on fingerprint or fiber evidence, so it made him uneasy, as if the honor and notoriety might be snatched away at any moment.

Len Jakowski set him straight. "Look, you located a major cache of firepower down there. If it belongs to the Subway Killer, so much the better. But whoever stashed it, they don't have it now—and if they come back for it, we'll nail 'em. Any cop sees that many guns going out of circulation, there's cause for celebration."

"But Jeff found the place."

Jakowski was shaking his head. "Yeah, he was a big help, but you're the one put us on to that location, right? All this by-the-map investigation, it's starting to pay off."

"I guess so," McRay said uneasily.

"You guess so." Jakowski shook his head and laughed. "I heard through the grapevine, the Cap is pleased. Very pleased. You've got a green light, Kev."

A green light. Bullpen jargon for permission to go full speed ahead in the approved direction. The problem was, McRay didn't know where to go next. He had a list of maybe a hundred possible locations, all culled from maps and work orders, and to check out so much area in a reasonable amount of time—say the next twenty-four hours—he'd need, at minimum, three hundred officers. And there was no way on earth that Captain Michael Francis Fucking Harnett would go along with that.

Len Jakowski reluctantly agreed. "We've got to narrow it down," he said. "What are the parameters?"

"Start from what we've got," McRay said. He unfurled a street map of Manhattan. "The weapons cache is right here." He touched the intersection of Second Avenue and 48th Street. "Say you're a demented serial killer," he said to Jakowski.

"Say what?"

"You're Marlon. A city engineer, master of the underground. You've got this special place where you keep your trophies."

"The Doll House."

McRay nodded. "You've got the Doll House. Also you've got weapons and supplies cached around the city."

"I get it," Jakowski said. "I was Marlon, I'd keep the guns nearby."

"How near?" McRay asked.

Jakowski shrugged, thought about it. "I dunno. Too close, if somebody stumbles on the cache, they'll be knocking on my door. Too far away, I can't get to the stuff when I need it."

"Now you're thinking like a serial killer," McRay said.

"Gee thanks."

"I agree. Not so close he gives himself away, not so far he can't get there quick. Let's pick an arbitrary number. A ten-block radius."

McRay picked up a red marker, drew a line along 52nd Street, down Sixth Avenue to 42nd Street, then all the way over to the East River.

"Quite a chunk of real estate," Jakowski said. "How many likely locations fall inside that area?"

"I'm going to start culling through them right now. Do me a favor and get on the computer. Pull everything we've got on John Chester Marlon."

"You already did that."

"So maybe you'll see something I missed. While you're at it, pull Ned Cody. See if there's any previous contact between them."

"You mean maybe he's not a hostage?"

"Anything is possible," McRay said. "Anything at all."

* * *

Supper was a take-out curry, eaten right from the box. And hot tea. He'd been ignoring the deep bruises all day long, and the congestion in his lungs, but after a couple of hours of desk work, it was all coming home to roost. He had, after all, checked himself out of a hospital against doctor's orders. And after the exhilaration of locating the weapons cache wore off, he was left with the aches and pains of being damn near drowned in the storm sewer.

Along with the physical letdown came a mental heaviness, a weight in his mind. Anna. The chances of finding her alive diminished with every passing minute. Marlon was a stone cold killer, he wouldn't keep the doctor alive any longer than necessary. And what was the point of holding a hostage if you'd made good on your escape?

The next bundle Jeff Roberge stumbled over might be her.

If only I'd had a gun with me, McRay chided himself. The hell with Annex security rules, I should have insisted on keeping my sidearm. Okay, never mind about the gun, they'd never have let you in there armed, but still you could have done something. What happened, you were hypnotized by that psycho, just like everybody else. He dared you, and you were afraid, here's what it boils down to—cowardice. Fear that he'd break her slim neck before you could stop him. If you could stop him. The guy outweighs you by at least fifty pounds of solid muscle, he's not going down easy.

He closed his eyes, sipped the hot tea. Forget about it. What's done is done. The reality is, he snatched her, and now it's up to you to find her, dead or alive. You owe her that much.

He was asleep in his chair when Jakowski tapped his shoulder. "Hey sleeping beauty."

As McRay jerked awake, his hand flew out, tipping over the cup of cold tea.

Jakowski shook his head, amused. "Kid, you look like hell. You need to go home, get a good night's sleep."

McRay shrugged off the suggestion. "Any news?" he asked.

"I been pulling computer files, like you asked me. Which includes everything you already entered on Marlon, by the way. And I tried this Ned Cody character, all he had was a prior drunk driving, and about a hundred parking tickets. So I checked with the Department of Corrections—so far as they know he never had prior contact with Marlon. I ask, does that include personal correspondence, they can't say."

"They can't say?"

"They don't keep a record of letters going out, unless there's a request to do so. But what I did, I checked with security at Sing Sing, and they did keep track of all the mail Marlon received, and he got lots of it, I guess. Being a famous serial killer and so forth. And there's no record of any mail from Ned Cody."

"It was a long shot."

Jakowski hesitated. "I did pull another file, Kev. I hope you don't mind."

"Why should I mind?"

"The shrink. Anna Kane."

McRay was fully awake now, alerted by the change in Jakowski's voice. He'd found something. "Don't tell me *she* corresponded with him."

"Only through official channels," Jakowski said. "Regarding the experimental surgery. No, this goes way back. Kind of a fluke I found it, really."

"Come on, Len. Spill it."

Jakowski sighed and took a seat. "You know what I heard once, this late-night radio show? That the reason shrinks become shrinks is so they can cure their crazy parents. Which is as good a reason as any, I guess. And Dr. Kane, she had more reason than most."

"How'd you find this, Len? What file?"

"The interborough murder file. You told me the lady came from upstate, right? Out in the boonies?"

"That was my impression."

"Anna Kane was born in Queens. Flushing, to be exact. Her old man was a Korean war vet, medical discharge."

"A section-eight?"

"That's about the size of it. He's in and out of vet hospitals, they don't know what to do with him. So one night he forgets to take his pill or whatever, and he goes nuts. Berserk. I got this from the incident report, by the way. The newspapers didn't have all the gory details, it was just another domestic violence. Happens every day."

"Come on, Len. What happened?"

"What you'd expect. He threatened his wife, told her he was going to kill her and their four-year-old daughter. That was Anna. And then he left the house. She called the cops, but before they got there the husband came back with a knife he'd bought at the corner store—stolen, actually—and he chased the mother around the house. Stabbed her in the face, cut her eyes. Then he cut his own throat."

McRay felt a great weariness return. He knew what was coming. "Where was Anna?"

"Hiding in a cupboard. She witnessed the whole event. Her mother survived, but she's been in an institution ever since. Anna moved upstate right after the murder, lived with various relatives. A tough start for a little girl."

"Yes," McRay said.

"Pretty remarkable, really, a kid like that gets all the way through medical school."

McRay nodded.

"And then what she tries to do is find out why men go nuts and kill their loved ones. Solving the great mystery, I guess. Very gutsy."

"She's a special person," McRay said. "I knew that."

"I hope she makes it," Jakowski said. "I really do."

CHAPTER TEN

Ned Cody had no idea what time it was, or for that matter what day. Living without light did that for you, it stole the hours and made them all a blur of darkness. He'd tried counting heartbeats, got up to a thousand, and realized the whole idea was insane.

Dr. Kane had had a watch, but it had been lost in the tunnels, snagged off her wrist. Probably a big sewer rat somewhere, sporting a nice quartz Seiko.

"It doesn't matter what time it is," she told him, an edge of impatience in her voice. "We're waiting, that's all that matters."

"Waiting for Godot," he said. "Ogunquit Playhouse. I was Estragon."

"Really?" she'd said. To his amazement, she actually sounded interested. "I didn't know you were on stage. I thought you were a TV actor."

Ned's laugh was sardonic—as if his whole life was a joke, an anecdote. "Daytime drama stars are very popular on the summer circuit. They ask for autographs, what they want is your TV character's name."

"You're kidding."

"Swear to God," he said.

One good thing about being marooned in the dark was that Dr. Kane let him get much closer than she would have otherwise. Something intimate about being blind, it made you want to whisper and touch, just to be sure the other person was really there. So far the touching had been of the hand-to-hand variety, and Ned wasn't pushing for more. Not yet—and maybe not ever.

"Will you go back to acting?" she asked.

"You mean if I survive this, and if I make parole?"

"I mean, if you could do anything, be anybody, would you still be an actor?"

"Hey, the fact is, I'm a phony," Ned said, after giving it some thought. "Fake people don't make great actors, but sometimes it gives them a life. Yeah, sure, I'd go back—but nobody would hire me."

Anna felt for his hand, patted it. "You're not a fake person, Ned. And why wouldn't they hire you?"

"Small problem," he said. "I killed my co-star, remember?"

Now it was her turn to pause. "I remember. I wasn't sure that you did."

"That's a game everybody plays," he said bitterly. " 'I can't remember.' Which is bull. Believe me, it's not a thing you can forget, no matter how hard you try."

"Do you want to talk about it?"

Ned laughed. "We're waiting for a guy to come back and kill us, and you want to know what I was thinking when I strangled poor Tracy?"

"He's not going to kill us," she said. "And sure, why not? I have a professional interest."

"You're not scared I might strangle you?"

"I'm not Tracy," she said. "Also I've got a weapon."

Indeed she did. A hunk of jagged steel from the broken can. It was a mean and nasty blade, and something about the way she handled herself convinced him that she was capable of using it.

"So maybe I should be afraid of you," he said.

"Don't be. You're not Marlon."

That's what it came down to, of course. Everything was about Marlon. Even his own desperate act of violence—killing a woman who'd made the mistake of loving him—only served as a basis for comparison.

"I was drunk," he said. "That's my first excuse. And I'd been snorting this really rancid coke for about five days. Cut with methedrine. It made me crazy. Not crazy-insane, but crazy-mean. Tracy was doing the coke, too, and it made her want to hurt me back. Which she did."

"She physically attacked you?"

"Not that kind of hurt. More the mental kind, like, 'You're a worthless hack with no talent and you'll never work again.' Which by the way didn't bother me, because it was true. So I agreed with her, and that's what made her really angry."

"Cocaine can cause temporary psychosis. That's been demonstrated."

Ned made a dismissive noise. "Yeah, well I know a thing or two about cocaine. And it wasn't the drug made me do it. And it wasn't because my mother didn't love me, either."

"Did she?"

"I don't know. Maybe. As best she could. But that's not the point."

"What is the point, Ned?" Anna asked softly.

"The point is I wanted to kill myself, but I was afraid, so I killed Tracy instead. I invited death into the room, and oh boy, it came right in and made itself at home."

"You were suicidal?"

"I was a fucked-up, out-of-work, drug-addicted mess. And for some reason, right at the moment I put my hands around her throat, killing somebody seemed like the solution to all my problems. And you know the sickest part? We'd been fighting for like three days, off and on, but when I did it we were kissing and making up. We were forgiving each other."

"You killed her because she forgave you?"

"Yes," said Ned. "No. I don't know. That's what I'm saying, I know I did it, but I don't know why."

The effort of discussing the murder made him feel a kind of dreamy lethargy creeping over him, as if he'd just donated too much blood. Light-headed, he was seeing pinpoint sparkles in the dark, imaginary stars.

"What's that?" Anna asked, in a hushed, urgent voice.

Cody listened. At first he heard nothing more than his own heart beating. And then, under that, a kind of faint, furtive scratching. "The door," he said, whispering directly into Anna's ear. "Either a rat wants in, or Marlon."

At the mention of the killer's name, she stiffened—he could sense an almost electric tingle as her muscles tensed. The noise was louder now—too loud for a rodent; the source was human-sized, the sound of someone prying at the sealed door.

"He welded it shut," Cody whispered. "He'll need a cutting torch."

The noise ceased. They waited. Cody focused all of his powers of concentration on the door, imagined his ears were like radar antennas, able to pick up any signal, no matter how faint. If he uses a cutting torch you'll be able to see it, he told himself, and he imagined what the faint red glow might look like as the steel heated, and he waited, willing his eyes to see it.

Suddenly there was another and much louder noise. A sound to stop your heart: feet hitting the concrete floor. And a visceral grunt, as a man might make who had just dropped from the ceiling.

Impossible, Cody thought, as Anna's hand clenched on his wrist, you're imagining your worst fear, that's all it is, you're sharing your fear with the woman and so she's experiencing the same unfettered panic.

A moment later he was blind.

The light was hot, and it poured through his fully dilated retinas, burning white, white, white, expanding like the flash of a nuclear detonation.

He heard Anna scream and then he was being shoved back and a stone fist was clubbing him into unconsciousness, and he went willingly, eagerly, seeking the soothing, intimate darkness as Marlon's flat dead voice said, "Did you miss me? I missed you."

DAY
6

The Doll House

CHAPTER ONE

In the dream McRay was sleeping at his desk, head down on his folded arms, as he'd napped in elementary school, and through the desk he could hear Anna Kane calling for help. Her voice was muffled, coming from miles underground, and he was unable to move, unable to help, unable to find her. What paralyzed him was not sleep, but the darkness gathering behind him, a malignant force boiling like a thundercloud, gathering power, ready to strike.

When he startled himself awake he was at his desk, head cradled in his arms, and someone was calling his name.

Not Anna, of course, but a detective he didn't recognize. Scrawny guy with a mashed-up nose, deeply pockmarked skin, and the kind of sad brown eyes that would make some women forget the homely mug, or maybe confuse him with Humphrey Bogart. Until he opened his mouth and out came that adenoidal buzz that marked him as a son of the Bronx.

"You McRay? Yeah? I'm Joe Pizzi, Homicide," he said, laying a printout on the desk.

"What's this?" McRay said, picking up the paper.

It was a little after midnight and the bullpen had that gritty, over-caffeinated, late-night feel. The city was beginning to howl, as expressed in frantic calls to 911, causing dispatches from fire departments, patrol cars, EMT, violent crime units, family intervention units, Homicide.

"Bulletin you put on the computer," Pizzi explained. "Any crimes reported, a ten-block radius."

"Oh, right," McRay said, blinking the sleep from his eyes. "Thanks."

" 'Cause, see, I caught this homicide, right there on Park Avenue, right in the middle of your area. Could be, I dunno, might be a possible connection."

McRay sat up straight, willed himself awake. "Marlon?" he said. "The Subway Killer?"

Pizzi scrunched up his narrow face. Looked like he was sucking on a lemon, but really he was thinking it over. "Long shot," he said at last. "Strickly a hunch, okay? What it is, this victim who got strangled. Residential apartment building, Park Avenue, you with me?"

"I'm with you."

"Victim is a fifty-three-year-old Hispanic male, Hector Rivera. He's the super, lives on the first floor, ground level. Neighbor called it in, this old lady lives across the street. Apparently, he drew the bolt and the assailant broke the chain. And whoever did him, we're talking a very strong individual, 'cause Hector's throat was crushed. I mean *crushed.*"

"Was anybody sighted in the vicinity? You said a neighbor—"

"Hang on, lemme finish." Pizzi was animated now, making shapes with his hands. "That's what made me think of your guy. Earlier today, there's this Transit cop got killed on post."

"I know about that. He was stripped—"

"Hey, you gonna let me tell it or what? I could; you keep interrupting, you can just read my report. I'll go on home and go to bed, which is where I shoulda been three hours ago."

"I'm sorry," McRay said. "It's been a long day for me too."

"Okay, like I say, this Transit cop gets killed—strangled—and his uniform gets stolen. Your guy the Subway Killer is a suspect. I must have this in the back of my mind, because when the old lady tells me about the cop—"

"What cop?" McRay couldn't help himself.

Pizzi sighed, threw up his hands. "Why is it nobody ever lets me finish a story? Never mind, feel free to interrupt, I'm used to it. Anyhow, the point is, the cop is why the old lady called in. She's a busybody, keeping an eye on the neighborhood. Regular crimestopper, you know the type. What happens, she sees a cop go into Hector's apartment and she gets worried. So she calls up the precinct, wants to know what crime has been reported that building. This is a lady won't take no, so eventually they send around a squad car, check it out, just to shut her up. Responding officer rings the bell, sees these feet on the floor."

"Just the feet?"

Pizzi smirked. "Not what you're thinking, no. The victim's feet were firmly attached to his legs, only it was just the feet they spotted from the door. Anyhow, they bust in, he's on the floor, dead as they get. That's where I come in. After the ME does his thing, I check with the phone company. No outgoing calls from the victim's phone for the last twelve hours."

"So he never called the police."

"Nope. And there's no record, any on-foot patrolman dispatched to his domicile. So we're looking for a large individual impersonating an officer."

"She said he was big?"

"Didn't I mention? Yeah, that's what made me think maybe it's your guy with the stolen uniform, out strangling citizens."

"You have the old lady's name and number?"

Pizzi tore a page from his notebook, handed it over. "So, did I do good?"

"I'll let you know."

"Yeah? Detective Joseph Pizzi. Two i's, two z's. That's if you get anything you can use. You don't, forget I stopped by."

When Pizzi strolled away, McRay snagged himself a mug of coffee and sat back down at his desk. What was it about Park Avenue? Some connection there, but he couldn't put his finger on it. He'd felt the same nagging sense of connection when he'd decided to set the ten-block radius for the Doll House search. What was it, a psychic type of thing? No way, he was a guy who never knew if it was going to rain, never had a vibe he'd recognized as a premonition. That ESP nonsense was for TV shows and publicity-crazed psychics. Had to be somewhere in the maps or the missing persons reports; his overtired brain was misfiring.

Len Jakowski and Jeff Roberge had both gone home, promising to return shortly after dawn. McRay had stayed on, napping at his desk, because he couldn't bear the thought of missing anything. The sheer number of troops assigned to the tunnel details meant the inevitable police bureaucracy had formed, a layer of fat around the heart of the investigation, and if you weren't right there, monitoring the information, something vital might easily be lost or overlooked. The captain's primary mission was to protect civilians—without exactly saying so, he'd kissed off on the idea that Dr. Kane might still be alive. McRay was practically the only assigned detective who believed in the possibility of her survival, therefore it was incumbent upon him to keep the flame burning.

Pizzi's report of a mysterious Park Avenue homicide invigorated him in a way the coffee could not—it gave him hope. If the killer was Marlon—if he'd come up from underground, at great risk—there had to be a reason. Find the reason, he might find Marlon, who would lead him to Anna.

It was a long shot, but McRay decided to take it. Besides, it was driving him nuts, hanging around the bullpen. He wanted to be out there, doing something, anything.

"I'm going out to a crime scene," he told the night desk sergeant. "If Jakowski or Roberge calls, tell them I'm at this address," he added, writing it down.

The last thing he did before leaving was check his brand new, just issued Glock 9-millimeter semiautomatic pistol. Hell with the old five-shot peashooter. Unlocking his desk, he slipped another fully loaded magazine into his jacket pocket. Ruined the fabric lines, but it couldn't be helped.

There was nothing shaking on Park Avenue at one o'clock in the morning. A few brave, possibly inebriated civilians strolling the sidewalks, a couple of dogwalkers on the median, that was it.

The first thing McRay did was roust the elderly woman who'd made the initial report. A Mrs. Elsie Goldstein, who occupied a small, densely furnished, fifth-story apartment that faced the avenue, and the crime scene opposite.

Mrs. Goldstein was not, as he'd anticipated, sound asleep. Nor was she inclined to allow a complete stranger access to her apartment at this hour of the night. McRay heard all this through an intercom phone in the lobby, where he'd been admitted by a uniformed security guard.

"The Subway Killer mean anything to you, Mrs. Goldstein?" he said into the intercom.

"I never take the subway, young man," came back the crackling reply.

"Okay," he said, deciding to try another tack. "Your security guard has seen my I.D. How about if he accompanies me up to your apartment?"

Mrs. Goldstein tried to change the subject. "Do you have a suspect?" she wanted to know.

"I just mentioned the Subway Killer," McRay said jauntily. "You weren't impressed."

"That horrible man who kidnapped the pretty doctor?"

"The very same."

There was a long pause, the noise of dentures being shifted into place. "What's your interest in this, Detective?"

He sighed. What was it with this old geezer, did she get a kick out of keeping a cop on the phone or what? "My interest? I'm investigating a homicide, Mrs. Goldstein."

"I mean what brings you out at this hour?"

She was angling for information and he decided, what the hell, give her some. "I think Dr. Kane may still be alive. There may be a connection to Mr. Rivera's murder, that's what I'm trying to find out."

"Oh?" said Mrs. Goldstein. "How interesting. And what is your relation to Dr. Kane?"

McRay, nonplussed, stared at the phone. Who was this old lady, was she a Gypsy? "Why do you ask?" he said uneasily.

"So you *do* have a relationship."

"She's a friend," McRay admitted.

"A friend? That's all?"

"Okay, okay," McRay said, sighing. "She's more than a friend. That's why I'm busting my ass at this hour, Mrs. Goldstein, are you satisfied?"

Mrs. Goldstein sounded amused. "Tell the guard to bring you up," she said. "I'll make hot cocoa, it fortifies the blood."

CHAPTER TWO

The view from Mrs. Goldstein's apartment was unremarkable. But it was considerably enhanced by the high-powered, tripod-mounted telescope she had aimed at the crime scene.

"I never look through bedroom windows," she said primly, setting down the tray of hot cocoa. "Amorous entanglements are of no interest to me."

"Mmmm," said McRay—his instinct told him the subject of peeping was a loaded gun aimed right at his cup of hot cocoa. Which, by the way, smelled delicious. He lifted the delicate china cup, blew gently, and sipped. "Hey," he said, pleasantly surprised.

Mrs. Goldstein understood. "I make it myself," she said. "Did you know that good cocoa has almost as much caffeine as coffee?"

"Is that right?" he said. As a matter of fact, he'd heard that about chocolate, but did not want to impress his host as a know-it-all. Better to keep her talking; it was amazing what people would tell you if you just kept them talking.

Elsie Goldstein was long-legged, slender, silver-haired, with bright young eyes glittering in an ancient face. Good bones, he could tell that much, the kind of high cheeks and poised, slender neck that had made Katharine Hepburn such a beauty. Intense that way, too. Matter of fact, she was staring at him with such intensity that he had to look away, take a break by glancing down at the saucer.

"Delft," she said. "My husband bought the set for our fiftieth anniversary. Our last anniversary."

"I'm sorry," he said.

She waved it away. "Years ago."

McRay had spotted a collection of framed photographs, neatly displayed over a built-in bookcase. "You were a dancer?"

Mrs. Goldstein shook her head. "A runway model. Before that, the Follies."

"The Ziegfeld Follies?"

She nodded primly. "So I'm at least ninety years old."

"Oh," he said.

"I'd have to be, wouldn't I?" She seemed amused by the idea, and then sat down in a wingback chair and crossed her ankles. "Lucky for you, I'm a night owl. Have been all my life. The most interesting things seem to happen at night, don't you agree?"

He perched on the edge of an upholstered chair, glanced at the telescope. "Some of them. But it was afternoon when you saw the policeman enter Mr. Rivera's flat."

"Was that his name, Rivera? Yes, I was having my first tea. Tea for daylight, cocoa when the sun goes down. Used to be I'd have a double whiskey at sunset, but I gave that up. Made me uncertain on my pins."

"Your pins?"

She admired her ankles, inviting him to do likewise. "Legs. Old word, I guess. Used to be gams, once upon a time, that was a gangster word. I heard them all, you were bound to, when you did the high kick for a living."

"Uh huh," he said, aware that the old bird was flirting, in her regal way. "So you saw a policeman enter Mr. Rivera's flat," he said, prompting her.

"I did indeed."

"Did this policeman arrive by patrol car, did you notice?"

"I did notice, and no he did not. He came strolling up the avenue, the way cops used to stroll up the avenue."

"How's that?"

"Free and easy, like he owned the world. That's why I noticed him, you see, because he reminded me of Officer Halloran."

"Excuse me?"

"Officer Halloran. Of course you wouldn't know him, he's been dead since, oh, just before the war. The Second World War, not the first."

"Oh," said McRay.

"Before you were born. It seems to me that all the policemen were tall, back then. This used to be a city of big men."

McRay sat up straight, put down the cup and saucer. "He was a big man, this policeman you saw?"

"Oh, yes." Mrs. Goldstein shifted, brought a curled hand up under her chin, and closed her eyes, as if that helped her remember. "It's difficult to tell through the scope, the lens can deceive, but he was tall. Taller than you, and very broad shouldered. The uniform was tight across his shoulders, I noticed that. I like a well-muscled man, don't you? No, of course you don't, what am I saying. And he had a thick neck, like John L. Sullivan. Walked on the balls of his feet like a prizefighter, too." She opened her eyes, and waited for his comment.

"Hat?" he asked.

"Oh yes," she nodded. "And a holster and a nightstick, too."

"So you couldn't tell what color hair he had?"

"No." She hesitated. "Not even sideburns, or I'd have remembered, because Officer Halloran had such nice full sideburns."

"Could his head have been shaved?"

She shrugged. "Possibly. I do remember that he had rather small ears."

McRay felt a current run through him, almost lifted the hairs at the back of his neck. Yes! It was an otherwise insignificant detail, nothing that could be used for legal identification, but it was a fact that John Chester Marlon had small ears. And McRay had seen the man pacing his cell and yes, he did walk on the balls of his feet, lightly, like an athlete or a boxer.

"You saw him go into the super's apartment, is that correct?"

She nodded. "He rang the bell. Then he had a short conversation with this man—Mr. Rivera, was it?—and he pointed up at the building, and then next thing I knew, the cop went inside."

"Rivera pointed up at the building? Could you see what he was pointing at, exactly?"

"I could not," she said. "After he went inside, I looked, that's the first thing I did, but there was nothing I haven't seen a thousand times. Oh, more than a thousand. Much more."

"But you had the impression he was inquiring about something in the building?"

30 day refund on all sealed music, book
and movies. Opened product cannot be
exchanged or refunded. Defective produc
will be exchanged for the same title.

Cashier 3   Receipt F2364031
  CHRISTY   2004/02/20 at 13:14

Sold To: CASH SALE

----

    1 MISC299BOOK @ 2.99   2.99
       SPE ASSORTED REMAINDER
                        Sub-total   2.99

                        G.S.T.   0.21

                        Total   3.20

Paid by: Cash   3.20
                        Tendered   5.20
                        Change Due   2.00

"Yes," Mrs. Goldstein said firmly. "That was my impression."

"And he never came out?"

She shook her head. "Not that I saw. For all I know, he may still be in there."

That was when the hairs did, in fact, lift from the back of Kevin McRay's neck.

CHAPTER
THREE

The entrance to the victim's ground-floor apartment had been plastered with yellow crime-scene tape. No surprise, the door was locked, and McRay did not have the key. Getting the key would require a trip to the Homicide unit, where you had to go through channels, obtain official permission to enter the premises. All of which could take hours, possibly days.

Using a flashlight, he examined the door—it was solid, steel-jambed, held in place by deadbolts. The ground-floor windows were covered by wrought-iron bars, a normal enough precaution, considering the fashionable address. Short of wielding a ten-pound sledgehammer, there was no easy way to break in.

He waved up at Mrs. Goldstein's building, confident that he was framed in her telescope at that very moment. He smiled and shrugged, as if to say, what can I do, being a law-abiding peace officer?

What he did was go around to the back of the building, out of sight of prying eyes. There he found a narrow service alley, once used by carriage tradesmen, he supposed. He perused the dark little alley for an unsecured window within reach from the ground.

There were no such windows.

Instead, he found an old basement bulkhead, looked as if it had been

torn apart for repair, and then left boarded up with plywood. He had no
way of knowing if there was an access from the basement to Rivera's
apartment, but it was the only shot he had, at this time of night, and on
short notice.

The plywood sheathing came up surprisingly easy, nails popping
free from the mildewed frame. Too easily, really; he was beginning to
have misgivings about entering the building on his own, at three in the
morning, when sensible people were sound asleep.

The flashlight illuminated brick steps going down. McRay hitched
up his belt, checked to make sure he could reach his gun easily. The last
time he'd gone below street level on his own, he'd damn near drowned.

So what was the big deal? This wasn't the subway or the sewer or
some unknown tunnel, it was just an ordinary basement in an ordinary
building, probably nothing more dangerous down there than a feral cat
or two.

Go ahead smartass, you're committed.

He took a deep breath and went down the steps quickly. Dive right
in, that was the only way to go. In his haste to get it over with, he skidded
on the last step, nearly lost his balance. A bone shaker, slamming hard
upon his heels.

McRay crouched, massaging his ankles, and swept the beam around,
taking it all in. The basement was a clutter of bins and boxes and storage
areas caged off for the tenants. Pipes, ducting vents, a small, coin-oper-
ated laundry, this was the guts of the building, unfinished and unadorned.

The light caught a glitter.

He pulled the beam back, and saw that he was focused on a human
torso. Not a real torso, he concluded after his pulse stopped hammering,
but part of a mannequin, or maybe it was a tailor's dummy. Just a thing, a
suggestive shape that came alive in the dark.

"Don't be an idiot," he said aloud, for the comfort of hearing his own
voice. Basements were spooky places, so what? He wasn't here to check
out the nooks and crannies, he was trying to get into the victim's apartment. Rivera had been the building super, it stood to reason his place
would have a back stairway, access to the utilities, the fuse boxes, and so
on.

A few minutes went by before he was able to get oriented, form a
sense of where the victim's apartment was in relation to the basement.
When the layout took shape in his mind, he walked carefully along the
row of storage cages, located a stairwell that undoubtedly led up to the

main hallway, and then another, much narrower set of wooden steps leading to a paneled door. All doubt was swept away by a small, faded plaque attached to the door: *Building Superintendent. Do Not Enter.*

The first thing he did was knock. Rat-a-tat on the panels, wanting to make sure that no one was home before he tried forcing the lock. When there was no response, he put his ear to the door and listened. Silence, dead silence.

Then, miracle of miracles, the knob turned in his hand. The door gave only an inch or so before the slack was taken up by a light chain. So either Rivera was not in the habit of deadbolting the inside basement door, or the homicide detectives hadn't bothered.

The chain broke easily, and McRay found himself in a small, railroad-style kitchen, bathed in the eerie, monochromatic light of a street lamp shining through a small-paned window over the sink. He saw a set of dishes left to dry on the sideboard, a towel neatly folded on the rack. Hector Rivera had been a tidy man, kept his little apartment spic and span: a nursery rhyme with a bad ending. What would he think, this neat gentleman, of all the fingerprint dust scattered on every smooth surface? Would he complain from the grave—those dirty New York detectives, how dare they leave their grubby powder all over my clean apartment?

McRay looked down, saw that he was stepping in the place where Rivera had died, or where his body had been left, as outlined in black tape on the linoleum floor. Died looking up at that dish towel, and the black and white tile pattern above the counters.

More likely, though, he'd died blind, blood cut off from his brain, fading to black. Powerful hands crushing his throat, pinching the carotid artery—unconsciousness would have come quickly, perhaps within seconds.

And Mrs. Goldstein had never seen the suspect emerge from this apartment. A minor point, overlooked by Pizzi and the other homicide detectives, who had dismissed her as an elderly crackpot, a busybody. Of course it was possible that the suspect had exited by the same door he'd entered, or by another door, or that Mrs. Goldstein's attention had strayed, that she had stepped away from her telescope, gone to the bathroom, made tea, any of a thousand chores performed automatically, and thus easily forgotten.

But what if she was right? What if the suspect—Marlon, it had to be Marlon, he felt that in his bones—what if he had remained in the building, somehow eluding the investigating detectives who would not, in any case, expect to find him here? Killers fled, that was the rule, and homicide detectives knew the rules, played by the book, crossed every t.

McRay stood there quietly, straining to hear. How did you muffle your own heartbeat, stop it from pounding in your ears? How could he hear anything with his goddamn heart slamming so goddamn hard against his goddamn ribs?

Goddamnit.

Finally he couldn't stand the oppressive silence anymore and he picked up a saucepan and banged it against the counter. Make a joyful noise. Let the bastard know the cavalry was here. The next thing he did was unholster his gun. Left hand for the flashlight, right hand for the Glock 9-mil, empty all fifteen rounds in the son of a bitch in about two seconds.

The next thing McRay did was turn on the lights in each room. Kitchen first, then the small TV room, the tube showered with fingerprint dust, then the bedroom, barely big enough for the bed, and finally the bathroom. No shower curtain, so he didn't have to sweep that back like they were always doing in the movies, ready for the bogey man to jump out.

Thinking: Mrs. Goldstein will be watching, she'll see the lights come on and she'll know I found a way in. Would she make another phone call, report him? Fine if she did, he could use the company.

After he'd searched all the rooms, he went back and looked under the bed, into the shallow closets, until he was satisfied that Marlon couldn't be hiding anywhere, unless he'd crammed himself into the refrigerator.

McRay checked the refrigerator. Found deli salsa, bottled sauces, salad dressings, carefully labeled Tupperware—Rivera planned his meals by the week.

"Poor bastard," he said aloud, stepping around the taped body outline.

What had brought Marlon here, impersonating a police officer? Why had he risked killing a cop in a crowded subway, or the even greater risk of walking jauntily up Park Avenue as if he owned the world?

The uniform would get him in the door, into the building. But what was here, that made the risk worthwhile? Surely not the thrill of killing a middle-aged apartment super and then leaving him splayed on the kitchen floor? This wasn't the thrill killing of a female victim he'd stalked in the tunnels, stoking his fantasies. No power or satisfaction could flow from such an ordinary death. There had to be a purpose beyond the killing part, a goal.

A reason, goddamnit. But who was he to provide a rational explanation for the behavior of a psychopath? Anna had attempted that, and look where it got her.

Okay, can the psychology. It came down to this: why pick on the super? What did Hector have, that Marlon might want? Deli salsa? Dish towels? TV? What did a building superintendent have that none of the other residents might have?

McRay had returned to the kitchen. He'd placed his gun on the counter and he had both hands in his pockets, an old habit that made it easier to think, and that was when it came to him. Keys. His fingers fiddled with the keys in his trouser pocket, and he knew, he absolutely knew what the super had that no one else had: keys to every door in the building.

Holy Jesus.

For a couple of glorious moments he was convinced that he'd solved the crime and nailed John Chester Marlon. The Subway Killer had come up from the underground and was hiding in an apartment in this very building!

Was it possible?

And then another thought slammed into the first, shattering his confidence. Marlon was smart, too smart to think he could hide out in a building where a murder had taken place. First thing homicide detectives did was interview all the residents—McRay had seen the reports confirming the door-to-door. Scratch the apartment hideout theory.

If Marlon had killed for the keys, it was the keys to something other than an occupied residential apartment.

He nearly jumped when it came to him. What about an *unoccupied* apartment?

McRay picked up his gun. He thought about holstering it, and then he thought, why not be ready? Just in case.

CHAPTER
FOUR

A crystal chandelier illuminated the ground floor hallway. It was a beautiful source of light, casting soft, flickering forms that moved as if alive, set into motion by the sudden opening of the superintendent's door.

McRay padded lightly along the oriental carpet runner. The last thing he wanted to do was wake up the tenants, have to explain why a plainclothes detective was wandering around with his gun drawn. He'd slipped his badge holder into his breast pocket, leaving the shield visible. Just in case some trigger-happy resident decided to challenge him.

More cops got shot accidentally than in the line of duty, that was an ugly fact of life. And here he was, violating a department order, interfering with a crime scene. It didn't matter that he was a cop, he was still breaking the law, when it came right down to it. Who could blame a frightened resident, shooting a plainclothes detective who barged in in the dead of night, unannounced?

His chief concern wasn't the tenants, of course. But it helped control his mounting anxiety. Too damn much caffeine in the last sixteen hours, that's what had elevated his pulse, made him feel like he'd just run a ten-mile road race, his head going light and his knees turning to liquid.

Because you could stop John Chester Marlon with bullets. No question about that. Hell, a feisty woman had gotten lucky, slammed him upside the head with a brick, and he'd gone down. Still, McRay couldn't help but think about how weak and ineffectual he'd felt in Marlon's presence, the look in the man's beady little eyes, like he knew what you were thinking, and found it amusing.

Shoot first, that was McRay's plan. As soon as he'd formulated it, he knew he couldn't do it. Kill Marlon and he'd never know where he'd taken Anna, and if she was alive or dead.

Okay, just wing the bastard, like they always did in the movies. Knee-cap him. Good plan, Kev, just make sure you hit him—and don't get too close; this is a guy can kill with his bare hands.

Other than the glide of chandelier reflections, nothing stirred in the hallway. Nice old building—what did they call that, wainscoting? Dark wood panels that came up waist high, yeah, that was wainscoting. Place had to be at least a hundred years old, and they'd kept it up. What was that wood, walnut? Rich-looking stuff, whatever it was, and the late Hector Rivera had kept it polished with lemon oil, the scent was unmistakable. Brass everywhere, too, the door handles, the stair rails, nice little touches that meant old money, rich folk, old New York in better days. Carriages, tradesmen, servants, every conceivable luxury available on demand. And delivered with a tug of the forelock, too, no surly remarks. Not to your face, anyhow.

The current tenants were listed under glass, in a frame just inside the heavily secured front door. Thirteen apartments, all with tenants indicated, and two ground floor business suites. Suite A was occupied by a certified public accountant.

Suite B was left blank. Neither an occupant listed, nor a "for lease" notification. Which raised the question of why such a valuable location had been left in limbo, neither occupied nor seeking a leaseholder.

Suite B.

Had a nice ring to it. Make a nice jazz piece, maybe a McCoy Tyner composition, or Miles in the right sort of mood.

You can't stand here all night musing on titles, Kev, you have to face the music. Suck it up and get to it.

Suite B was in the rear of the building, the door located under the grand staircase. The top panel was frosted glass, and he could see where the lettering had been removed. He couldn't make out the name. Maybe a *D* something, or a *B*, it was hard to tell.

He put his ear to the door. Total silence. A silence so absolute it made him want to curl up on the carpet and sleep for a couple of years.

Let somebody else check out sweet old Suite B, see what kind of surprises it contained.

The pane of glass was so thin that it shattered like milky peanut brittle under the butt of his pistol. Breaking and entering, a textbook example. Tapping the shards from the frame, he reached through, drew back the deadbolt. Very little light here, under the stairway, so he turned on his flashlight, almost immediately located a switch just inside of the door frame.

McRay clicked on the light and found himself standing in a dentist's waiting room.

Anna was aware of two things. A great weight pressing down, and the bump of wheels right under her head. The weight was Ned Cody, bound and gagged, as she was. He seemed to be unconscious. The noise made by the wheels, that was harder to figure out. After a while she decided it had to be something like a canvas laundry cart, moving steadily along, alternately over a smooth surface—the wheels hummed—and over rough—the wheels banging.

She and Cody had been dumped into the cart, and now they were on the move. She couldn't see who was pushing the cart—she couldn't see much of anything—but it was Marlon, no doubt about it. Listen hard and you could hear a kind of tuneless whistling. So he was in a good mood, back in control, and Anna remembered the last thing he'd said, as he placed his hands over her face and shoved her down into the darkness: *What were you thinking?*

What *had* she been thinking, scheming to overpower him with nothing more lethal than the jagged edge of a tin can? Had she really believed she might succeed?

A bigger question was this: why was she still alive?

Marlon had had numerous opportunities to kill her, as he'd undoubtedly killed more than a dozen other, similar-looking females. Was it possible that the implant was actually functioning, on some reduced level? Did he fear being rendered unconscious while in the throes of violence? Nothing about his manner suggested such fear on his part—there had to be some other reason why she was being kept alive. Because he did intend to kill her eventually, that much was clear.

What? he'd said, responding to her direct question. *Are you in a hurry?*

The unthinkable truth was this: if it was going to happen, she wanted it to happen quickly. In that sense, she *was* in a hurry. Above all, she did not want to share her death with him. That was her greatest fear, that he would seek some intimate connection, delve into her mind in the final moments, strip away the last few shreds of her dignity. She was determined not to let that happen, no matter what.

"We're almost there," he said. "Home at last."

The wheels hit a rut. Above her, Ned Cody groaned.

"You're going to be surprised," Marlon said, and she could feel him looming over the cart, directing his comment to her. "It's not what you think, Dr. Kane. It's much, much better. Or much, much worse, depending on your point of view."

Anna heard a gate being closed. And then the bottom dropped and she was falling. No, not falling—they were on an elevator, she could make out the whir of an electric motor, the hum and scrape of cables descending. It sounded old, creaky.

"Freight elevator. Rated for ten thousand pounds," Marlon said in a conversational tone. "Had it right at the limit a few times. Of course that was several years ago, when I was first starting out. Dealing in quantity."

Ned Cody was starting to squirm.

"Careful now," Marlon warned him. "You'll bruise Dr. Kane, and we wouldn't want that, would we?"

Cody stopped squirming. He was fully conscious now, she could feel his muscles tensing in response to Marlon's voice. Vibrating was more like it.

The lift bumped to a stop, and once again she was aware of a pneumatic hiss. Then the cart was trundling forward, the wheels humming on a smooth surface. She was aware of light and shadows alternating rapidly. The cart accelerated down an incline and she heard Marlon's feet pitterpattering, hurrying to keep up. There was a distinct echo, as if they were in some vast, cavernous place.

"Let's not leave the barn door open," said Marlon cheerfully.

There was a heavy click, followed by the sound of a garage door descending, locking down.

"Let's sit up, shall we?"

Hands reached into the cart, lifting Ned Cody, and then she was being shifted upright so quickly that the blood rushed from her head. White dots in her eyes, phantom fireflies swimming in her field of vision. Blurred human shapes, and looming close, Marlon himself.

"Now, that's better," he said. "Welcome to the Doll House."

The gag couldn't stop her from screaming inside.

CHAPTER
FIVE

McRay's first impression was of dust. Time had settled over the waiting room in the form of a fine layer of dust. Dust on the small couch and the matching chairs, dust on the magazine table and the magazines, dust on the floor, where he could make out several trails of footprints, some more recent than others—you could see where the dust was starting to fill back in.

Decades' worth of dust, he decided. The most recent magazine on the table was a *National Geographic* dating from twenty-three years ago, so maybe that was an accurate marker. Was it possible that Suite B had been shut up for more than two decades, and never once disturbed—or cleaned—by the meticulous building superintendent? If so, the lack of attention wasn't coincidental, it had to have been by design. Access forbidden. Except for the man who left the footprints.

A large man, size twelve shoes at least.

McRay followed the prints into a small, interconnecting room, found a metal desk, drawer files, an old rotary telephone, all of the edges softened under archaeological layers of the dust and grime, laid down over the years.

This was, he realized, a dentist's office. He used his thumb to clean the obscuring dust from a nameplate, and felt his heart pause in midbeat.

Stephen J. Marlon, D.D.S.

It was like opening a door in a nightmare and being suddenly awakened by a blast of cold, dirty wind.

That's why he'd been nagged by the idea of a Park Avenue address! Because in the back of his mind was the knowledge that John Chester Marlon's late father had been a Park Avenue dentist. The family lived in Brooklyn, which was where the background checks had been conducted by detectives, but dear old dad had practiced in upscale Manhattan.

Yes, yes, yes.

Dead and gone for twenty years, and nowhere in the Marlon investigation had there been any information that the father's place of business still existed. How was it possible? A man died, his practice was closed, or sold—nobody just shut the doors and let the dust accumulate for decades, not with real estate *this* valuable.

And yet it had happened.

The office had been preserved, and therefore had special meaning for Marlon, who as his father's heir must have made the decision to keep the place exactly as it was. A place so important, so crucial, that Marlon had risked at least two murders to gain access to this place.

McRay became aware that he was perspiring. Sweating so profusely that his sleeves were wet and his hands were slick. Slick on the pistol. There it was, clenched in his right hand, and he didn't even remember how it got there. Had he come in here holding the thing? The place was empty, not a creature was stirring, shouldn't the gun be returned to his holster?

Answer, no. Those were Marlon's footprints in the dust, had to be. So he'd been here. He'd killed not ten yards from this very spot.

McRay forced himself to breathe more slowly. He was hyperventilating and it was making him light-headed. Slow it down, take it one breath at a time.

This discovery was the biggest break thus far in the Subway Killer case. Even bigger than the weapons cache. Unlike the cache, this mausoleum of a place was intimately connected to Marlon's past. He'd killed to come here, it *had* to be important.

With his gun steadied in both hands, McRay explored the suite. So hard to concentrate, process what he was seeing. A waiting room, the receptionist's office, a small storage room, and finally the boxy, arsenic-green examination room where Dr. Stephen Marlon had practiced dentistry.

Something wrong, that was his first impression. Then he saw the round, circular shape on the floor and he realized what was missing. The dentist's chair. Recent footprints disturbing the dust on the rest of the floor. Marks from where the chair had been dragged from the room.

McRay followed the trail, noticed that the beam of the flashlight was trembling. Silly. Empty rooms, why was he shaking all over? Pull yourself together, man, you're doing good work here. This is the big break you've been waiting for—don't lose your focus.

He closed his eyes, again forced himself to breathe normally. Amazing how much courage it took, closing his eyes in this situation. But he had to prove that he could do it, take that risk, because self-confidence was bleeding out of him like thin blood from a mortal wound.

McRay counted to ten and opened his eyes. Nothing had changed. He was alone in this place. The emptiness was a hollow chamber inside him, an echo of fear that seemed to originate under his diaphragm, making his stomach feel clenched and cold.

Follow the footprints, Kev. Do what a detective does.

And so he followed the imprints in the dust, the unmistakable evidence of a large man dragging a heavy dentist's chair. A trail that led directly—and this was what he'd been avoiding—directly to a paneled storage closet built into the corner of the small room. The footprints became blurred, as if there had been some increase in activity just outside the closet door.

Opening the door was even more difficult than closing his eyes. Because you never knew, did you, what lurked in closets?

He centered the pistol on the door, lifted the latch, and took a step back as the door swing open. The relief was so intense he almost wept. The shallow closet was filled with narrow shelving—there wasn't room in there for a cat, let alone a man as big as John Chester Marlon.

But what about the footprints in the dust? The trail led to this closet. Were they the imprints left by a ghost, a creature who could melt through walls?

McRay didn't believe in ghosts. The prints were as real as the gun in his hand. He pointed his flashlight at the shelving, took a good look. The beam of light skittered over a black edge. Hold it. The dark edge was a gap in the paneling.

He held the flashlight with his teeth—no way was he going to holster his sidearm—and lifted out a section of shelving with his left hand. There. Now he could make out the form of the whole panel. As if, he suddenly realized, the storage closet had been built up later, to cover an existing doorway.

He worked quickly, pulling away the shelving. Yes, there it was, a door. A moment later he had pried the panel open and his flashlight was illuminating a narrow, curving stairway.

A stairway going down.

CHAPTER SIX

Gently Marlon untied their gags, patted their cheeks. "There," he said. "Feel better?" He waited a moment, did not seem surprised that his captives were unable to respond.

All around them, the dead screamed in silence.

This was Marlon's gallery of corpses. The chamber, fully three stories high, had been divided into several levels. It looked, at first glance, like a full-scale doll house cut away to reveal the interior. Theatrical spotlights had been carefully focused on the occupants of each of the many "rooms."

Human trophies on display, dead but somehow alive.

The cadavers had been preserved intact, as if frozen in their own time-stilled moments of death. Their open mouths screamed silently. Expressions of unspeakable fear were imprinted on each face, and lifeless hands reached out, as if to ward off some terrible, incomprehensible evil.

Anna shut her eyes, but the nightmare images remained burned into her brain.

They'd all been wrong about John Chester Marlon. His trophies weren't limited to attractive young women of a certain age. His tastes ranged over both genders, extended to all ages. Displayed in the chamber, starkly illuminated by the numerous spotlights, were dozens and dozens of victims, victims preserved in grotesque poses. Men, women, children.

Some of the Doll House "rooms" held only a single victim; in others there were several cadavers, carefully displayed in eerie, hideous arrangements that had no pattern or meaning, beyond evoking a numbing sense of horror.

Even with her eyes squeezed shut, Anna couldn't stop the silently screaming images from slamming into her mind like hammer blows. Nor could she stop the sound of Marlon's smug, self-satisfied voice.

"I never meant to call it the Doll House," he explained. "That nasty little cellmate they sent to spy on me was so dense I couldn't make him understand, and when he finally said, 'Oh, you mean like a doll house,' I let it go." He gazed about the chamber with an expression of immense satisfaction, nodding to himself. "Not that I expect anyone alive now to understand. A work of art this advanced, breaking through into a new vision, it will take a generation even to *begin* to comprehend what I've made here."

More than anything, Anna wanted to put her hands over her ears, block out his insistent voice, but her hands were bound with the plastic twine. She had to listen.

"What I have done here is make a world unto itself," Marlon said, sounding enormously pleased with himself. "It stands alone, terrible to behold, and uniquely beautiful. You can't help but be amazed and terrified—and that is why my transcending genius will eventually be celebrated. Picasso, Matisse, all the so-called geniuses of the twentieth century will pale in comparison with John Chester Marlon. This is *my* century. My millennium. A thousand years from now the enlightened will still be visiting this place to bask in my genius."

Beside her in the laundry cart, Ned Cody was being violently ill.

"I take that as a compliment," Marlon remarked serenely. "You're overwhelmed. My work is beyond the comprehension of a failed, second-rate actor. And a third-rate killer, I might add. That's but one of our many differences, Mr. Cody. You killed someone you thought you loved because you were afraid to kill yourself. Murder for you was a form of suicide. For me it is life affirming. Each time I take a life, that small death becomes eternally beautiful. It becomes part of the whole, transformed, improved."

Anna felt herself drifting into a fugue state, cut off from unbearable reality. She was forced to make a decision. Either open her eyes and face the unfaceable, or retreat so far into her mind that she might never return.

At first the temptation to escape was overwhelming. She allowed her mind to close down, narrowing focus. She was no longer with Marlon, she was drifting back in time, becoming smaller, younger.

By the time she realized she was heading inevitably to another, deeper place of incomprehensible horror, it was too late.

Anna in the cupboard.

Four-year-old Anna, waiting for Daddy to come back and take her to heaven.

Daddy whom she loved. Poor crazy Daddy. Driven mad by forces beyond his control—even as a small child she had instinctively understood that her father couldn't help himself. No one could help him.

Crazy Daddy who loved her—that much she knew. Because when he came back into the house, the candles of jack-o'-lantern madness glittering in his eyes, she had been watching.

Little Anna crouching in the cupboard, spying through a crack in the door to see what Daddy would do, who he would hurt.

Oh, the things she saw.

She saw Mommy throwing herself at Daddy, trying to protect her.

She saw the flash of that terrible swift knife, heard her mother scream and bleed. And then. And then.

And then she saw Daddy look her way, catch her watching. Peekaboo.

Oh yes, he'd seen her peering from inside the cupboard, and the spark of connection seemed to wake him, as if in his insane rage he'd been asleep.

He came knife in hand to the cupboard.

He opened the door.

He saw her crouching, terrified, unable to speak.

Good night, my little angel, he'd said. *Remember that I loved you.*

And then he closed the cupboard door and went into another room and killed himself. Anna did not look at Daddy dying, she ran directly from the cupboard to her wounded mother and took her by the hand into the street, where the blue lights were already flashing.

Remember that your father loved you, Anna told herself as the events replayed in her mind. Your mother loved you, too. All the terrible things you saw, what really matters is that Mommy and Daddy loved you, even if they didn't love themselves, or each other. That love is what gave you strength. It made you what you are. The little girl in the cupboard survived. No one can take that away. No one. And if you can survive the cupboard, you can survive anything. Anything at all.

Anna opened her eyes.

"Good," said Marlon approvingly. "You have courage."

She made herself look around the chamber. "You killed so many. Why?"

"You're surprised," he said, sounding pleased. "You thought I was just a common psychopath, fixated on particular females. A dime-a-dozen serial killer. But as you can see, my interests range as wide as the human race."

This much was true: the victims were of both sexes, and all ages and races. Long-haired brunettes were just one of many physical types he'd collected, male and female. His fantasies about being an artist were obviously insane, but whatever Marlon was, he was not, as everyone had assumed, a typical, sexually obsessed serial killer.

"Less like tomb sculpture than *tableau vivant*," he said grandly. "More accurately, *tableau morte*," he added with a wry chuckle.

Tableau vivant. Yes. Anna remembered that as a girl she'd once seen, and been fascinated by, a photographic album of "living tableaux"—people frozen in a collective pose of a famous work of art. In some of the old photographs, the participants had draped themselves in sheets, and paled their exposed flesh, attempting to emulate marble sculpture. There had been a craze for such *tableaux vivants* in the nineteenth century, possibly because of the frankly erotic exposures made in the name of art.

There was nothing remotely erotic or sexually suggestive about Marlon's ghastly tableaux. Although not mummified or obviously decaying, his "sculptures" were unmistakably dead. To make it worse, the frozen facial expressions of the cadavers ranged from silent screams to tormented grimaces.

His theme, if he had one, was limited to fear, horror, revulsion.

"Rodin used armatures, when he brought clay to life," Marlon explained. "The skeleton is my armature, and flesh itself my clay."

"You're not insane," Anna said. "You're evil."

"I call it 'transformation,'" he said, ignoring her loathing. "The technique is very delicate, and extremely difficult. First the body must be saturated with thin, transparent epoxy resins."

He indicated his work area, a mortician's slab. Several large resin barrels and a drum of solvent were near at hand, along with a rack of intravenous tubing.

"Once the saturation is complete, the body remains pliable for less than thirty minutes. Think of it! Not only have I created a new medium, but I had to learn to work quickly, like a fresco painter. My first efforts were rather ghastly—I had to destroy them. Did you know that Cezanne destroyed dozens of his paintings? Anything that didn't measure up to his standards. That's the mark of a true artist. Leave nothing behind but your best work."

Cody's voice was faint. "You're no artist," he said. "You're a monster."

"Come now," Marlon said. "Was Caravaggio a monster? The supposedly mad painter Francis Bacon? Men of transcendent genius are not bound by ordinary law, or perceptions of conventional sanity. What matters is their work."

"This place is hell," Cody gasped.

Marlon nodded thoughtfully. "An astute observation," he said. "But if it is Hell, it is the Ninth Level of Hell. That place where souls are frozen in Eternity, caught forever in the moment of death. Dante wrote of it, but I have made it real. A place so powerful that its terrible beauty will blind the eyes of the ignorant, and inspire the enlightened." He smiled. "I see that despite your apparent revulsion, you can't take your eyes off what you see before you. Admit it, Ned, you're fascinated."

The actor made a weak choking sound and was sick again.

Marlon turned his attention to Anna. She really focused on him for the first time since entering the lighted chamber, and saw that he was, inexplicably, wearing a policeman's uniform.

"I've decided to make you an offer," he said. "Remove your little computer chip and I'll let you live. Both of you."

Anna wanted to believe him. The yearning burned under her skin, made her blood hum. To go on living, what a remarkable stimulant. Oh, yes, she wanted to believe with every fiber of her being. At the same time she knew he was lying. The lie was as fat as a ripe peach. A ripe, rotting peach corrupted with the sweet stench of epoxy resin, and death.

"You think I'm lying," he said. "But think about this—what difference does it make if I am? Would you know the truth if you heard it? Might I not make a promise and then change my mind? So whether I'm lying or not is immaterial, because there is one fundamental truth: if you don't remove this ugly little bug from my neck, I'll cut off your eyelids and make you watch while I transform your companion into a work of art. I'll make him howl for all of eternity."

Ned Cody had finished being sick, and he turned to Anna with an expression of such intense loneliness that she wanted to weep. Wanted to cry but could not.

"I'll do it," she said. "All I need is a scalpel."

"Did you hear that, Ned?" Marlon said. "Your true love comes to the rescue. You weren't looking, but her eyes really lit up when she said the magic word. Scalpel."

"No," Anna said.

"Yes," said Marlon. "She wants to cut my throat. She wants to become what we are, Ned. A killer. Why not? She's in good company."

"I won't," Anna said. "I promise."

"We both know what promises are," Marlon said. "I know a way, if you have the nerve. Do you have the nerve, Dr. Kane?"

"Yes," she said.

CHAPTER
SEVEN

"This is Detective Kevin McRay," he said, speaking into the super's telephone. "I'm requesting backup."

He was surprised at how steady his voice was, how calm he must have sounded, giving the Park Avenue address and explaining who should be notified and why.

Amazing how calm he sounded, because he wasn't calm on the inside. Not even close. His stomach felt like it was ratcheting up the incline of the Coney Island roller coaster. That keen, nauseating anticipation. The waiting to plunge.

Because he couldn't wait. Waiting was death, if not for him, than possibly for Anna. And so Detective Kevin McRay violated yet another departmental rule.

He didn't wait for backup to arrive. He went ahead.

There was a surprise at the bottom of Marlon's secret stairway.

An old train tunnel that came right into the sub-basement.

McRay knew about the old system of private railway cars for wealthy East Side residents. For a couple of decades before the turn of the century it was the height of fashion for private mansions to have small-gauge rails feeding directly into Grand Central Station. As the major luxury hotels had direct underground access, so did the bankers and robber barons of Park and Lexington avenues. Rather than venturing out into the horse-clogged streets, a man of means could step into his own basement and journey by privately owned electric coach right into the train station where, presumably, his own full-size railway car awaited.

The system had long since been abandoned, but a few of the tunnels still existed, undisturbed by more recent excavations. Dr. Marlon's office, located in a converted Park Avenue mansion, had been situated above one of these old connections. Had the dentist's son discovered the paneled-over stairway and tunnel as a child—was that what had originally spurred his interest in the world of subterranean Manhattan?

John Chester Marlon as a child, exploring the secret underzones of the city. It was a chilling thought, but it made a kind of twisted sense—the doll house reference, that was something from a child's imagination, right? And sociopaths had in common an overwhelming, infantile perception of self that made empathy with other human beings inconceivable. Was that where the boy's obsessions had begun, there in his father's place of business?

And why had Marlon hauled away his father's dental chair, what was *that* about?

McRay nervously played the beam of light around the narrow tunnel. The walls were of tightly mortised brick, with supporting arches every ten yards or so. The narrow-gauge rails had been taken up, but he could see where the spikes had pierced the gravel-embedded cross-ties that remained underfoot. The private cars must have been quite small, he decided, barely wide enough to sit two abreast.

When the old gaslight fixtures were functional, the private rail line must have had a warm glow as the little cars clicked along the tracks. Now it was cool and damp and as black as the inside of a hat. The tunnel curved, restricting visibility to less than a hundred feet, despite the powerful flashlight beam. The arches weren't wide enough to hide a man of Marlon's size, but the interplay of shadows kept McRay guessing.

The Glock 9-mil was by now an extension of his hand. The phrase "fire when ready, Gridley" came to mind—where had *that* come from, was it an old movie? No, something out of American history. Fire when ready, McRay. Better yet, fire the moment you see him, fire at any son of a bitch who steps out of those shadows.

Might be an innocent victim, he cautioned himself. But his fear said: nobody is innocent, just pull the damn trigger.

Beneath his feet the hard, earthen floor of the tunnel was beginning to hum. A deep, steady vibration. Something very large up ahead. Dynamo, power plant, that order of magnitude. Which made sense—Grand Central Station was like a small, self-contained city. The station had its own generators, pump rooms, heaters, its own refrigeration plant, and a massive electrical conversion system that switched city-supplied AC over to direct current for the shuttle to Times Square and other subway lines.

McRay advanced, aiming his gun and his flashlight. He was no longer afraid. Afraid didn't cover it. He'd entered a more advanced state of anxiety, somewhere beyond fear.

The truth was, he was so scared he wanted to kill somebody. That would make it right, killing somebody.

Len Jakowski was dreaming of fish. He was underground, walking under the city, and fish were swimming by, languidly flicking their tails. The fish glowed, they were like floating lanterns in the dark.

His wife made the fish-lanterns go away. "Didn't you hear the phone?" she said, her voice thick with sleep. "You never hear the damn phone."

"Huh?" he said. "Huh?" and then the phone was at his ear and a voice was telling him to pay attention, this was important.

"What?" he said. "What? You're kidding, he did what?"

Ninety seconds later he was wiping his face with a towel soaked in cold water. An old patrolman's trick, when you didn't have time for a wake-up shower.

"This isn't supposed to happen," his wife said. Not complaining, just stating a fact. "You've got seniority."

"That crazy bastard McRay," he said. "He's gone down alone."

"You mean he's been shot?"

"Not yet," Jakowski said hastily. "He's supposed to wait for backup, but he went ahead. Into the tunnels. Marlon's tunnels."

"The woman," his wife said. "The lady head-shrinker. So it must be love, huh?"

"I guess," Jakowski said. He was stepping into his trousers, looking for his shoes.

"Cutey-pie Kevin in love. This is the first time, that I'm aware of. I'll bet he brings her deli sandwiches."

"I wouldn't know."

"Ask him does he bring her food from the deli."

Jakowski located his sidearm, slipped it into his coat pocket. "Now why should I do that?"

"You used to bring me things, Len, remember? Little treats?"

"Sure I do," he said. "Those were the days, huh?"

"You don't remember."

"Hey, we're still married, doesn't that count for something?"

She kissed him at the door. "It counts," she said. "Of course it does. Wait a minute, where's your vest?"

"Aw nuts."

"I'm not letting you out that door until you put on your vest."

He didn't fight her. Hell, he *wanted* the Kevlar vest, he was naked without it. Who knew, these days, what might come his way?

The air was humming. It was warm and moist and it was humming. There was faint light, too, or was that his imagination?

McRay switched off the flashlight, satisfied himself that yes, indeed, there was light at the end of the tunnel. The constant drone had to be coming from Grand Central—maybe it was just the background noise, all the trains and human activity, all those tramping feet setting up a vibration.

But the hum kept getting louder, until it had substance, like the air. You could inhale the noise, absorb the drone like oxygen. And the light became stronger, softening the whole tunnel like a false sunrise.

He emerged, finally, into a cavernous area where a number of spur lines converged. Overhead, arc lights burned like stars against a soot-blackened ceiling. There was not a soul in sight, not so much as a rat moving on the old track beds. What had he been expecting, the ghost of Cornelius Vanderbilt, boarding his gold-plated railway car? John Chester Marlon waiting to take his ticket? What?

McRay leaned against a wall and took a deep breath. What had he been so frightened of, back there in the tunnel? Marlon wasn't bulletproof. He couldn't walk through walls or make himself invisible. He couldn't, damn it, the man could not read minds. That was an old parlor trick, a head game he played with potential victims. The prison guard he'd shot, she'd simply been immobilized by fear, it wasn't as if the crazy son of a bitch had hypnotic powers. No way.

When his heart was beating at something like a normal rate, McRay followed the spur lines until they abruptly ended at a cinderblock wall.

The wall was a fairly recent construction, probably installed as a means of keeping out the derelicts who had been setting up crude camps throughout the subway system, burrowing like human weevils into the underbelly of the city.

So, a dead end.

He retraced his steps in the opposite direction, and became aware that the dynamo hum was considerably louder here. Follow the noise, he told himself, and by doing so he discovered the freight elevator he'd missed on the first tour.

This was no ordinary freight elevator. Behind a slatted gate was an old timbered platform that had to be twenty feet wide, thirty feet deep. Large enough to lift huge pieces of machinery. With the spur lines walled off, there was no reason for it to be left in functioning condition, but when he pulled back the gate, the cables were activated. The floorboards vibrated. And when he pushed the brass lever, the machinery engaged and the whole thing began to move at a snail's pace.

Going down.

It wasn't until the freight elevator was halfway down to the next level that he realized how exposed he was. Trapped between two levels, he was an easy target. Backing up against the sidewall, he crouched with his gun extended. Squinting against the growing darkness—the lower level was not illuminated.

Finally the elevator clunked to a stop. He waited where he was, letting his eyes adjust. No point in turning on the flashlight right away, it would only pinpoint him as a target. When he was satisfied that there were no forms lurking in the immediate vicinity, he pulled back the gate as quietly as he could. Probably didn't matter, the hum was now so loud it absorbed most other sounds, including the slap of his feet against the concrete ramp that led off the freight elevator.

It was much warmer at this level, too. More evidence that a generator or turbine was nearby. The flashlight revealed a corridor fully as wide as the freight elevator. A world of concrete down here, thick walls and high arched ceilings, holding up tons of earth. Had to be seven or eight levels down, well below the deepest subway lines.

Had Marlon come this way? There seemed no other alternative, unless he had some hidden passage not readily visible to the naked eye. Which was, come to think of it, a distinct possibility.

What kept McRay moving was the idea of the dentist's chair. The damn chair had to be somewhere down here. An innocent building superintendent had been murdered for that chair, so it had to be important to Marlon. Maybe the big guy had a toothache, huh? Right, and King Kong was just a misunderstood ape.

McRay was thinking about that when his flashlight beam found a corrugated steel door. A warehouse door, sealed and locked.

He decided it was important to find out what was behind the door.

CHAPTER EIGHT

"**Y**ou want to kill me," he said. "We both know that."

Anna found herself wedged against the cushion supports of an old dentist chair. Marlon had his back to her, pinning her legs against the armrests. The hair had begun to grow out on his pale, translucent scalp, black stubble coming up through the bone of his skull. He was so close his odor filled her mind, a scent redolent of maleness, of an immense physical presence that made her feel weak-limbed and light-headed.

"We have that in common," he said. "All three of us. Scratch a human, find a killer."

Marlon held the actor immobile in his lap, a scalpel poised over his neck, just above the carotid artery. Moments before, he had presented Anna with a matching scalpel, placing the handle firmly into her sweating palm.

"Ned knows," Marlon said. "Tell her, Neddy boy." The big man relaxed his grip enough to allow Ned Cody to speak in a hoarse, strangulated whisper. "Do it," he urged her. "Kill him."

"Admit it, Dr. Kane," Marlon said. "The only thing that prevents you from trying to cut my throat is fear. You're not afraid of becoming a killer—you've wanted that all your life. You're just afraid that you won't succeed."

Anna ignored the taunt, determined not to play his mind games—a willingness to save her own life by snuffing out John Chester Marlon did not make her a killer. She had not crossed over into that dark place where the soul became psychotic, where murder became desire. Not yet.

"I can't do this."

"Oh, but you can," he said. "You gave me your word."

"I was mistaken," she insisted. "This should be done by a surgeon, in antiseptic conditions."

Marlon's bulk shuddered against her and she realized he was laughing silently. "Oh please," he said. "I might get an infection? Did you hear that, Ned? Gallows humor from our pretty doctor."

He had torn away the surgical dressing, exposing the fold of flesh on the back of his neck where the MSD had been implanted. Healing had already blurred the original incision.

"It's not that simple," Anna said.

"At the count of three, you will make the incision," he insisted.

"What difference does it make?" she asked. "You're not trigger-reactive, so the device doesn't work. You proved that by escaping. You're proving it right now."

"Think of it as a bad tooth," he said evasively. "I want it pulled."

This, she realized, was why he had brought her to this place, why he had kept her alive. "The battery contains a radioactive material," she warned. "It may leak."

"I'll take that chance. One."

"But—"

"Two. At the count of three," he warned, "you either make an incision, or I will."

He meant Ned Cody, of course, and he was quite right about her fear. Yes, she wanted to kill him and yes, she was afraid of failing. Even if she did manage to inflict a fatal wound with the blade of the scalpel, he would still have time to finish off Cody and turn his wrath on her. A wrath so awful, so unthinkable that it was worth delaying at any cost. The sight of all those eerily preserved cadavers had burned this thought into her brain: every minute left alive was precious, even in this terrible place.

"Three," he said.

Anna drew the blade along the original incision, releasing a crimson thread of blood. The flap of skin opened. She twisted the blade and the small, wafer-shaped implant slipped out, exposed to the light. She nicked the thread of wire that held the wafer in place and it was done. Marlon was disconnected. Free to kill without fear of activating the device.

He hadn't reacted to the blade. It was as if he did not register pain.

"Drop the scalpel to the floor," he said softly.

She did so.

"Now the bug."

She dropped the implant into his open palm and raised both hands above her forehead. "Let Ned go," she said. "That was the deal."

"Deal?" he said. "And what will you do if I don't let him go?"

"I'll claw your eyes out."

"I could still do both of you."

"Maybe so," she said. "But you'd be blind."

And blinded, he wouldn't be able to admire his handiwork. His hideous "dolls." That, Anna believed, was the only credible threat she could make. She felt his muscles stiffen, trapping her even tighter against the confines of the chair, and then Ned Cody was slumping to the floor, his hands still bound with the plastic strapping.

"Fair enough," Marlon said, rising from the chair, turning to face her. He extended his right hand. "Shall we dance?"

Ned lay motionless on the floor, watching Marlon reach out for Anna. There was nothing he could do and it was driving him crazy. Anna, sweet brave Anna had just risked her own life, and probably sealed her fate, to buy him a few more precious minutes of life. Why? She knew he was guilty. Even worse, she knew he was a coward, and yet she had not hesitated.

True, he'd jumped into that elevator car when Marlon seized her as hostage. He'd put himself at risk, but it hadn't been an act of courage. Far from it. He'd *wanted* to follow Marlon into the darkness. Wanted to feel his power, see where it could take him, over the edge into the realms of nightmare and forbidden fantasy. Like poor pathetic Arthur Glidden, Ned had wanted desperately to believe that there was no right, no wrong, no good or evil, no guilt or innocence, that his soul was not damned for all eternity.

It was all a lie, he knew that now. Evil existed, it was here right at this very moment, reaching out for Anna Kane, proposing a dance of death. And if there was good in the world, it was personified in Anna. Ned believed this as strongly as he'd ever believed in anything.

If there was good and evil alive in the world, were there miracles, too? Because he needed a miracle right now. A miracle that would give him one more chance to make up for all his lost chances. Up to now, everything had been playacting, even Tracy's murder had been a kind of playacting.

Send me a miracle, Ned Cody prayed, straining at his bonds. I want to do something real, for once in my life. Even if it costs me my life.

"Dance with me," Marlon said, reaching for Anna. "I'll make you live forever."

They heard it then, a noise coming from the other side of the sealed, overhead door. The methodic thump of metal on metal.

Someone was trying to get in.

CHAPTER
NINE

McRay heaved against the length of iron pipe, using it as a pry bar wedged under the lip of the corrugated steel door. The damn thing would lift an inch or two—and then nothing. Locked from the inside, apparently, since there was no outside bolt or mechanism. Which made him all the more suspicious.

He dropped the pipe, backed away from the door. Was there another way in? Pacing along the dark passage, he played the flashlight beam into every crevice, searching for an alternative access.

Nothing.

There! Was it his imagination, or had he heard a muffled sound? Moving quietly, he returned to the sealed door and placed his ear against the rippled steel. There it was again. A faint murmur—was that a human voice, or his mind playing tricks?

He knocked softly against the steel, heard it boom inside, a lingering rumble. As if the space beyond the door was quite large, big enough to produce an echo. He was reminded of what happened when a seashell was placed next to the ear—the sound of distant waves was supplied by the imagination, a trick of the ear. And yet surely he'd heard *something* in there.

McRay was trying to wedge the pipe into the side of the panel, maybe spring the door from its tracks, when he heard a sound that froze him: the blood-chilling snick-snick of a weapon being cocked.

Instinct made him drop the pipe and move to one side of the door, but not so fast that he missed seeing the first row of holes exploding through the corrugated steel at a level just above his head. The distinctive *brrrapppp* of a full automatic followed, and he was jolted by the spark-dust of lead pellets in high-speed impact with hardened concrete.

Slugs stitched through the door, ricochets whining, concrete chipping, until the magazine was empty. Five or six of the longest seconds in his life.

It was strange, experiencing terror and elation in the same heartbeat. Terror because he'd found Marlon's lair, elation because that meant Anna might be nearby. She was in there, had to be! He very deliberately didn't allow himself to entertain the next logical thought—that Anna was in all probability already dead.

McRay suddenly tasted blood, frantically explored his face and neck for a wound, and then realized he'd bitten his tongue.

Maybe it was the self-induced pain that gave him the idea.

"God!" he moaned, lifting his voice. "Oh Jesus! Oh God!"

Screaming in pain was fun. He crouched by the side of the bullet-riddled door, gripping the Glock 9-mil pistol with both hands while he moaned and coughed and shouted incoherently.

The trick was to sound wounded and terrified at the same time. Sounding terrified was easy. Nothing to it.

Jeff Roberge clicked off his lantern, craned his long-limbed body, and said, "You hear that?"

"I hear all kinds of stuff," said Jakowski. "Why'd you douse the light?"

"Hear better in the dark."

"What are you, a freakin' bat?"

"Might have been gunfire."

"I'd know gunfire," Jakowski said. "All I hear is that fucking rumble."

"Transformers," Roberge said.

"I thought it was trains."

"Trains, too, but mostly transformers. Power for Grand Central."

"Right," Jakowski said uneasily.

"Now I don't hear it no more. The shots."

"Turn on the light," Jakowski pleaded. "What I'm hearing is my frigging heart. Banging hard enough, you probably hear it, too."

Roberge clicked on the lantern, illuminating the brick-vaulted tunnel. "Kevin must have come this way, huh?"

"How the hell should I know?" Jakowski said. "It's not like he's dropping bread crumbs, leaving us a trail."

He was so mad at McRay he was ready to pop the son of a bitch. Who the hell did young Kevin think he was, going off alone and then expecting to be backed up in the middle of the freaking night? Underground in the middle of the freaking night. Underground and in the dark and stalking a crazed killer in the middle of the freaking night.

Unless, of course, the killer was stalking *them*. Jesus, that was a hell of a thought.

Going into that dusty old dentist's office, that had unnerved Jakowski more than he cared to admit. Seeing that nameplate, *Stephen J. Marlon, D.D.S.,* why he'd been ready to crawl out of his skin. But nothing was as bad as following the mess of footprints through the cupboard and down into the sub-basement. Roberge seemed to know what it was all about— an old railway connection—but Jakowski was convinced the darkness harbored a secret so terrible that it would stop his heart.

Good thing Roberge had held the lantern, because Jakowski's hands had developed a sudden palsy, and he'd had to stop right there in the tunnel to take a leak, or risk pissing his pants like some nervous rookie.

Damn McRay! He wanted to risk his own life, fine, but this was beyond the bounds of friendship.

"We could wait here," Roberge offered. "Wait for the others to catch up."

An elite pursuit unit had been dispatched by the Transit Police— supposedly guys who knew the tunnels, and in particular the complex under Grand Central Station.

"Fuck that," Jakowski said, barging ahead. "Hell, those boys are as likely to shoot us as the freakin' Subway Killer, it comes to that."

"They know we're going ahead, right? They're aware of us?"

"Don't kid yourself," Jakowski said. "By the way, you wearing a vest?"

"Huh?"

"A bulletproof vest. You got one?"

"Uh, no," Roberge said uneasily.

"Better give me the lantern."

"Why's that?" he asked, handing it over.

"They like to shoot out the light," Jakowski said.

"The cops or the killer?"

"Both," he said.

McRay gradually stifled his moans, trying to sound like he was a man dying, or passing out. No longer a threat.

He waited, straining to hear, not willing to move from where he crouched with his back to the thick concrete.

A sound from inside, a furtive scuffling. Might be footsteps.

An electric motor suddenly kicked on, very close, and it was all McRay could do to stifle a real scream. He held his breath, forced himself to concentrate.

The door was lifting, clattering as it rolled up the tracks.

The mechanism jammed, and he heard a fist smash the corrugated steel in frustration.

McRay figured he was no more than a yard from where the fist hit the door. Very carefully, he shifted on the balls of his feet, bringing his gun to bear. Anybody stepped through the opening, he planned to empty the magazine—if he could see well enough to find a target.

Without the flashlight it was pitch black.

A soft, seductive voice spoke from behind the door. "Hey? You hurt out there? I can help."

McRay's bowels clenched. He knew that voice.

A beam of light painted the opposite wall. Slowly and deliberately it began to explore the area of floor beyond the door.

"I'm a doctor," Marlon said. "I can help."

The weird thing was, he sounded so damn convincing. The voice cared, it wanted to help. Had McRay actually been delirious with pain, he'd have been drawn to that voice, no question.

"If you can't talk, make a noise."

The voice had a shape and substance all its own. So close he could almost reach out and touch it. Strangely enough, it made McRay want to sleep. Just relax and let himself drift off. What was he so afraid of?

Another voice brought him back to life: a shout from deep inside. "Run! Don't listen, he'll kill you!"

Anna. The echo made it hard to identify, but his heart told him the warning came from Anna Kane. Anna or not, someone was alive in there.

Things started happening so quickly he never had time to let it sink home: she was alive.

The beam of light was snaking sideways, searching quickly. McRay knew he had to make a move before it found him. He took a deep breath, held it, and rolled away from the wall.

Lying prone, he could see under the partially lifted door. He fired three shots in the vicinity of the flashlight and saw the light shatter. The muzzle flash put sparks in front of his eyes, and raw fear made him continue firing in the same general direction, counting and squeezing, five-six-seven-eight-nine-ten.

What stopped him from emptying the magazine was the sudden realization that he might be endangering Anna. Jesus God, don't let me shoot her! And God, please make him be dead!

His lungs were tight, burning. He'd forgotten to breathe. As he gulped fresh air he scrambled forward, still prone, and crawled under the jammed door, into the larger space. Pitch black.

"Anna!" he screamed. "Is that you!"

His voice boomed through the cavernous space.

"Hide!" came her reply. "Hide!"

Her voice—she was alive! McRay wanted to call out, reassure her, but did not dare reveal his position in the dark.

He heard feet skidding on the concrete. Impossible to pinpoint location. And he became aware of strong, oppressive fumes. A powerful chemical stink like glue or solvent. What the hell *was* this place?

Snick-snick-snick. A full automatic being cleared and reloaded. McRay hastily decided the sound came from slightly to the right of where he lay, belly down on the concrete. He aimed in the general area. Held his fire, waiting.

Waiting.

Aware that he was drenched in fear-sweat. Had he wet himself? Couldn't be sure—and he didn't care. Was this what it felt like in a battle situation? Waiting in clammy, stifling darkness to return fire from you knew not where, you knew not when? And discovering, much to your surprise, that you didn't really care what happened next?

McRay knew he was going to die. The other thing he knew was that there was nothing he could do about it. It was not a question of courage or cowardice, it was simply a place he had entered from which there was no escape.

He saw the small blue muzzle flash before he heard the soft, deadly *brrrrp* of the weapon and watched with amazement as his body functioned, squeezing off rounds, aiming for the flickering muzzle flash. Any moment now the tumbling slugs would find him and this unendurable tension would end.

That's when the world blew up.

It was more sudden than the death he'd been expecting. Out of the darkness a faint pin-prick of orange came to life and bloomed instantly, filling his whole mind with an incandescent burst of white light.

Before his heart went to the next beat there was a floor-shaking *WOMP!* that sucked the air from his lungs, and then the hot dragon-breath of the explosion washed over him, parching the moisture from his eyeballs, and setting his hair on fire.

He was burning from the top like a goddamn Roman candle.

CHAPTER
TEN

Three minutes before the world exploded, Anna found a treasure. It was better than finding a diamond as big as the Ritz.

The scalpel.

Marlon's first reaction to the banging on the door was to douse the lights. With the Doll House plunged into darkness, Anna dropped to the floor, frantically searching the area where she'd been forced to drop the scalpel, and, miracle of miracles, finding it almost immediately.

And then she quickly located Ned Cody where he'd been unceremoniously dumped. In the dark he trembled at her touch, no doubt convinced that Marlon had returned to finish him off.

Anna put her lips to his ear and breathed, "It's me," and felt the tension wash from his body.

She touched his bound wrists and he held completely still while she slashed at the plastic binding straps with the scalpel. Tough stuff, the plastic, but the blade was true, and while Marlon concentrated on arming himself against the intruder, Ned and Anna scuttled away.

"I've got an idea," Anna whispered. "The solvent drums. We can make a fire." Acetone was a volatile solvent used in many laboratory procedures—every medical student knew it was potentially as explosive as gasoline.

Cody did not hesitate. "Burn this place," he said. "Yes."

"We might burn, too."

"I don't care," he said firmly. "Let's do it."

Finding the solvent drums wasn't as easy as all that, despite the palpable fumes. Marlon was firing his weapon at the door and the echoes were disorienting—were they heading in the right direction?

"This way," Cody insisted, reaching out to make sure she was nearby. "It's not far."

Scrambling along on all fours in a blind panic, he banged head first into the drum of acetone, stunning himself.

Meanwhile Marlon was cranking the door open, searching for the intruder, using his most seductive persona.

"I want to help," he crooned.

Right. Anna could just make him out as he held the flashlight and crouched by the partially opened door. No way to get by him—he wouldn't hesitate to shoot her, even if it meant spoiling a potential "doll."

With Ned's help, she pushed her full body weight against the drum, expecting resistance. Discovering, to her surprise, that the solvent drum was strapped to a dolly and therefore fairly easy to upend. But having tipped the drum over, she still had to find a way to open the damn thing, releasing the contents—the plug was sealed with a rubber gasket and normally cranked open with the aid of a wrench.

Maybe there was a wrench nearby and maybe there wasn't—no time to search around. Just do it. She locked her fingers on the plug and twisted with all her strength.

It did not move.

Marlon was crooning away, trying to seduce the man he'd wounded. At any other time in her life those pitiful screams and moans would have been heart-rending. Now, it was just another welcome distraction for Marlon to deal with.

Until, that is, she recognized the detective's voice. A voice from another lifetime. Kevin McRay, with the gap in his teeth, worried about her plan to pacify a convicted serial killer. If only she'd listened. "Anna!" he cried. "Is that you?"

The answer, resounding in her mind, was *yes*. Yes, she was Anna Kane, and yes it was important that she remain alive. That was as far as her reasoning went, a simple desire to live, but it was enough to give her the strength to bear down and loosen the plug on the solvent drum.

A moment later, as Marlon deliberately cleared and reloaded his weapon, a rush of liquid gushed through her hands. Icy cold because it was instantly evaporating, filling the air with noxious fumes.

"We've got to get away," she urged Cody. "Run."

"Lead on, Macduff," he said, coughing at the fumes—his shirt was drenched with solvent.

Linking hands, they both ran, stumbling in the dark. A moment later there was an intense flash of light and then the shock wave lifted them and they were airborne.

Anna remembered flying. And then McRay screaming, "Anna! This way!"

She sat up, shaking her head, and realized she'd been momentarily knocked out by the blast. Sprawled all around her were Marlon's "dolls"—she'd been slammed into the bodies by the blast. Limbs and heads, torn loose from brittle torsos, littered the area, but Anna didn't have time to be repulsed; the flames were racing in her direction.

"God help me," said a hollow voice. It was Ned Cody, lying right beside her in the tangle of limbs. She'd mistaken him for one of the preserved bodies.

His shirt had melted, scorching his back and shoulders.

"I must be dead," he said.

"You're not dead." Anna stood up, grabbed both his hands, and yanked him to his feet. "Can you walk?"

"I think so."

A wave of heat forced them to turn away. A wall of fire was advancing rapidly. Saturated with epoxy resins, Marlon's collection of victims exploded into flames, burning hot and white. The air was searing—Anna knew that if they didn't move fast, all the available oxygen would be sucked into the inferno.

McRay was still screaming her name, but she couldn't see him through the sheets of fire, nor could she hope to reach him on the other side.

"The smoke," Cody gasped. "Follow the smoke!"

Was the man delirious? But he was clutching at her, pointing frantically, and he finally made her understand. A column of black smoke roiled upward, but not *straight* up—it was being diverted to one side, where a steel catwalk and stairs had been bolted into the concrete.

There was an opening up there, and the rising heat had found it.

"Come on, we've got a chance!"

Sure they did. The same chance a flame had, of escaping up the chimney.

"Okay," she said, taking his hand. "Go for it!"

McRay never saw what happened immediately after the initial blast. He was too busy pulling his jacket over his head, desperate to snuff out the flames. Then the stench of burning hair turned his stomach and he vomited into the smoldering jacket, and by the time he'd come up for air, Marlon was nowhere to be seen.

Had he been consumed by the flames? Had one of McRay's bullets found him?

All such concerns became secondary when he realized that Anna had not, as he had hoped, used the explosion to make her escape. She was still in there somewhere.

He stood under the corrugated steel doorway, screaming her name and watching in horror as dozens of human figures exploded into flame. As the intense heat consumed the bodies they seemed to come back to life for a few terrible moments, writhing and then melting away.

For all he knew, any one of the figures might have been Anna, trapped in the flames. What was alive and what was dead, how could anyone know?

He called her name until the steel overhead began to buckle and snap, until the heat drove him back and turned his tears into steam.

CHAPTER
ELEVEN

It sounded like popcorn going off in a tightly enclosed space.

"That what I think it is?" asked Jeff Roberge.

"Oh, yeah," said Len Jakowski. "A full automatic. Maybe an Uzi or a Tech-9, something like that."

"Kevin have one of them?"

"Not to my knowledge."

"Well, shit."

They ran toward the sound of gunfire. Heard a flatter pop that Jakowski recognized as a 9-millimeter semiautomatic pistol, the police standard. He tried counting and lost track, but it sounded like a whole fifteen-shot clip.

At the qualifying range they told you to aim each shot, squeeze off one at a time, but in a live situation the impulse was to empty the damn clip as fast as you could pull the trigger.

So it was a panic situation, and to make it worse Kevin McRay was, to his certain knowledge, a barely adequate marksman.

Roberge, lithe and athletic, not to mention a decade younger, was loping along like a track star. It was all Jakowski could do to keep him in sight.

"Wait up!" he panted. When that didn't work he shouted: "I've got the gun!"

That stopped Roberge in his tracks. You didn't rush toward gunfire unarmed.

"You call it in?" Roberge wanted to know when Jakowski caught up to him.

"No use," said Jakowski, indicating the transmitter clipped to his belt. "We're too far down. There's plenty of Transit cops at Grand Central, they'll call it in."

"If they heard it," said Roberge. "Which way?"

They had emerged from the private railway tunnel into the cavernous space that had housed the old spur lines. Jakowski, grateful to be out of the dark, confining tunnel, discovered he wasn't all that pleased with the wide open spaces. He kept wanting to flinch, find cover.

They felt the explosion under their feet before they heard the WOMP! of the acetone fumes igniting.

"Aw, shit," said Jakowski. "That's another level down."

"Smell that? Kind of a chemical smell. Not gas."

"What are you, a bloodhound?"

"I got a full range of odor detection," Roberge said proudly, demonstrating. "I'm smelling heat. Something big on fire, man, even you can sniff it now."

True enough. There was no more gunfire, so they ran toward the smoke, which was just beginning to make itself visible, rising to form a sooty inversion below the high ceiling.

From above they heard alarm bells going off.

"Company on the way," said Jakowski, relieved.

They got as far as the freight elevator. Dense black smoke poured up the shaft. Jakowski covered his mouth with the sleeve of his jacket, his eyes watering. No way could they go any further, not without breathing equipment. You could already feel the heat building in the shaft.

"What do we do now?" Roberge wanted to know.

"The fuck I know. Wait here, I guess."

The elevator kicked on.

"Maybe a short circuit, huh?"

"Maybe." Jakowski unholstered his own 9-mil, checked that he had an extra clip in his trouser pocket.

"How you gonna see who to shoot?" Roberge wanted to know.

Jakowski didn't have an answer for that. Nor did he have time to think about it. The elevator cables were slapping—he could hear that much. Maybe the damn thing was going down, headed for the center of the earth, halfway there already. But in his gut he knew the elevator was rising, and that it probably wasn't a short circuit that had activated the motor.

Somebody was coming, as sure as Satan dwelled in Hell.

He found that it wasn't easy, coughing and keeping his aim at the same time. The fuck he was aiming at he had no idea, but if anybody came roaring out of that smoke, he intended to shoot first and go to confession later.

That's what he told himself.

The truth, when it happened, was that he held his fire as the occupant staggered out of the elevator. Even with the man's hair all frizzy and singed and his face blackened, he recognized young Kevin McRay and felt his heart lighten.

The detective was out of it, didn't seem to recognize them, and he was so racked by fits of coughing that he couldn't make himself understood.

"Air! Get him air!"

They grabbed him under the arms and ran back up the incline to the spur lines, where the air was better.

When he'd gotten his breath back, the first thing McRay managed to say was, "She's alive."

Ned Cody was giddy, he didn't feel a thing.

"Burn the fucker out," he said. "Didn't we? Didn't we?"

"Sure we did," said Anna.

Cody was giddy because of shock, the body starting to shut down, protect itself from pain. Anna had very little experience with burn victims, but she knew the reaction was not uncommon. If the burns went deep enough, the nerve endings went dead. Smokejumpers described mortally burned comrades laughing and singing as their flesh peeled away. Cody's burns weren't that deep, but it was obvious he wasn't experiencing any pain. Not yet.

"How's my face?" he asked jauntily. "Am I still handsome, or is it Lon Chaney time?"

"Your face is fine."

"That's not what I asked, Doc. I asked am I still handsome."

"You're still handsome, Ned."

It was true, the burns were confined to his back and torso; his face had been untouched.

The exit they'd discovered had taken them several levels up, to a sealed-up tunnel area that seemed to have been abandoned while under construction. The only source of light was a couple of ghostly bulbs protected by wire cages, but it was cool up here, and so far it was relatively free of smoke. Ned Cody was running like a man made of pure adrenaline—Anna had to beg him to rest while she did her best to dress his wounds.

"Know what this is?" Cody said, looking around. "Supposed to hook up to the Second Ave., bet you anything."

"I didn't know there was a subway on Second Avenue," Anna said, trying to humor him.

"That's because it never got finished," he said. "They started digging up the avenue, all these filthy rich East Siders went ballistic. Cracking the crystal or whatever."

"So they stopped?"

"Nah, that wasn't it. They ran out of money to steal. Pouring Mafia concrete. You know what Mafia concrete is?"

"Tell me."

"Sand and water. They dump it one day, then they come back the next and charge to take it away. That's what keeps clogging up the arteries of this city, Mafia concrete."

"Hold still."

"We got to get out of here," Cody said suddenly, trying to stand up. "Hear those trains?"

Anna didn't hear any trains.

"All aboard for Grand Central Station," said Cody. "First class all the way."

"You've got to calm down and keep still, Ned. You're losing body heat."

"Shuffle off to Buffalo. You and me, kiddo."

"Ssshh," she said. He grinned, made a show of zipping his lips. She concentrated—damn, but that *did* sound like distant trains. And then, faintly she heard what might have been alarm bells.

"Jack Lemmon and Marilyn Monroe in *Some Like It Hot.* On the train, get it? Hot like the fire, that's beautiful."

"Beautiful, Ned," she said. "Come on, I'll help you walk."

"Where we goin'?"

"Maybe we'll catch that train, wouldn't that be nice?"

He sang: " 'Dreamt last night, I got on the train to heaven.' That's *Guys and Dolls*, sort of. Only it was a boat, not a train. Can we get a boat, Grand Central?"

The faint sound of the trains seemed to be slightly stronger at one end of the blocked-up tunnel area. Cody was very unsteady on his feet, but he didn't weigh all that much, and Anna was able to pick up the slack, maintaining balance for both of them.

"Bells," said Cody. "I hear bells. Bells, bells, bells. Edgar Allan Poe, right? Poem?"

"Fire bells," Anna said.

"Ding dong the witch is dead, the wicked witch, the mean old witch," he sang. Then, "Do you like me, Dr. Kane?"

"Of course I do, Ned."

"No, no. Really, *really* like me?"

"I really like you, Ned."

"Cause I'm nuts about you, Doc. The whole four-letter thing. L-O-V-E."

"See that door, Ned? We're going through that door and we're going to get you to a hospital."

"But you'll be my doctor, right? That's the deal."

"Sure," she said. "That's the deal."

The door was steel-jacketed, and either padlocked or deadbolted from the other side. Anna eased Cody down and noticed him wincing— he was starting to feel it now, and under the soot smudges his skin was the color of moldy flour. Not good. She ran her hands around the jamb, looking for a place to pry, but it seemed as solid as a bank vault.

"Hinges," Cody said.

"What?"

"Hinges," he repeated, sounding out of breath. He lifted his hand and she saw that he was holding a rusty nail, something he'd picked up from the ground.

Hinges. Of course. He was suggesting that she use the nail to pop out the hinge pins.

With no hammers readily available, she made do with a rock, banging the pins lose. But even with the hinges unpinned, the damn thing still would not budge. Finally she hit the door at a full run, slamming the weight of her body against the panels. On impact the door sagged inward, and she was able to pry it open enough for them to pass through.

The doorway opened onto a stairwell. A very steep, narrow stairwell, enclosed by water-mottled concrete. She couldn't see all the way to the top, but the noise of the trains was considerably louder.

Ned Cody was having a lot of trouble getting up the steps, and she had to take most of his weight. "Ooh baby," he said. "Tell me, Doc, is that awful smell me by any chance? Kind of a charred pork thing?"

"No," she lied as they bumped up the steps. "You're going into shock, it messes up the senses."

"Did I tell you I love you?"

"Yes," she said.

"I must have been delirious. Otherwise I wouldn't have told you. My little secret."

"Uh huh."

"So what about your little secret, Doc?"

"I don't have any secrets," Anna said. Escaping from the fire and the horrors of the Doll House had energized her, but that energy was fading, heartbeat by heartbeat, step by step, and the top of the stairway seemed miles away, an impossible distance.

"Tell me what happened when you were a little kid," Cody insisted "To make you interested in guys like me."

"We'll talk later."

"Marlon guessed right, didn't he? Your Daddy killed your Mommy."

"My mother is alive," Anna said. "Do you really want to know what happened? If I tell you, will you be quiet until we get you to the hospital?"

"Cross my heart and hope to die."

"My father had an organic brain disease. He became extremely violent. He assaulted my mother and then he killed himself."

"And you saw it."

"Yes," she said.

"And that's why you do what you do."

"If you say so."

They were more than halfway to the top. The trains were much louder here, and she felt that once they emerged from the stairway, they would be safe, among passengers. That hope gave her the strength to carry Ned Cody, to keep going even though her body was telling her to stop.

"Look at me, I had a dull, normal childhood," Cody said, sounding faintly amused. "I'm the one who messed up. Go figure."

"Hang on," said Anna, taking it one step at a time. "We're almost home."

CHAPTER
TWELVE

Captain Michael Francis Harnett was not easily convinced.

"He had a back way out," McRay insisted. "Guaranteed."

"That's your theory," said the captain. He wiped his brow, leaving a worm track of ash across his forehead.

"He probably had three or four possible exits," McRay insisted. "That's the way he operates. That's how he thinks."

"But you didn't see him leave."

"Hey, I was on fire, okay? So, no, I didn't stop to take notes."

"All I'm suggesting, Detective, is that the suspect may have perished in the fire."

"Not a chance," McRay said.

All civilians had been evacuated from the various train and subway levels of Grand Central Station. McRay was being debriefed in the Suburban Level Pumping Station, where the Special Response Unit had set up a temporary command post. Already the station's huge reserve tanks were being tapped to help fight the fire still smoldering forty feet below, and the last of the passenger cars were being moved from the great, two-level loop that enabled trains to clear the station without having to back out. The subway shuttle to Times Square was off-line, as were sections of the Lexington Avenue subway and the Queensboro line. Because of the early hour—it was not quite dawn—all of this had been accomplished without significant problems.

Harnett wasn't just busting McRay's chops, he seemed genuinely perplexed. "How can you be so sure the perp survived?" he asked.

"I just know, is all."

McRay's belief in the killer's survival was partly based on the fact that John Chester Marlon was a cunning strategist—of *course* he had an escape route. But mostly it was because McRay refused to consider the possibility that Anna Kane had perished in the inferno: if Marlon could get out of there alive, so could she.

Hours would go by before the Doll House was cooled down enough to sift through the wreckage, and in all probability it would take weeks or even months to identify the numerous badly charred remains. In the meantime, the search had to go on, for Marlon and for Anna. Hell, even for Ned Cody, if he'd managed to get away.

"He's still down there," McRay said. "Believe it."

"If he is, we'll get him," Harnett said. "The Transit Police have two hundred officers deployed throughout the station, and they'll double that within the hour. My own squads are guarding every known exit. We've got the place so tight a fucking flea couldn't escape, let alone a psycho like the Subway Killer."

"He's a very smart psycho, Captain. He knows the underground like nobody else."

Harnett gave him a tight smile and patted him on the back. "You just rest easy, Detective. If your girlfriend got away, we'll find her, too."

"She's not my girlfriend."

"Whatever. There's an ambulance waiting for you at street level. Can you make it that far, or should I send for the EMTs?"

McRay shook his head. "I'm on duty, sir."

"Let the special teams handle it. You go be a hero."

McRay shrugged wearily. "Maybe you're right," he said. "I'm beat."

"Sure you are."

"I'm okay to walk up." McRay made a show of coughing. "Check out my lungs, right?"

"They'll take good care of you, son."

Once he was out of Harnett's sight—and presumably out of his mind—McRay ducked around a corner and picked up his pace.

"Hey, Kev!"

Jakowski was there, holding out a container of coffee. "Where do you think you're going?"

"You go on home, Len, I'll be fine."

"The fuck you think you're talking to, Kev? You're heading back down there, am I right?"

McRay shrugged.

"You're as crazy as he is, you know that? Your buddy Marlon."

"You're right," McRay said, turning away. "I'm crazy."

"Wait up," Jakowski said, tossing his coffee. "I've got your goddamn weapon, remember? And you can't shoot straight, anyhow."

"So? What are you, Wyatt Earp?"

"Close," Jakowski said.

By the time Anna managed to lug Ned Cody all the way to the top of the stairwell, the noise of the trains had diminished, and with it the sense of well-being that had accompanied that familiar sound.

She became aware of a strong odor—a stench of human waste and rotting garbage.

"I know that's not me," said Cody. "Bad as I am."

He leaned heavily against her, his whole body radiating a burn fever, as they emerged into a dark grotto of brick archways. The vaulted ceilings were low overhead, and visibility was extremely limited. Underfoot was sticky gravel, railroad ties, littered debris.

"Where are we?" Cody muttered. Before she could frame a reply he collapsed in her arms, still breathing but semiconscious.

Through the brick vaults and pillars, Anna saw open flames and reacted—the fire had followed them! A moment later, however, she realized that the flames were actually quite small. It was a kind of campfire. People had gathered around the orange flames, warming their hands, and Anna's heart lifted.

"Help!" she called out. "Over here! We need help! We need an ambulance!"

The only source of light was the fire, so it was hard to focus on the figures who turned toward the sound of her voice. Were they railroad workers? The light was obscured as the figures moved, shifting in silhouette, and then suddenly Anna and Cody were surrounded, and the stench of ripe garbage and filth was overwhelming.

"Hey lady, what you got there?"

"Check for her purse! Does she got a purse on her?"

Hands touched her, fumbling over her body. "Please," she said, squirming away. "We need help. My friend needs help."

Somebody laughed, breathing the fruity smell of cheap wine right in her face. "We all need help, bitch. Whole world needs help."

In the press of bodies, Cody stirred to consciousness. "Back off," he implored as his arms flailed around, not connecting.

More laughter. "The man say back off! Looks like he's dead man, all twitchy inside, but he say back off."

The derelicts were pushing closer, groping her, when someone carrying a torch shoved through the little mob, heading right for Anna.

"Give her room," said a deep baritone. "Hands off the lady!"

Suddenly the groping hands dropped away.

The man with the torch wore a hooded sweatshirt, and she could make out only his yellow, owlish eyes. "You're in the wrong place," he informed her. "No women down here. We got us some females, you peel away a few layers, but you wouldn't hardly call 'em women."

"We need help. My friend has been injured. Burned."

He raised the torch, got a good look at Ned Cody. "Heard the alarms go off," he said. "That was you?"

"That was us."

"What you want. Police?"

"Just help. A way out."

The torch wavered. "Ain't a cop alive who'd come down here, lady. This is mole country, you know?"

"What?"

"We the mole people, ain't you heard? Mostly they leave us alone, we stay deep enough."

"You mean you're homeless."

"Oh no," he said. "Don't be calling us homeless. We got a home. This our home, see?"

He raised the torch, illuminating a row of crates and boxes formed into crude habitations. The place was an encampment, and in the faint, flickering light Anna saw that there were hundreds of people living among the crates, an existence so degraded, so feral, that it was scarcely human.

"You need to see the man," said the torch. "The man know what to do."

The crowd around her had swelled, until there was no resisting the pressure. She and Cody were carried along, following the torch, until they came to a decrepit, time-ravaged subway car.

The subway car was off the tracks, most of the windows were missing, and the doors had been pried off, but compared to the old wooden crates and the cardboard boxes, it was a mansion, a castle.

A kerosene lamp hung from a handrail inside the car, faintly illuminating the interior. The man with the torch approached the subway car cautiously, his whole posture deferential, as if he were in the presence of royalty.

"Lady to see you, boss. Real fine lady."

Anna felt the malignant presence before he came into view, but there was nothing she could do, no way she could work free from the mob that had surrounded her. It was as if a fist had reached inside her chest and clenched her beating heart. He was here.

"Hello, Dr. Kane."

Marlon held up the lantern, inspecting the scene before him. He was still wearing the patrolman's outfit, had taken the trouble to clean himself up, although from close range it was apparent that the uniform had been singed in the fire, and that the seams were giving out.

"I've been thinking about you," he said. "You're on my mind."

"Help us, please!" Anna pleaded to the surrounding mob. "He's insane. He's a monster!"

Marlon's laughter echoed, and was mimicked by several of the mob.

"Save your breath, Dr. Kane," he said, holding his lantern out to the crowd. "Down here we don't believe in monsters, do we?"

The mob cried, "Nooooo!" and Marlon gave a short bow, acknowledging the response.

"We're all of us human, more or less," he continued. "All of us killers and lovers. All devils and gods. All creators and destroyers. We're everything, and the other thing, and all that is in between."

"You the man, Marlon! Nobody stop you!"

"Do you see, Dr. Kane? To these good folk I am a legend. Years ago I began to leave things for them. Stocks of food, clothing, whatever came my way. And they have not forgotten. They have been cursed as I was cursed. They have been shunned as I was shunned. And they will not betray me now."

"The cops know you're here!" Anna said, raising her voice to be heard.

"Of course they do."

"You can't escape."

"Oh, but I can, Dr. Kane. You should know that better than anyone. I'll escape, and with your help. I'll start over, and this time I won't make so many early mistakes. Beauty will rise again from the ashes, in another place. The work goes on, dear girl, the work must go on."

"I won't help you," said Anna. "I'd rather die."

"Oh, you'll die. First you'll help, and then you'll die."

He came to her for the last time, raising the lantern, and grinning like a tiger in the moon.

"What happened to Jeff?" McRay wanted to know.

"Sent him home. Unlike you, he's smart enough to know when to quit."

"I have to do this," said McRay. "Just to make sure."

They were making their way down a frozen escalator, heading for the subway tunnels that eventually connected under the Waldorf-Astoria. McRay looked drawn, on the verge of collapse, but his eyes burned brightly. He'd seen the light and he couldn't forget it. Frozen figures burning, burning.

"What was it like, the Doll House?"

"You don't want to know."

"That bad, huh?"

"It was hard to see with all the smoke, but I think he was taking more than just the women who fit the profile. That's what we missed. He was taking everybody. Men, women, and children."

"Children?"

"Let's drop it for now, okay?"

"Anything you say, Kev. I just want you to know, I get a shot at this guy, I'm taking it. I don't care if he puts his hands up and surrenders, I'm still taking the shot."

"That's murder," McRay pointed out.

"Is that right?"

"Just make sure he's dead."

They came to the bottom of the escalator. "Where are we going?" Jakowski asked.

"The Lexington Avenue subway passes within fifty feet of the Doll House. If they exited from the top—and they had to, I think—his connection has to intersect with the tunnel."

Jakowski nodded. "I'll take your word for it. But they've got that tunnel cut off from either end. Why not wait for the search teams? They'll flush him out."

"Maybe," said McRay.

"You think he's got another hole to hide in?"

"I'm sure he does. But he has to get there first. And he'll want to be well clear of the area."

"You want to walk the tracks, is that it?"

"That's it."

They'd come to a deserted subway platform under the hotel. Elevator access had been blocked off from above, to prevent any of the Waldorf-Astoria guests from venturing down to observe a manhunt in progress.

Jakowski was the first one to climb down from the platform and stand in the tracks, well clear of the third rail. "Every cop instinct tells me this is wrong," he said.

"Wait here, Len. I get in trouble, I'll call you."

"You're already in trouble, kid. You should see yourself."

"I'm okay," McRay insisted, hopping down from the platform.

"Like cancer is okay."

Complaining every step of the way, Jakowski insisted on walking in front. He was the better shooter, and he had the Kevlar vest.

The mole people flowed through the tunnel, keeping a fairly tight formation. Marlon controlled Anna with one strong hand encircled around her neck—in his other hand was a Tech-9 machine pistol loaded with a full clip. Even if she managed to break free and avoid being shot—extremely unlikely—she was completely surrounded by the ragged derelicts, who seemed to hold the killer in awe, responding to his commands.

As they moved along, he spoke to her, using an intimate, soothing tone that made Anna want to shed her own skin. "Think of it, Dr. Kane. After transformation, you'll be as immortal as Venus de Milo, or the Mona Lisa. For generations to come the enlightened will stand before you. 'She was the first transformation of the Second Coming,' they'll say. Isn't that perfect? The Second Coming, that's what my new work will be called."

Although he tugged at her, expecting an answer, she refused to respond. He wanted to engage her in conversation, acknowledging his dominion. The only thing left for her was to deny him that small measure of satisfaction.

Ned Cody had been left by the subway car, delirious and barely able to move. It was obvious even to the inexpert eye that he could not survive for long without immediate medical treatment. To Marlon he was already dead, and so spoiled he couldn't be "transformed."

"I'll tell you a secret," Marlon crooned, marching her along. "I can't be killed. They can fire bullets directly at me, and still I can't be killed."

Something had happened to him in the fire, she realized. His mental state had apparently deteriorated into a severe form of psychotic mania that made him, if anything, even more dangerous. Many psychopaths believed they were immortal, indistinguishable from God. Their acts of irrational violence—bloody public rampages—were a demonstration of that belief. *I am God, therefore I have the power of life and death*—and it was almost always death they chose to demonstrate. The most extreme cases went on demonstrating that power, killing and killing and killing, driven by the psychotic impulse, until finally cut down.

Marlon had finally crossed over and become a trigger-reactive, Anna realized, and a trigger-reactive serial killer was perhaps the ultimate killing machine—he had intelligence, cunning, experience, and he was in the throes of irresistible compulsion. That was the precise state her Microcomputer Sedation Device had been designed to control, but it was too late, she'd already removed the implant, and there was no way to stop him now, short of a bullet to the brain.

"I know what you're thinking," he confided as they surged through the tunnel, gathering a mob momentum. "You think I'm God. But I'm not God, I'm something more. God was the question, I am the answer."

Ahead of them was darkness, the void into which the tunnel vanished. To Anna that darkness was her own impending death, and she was being forced to march right into it. Maybe poor Ned Cody had it easy, succumbing to a feverish delirium as his body passed through the final stages of shock. At least he was alone, out of Marlon's domain.

The killer sang to himself as they marched. His voice was pitched high, a clear boyish tenor. At first she couldn't make out the words, but gradually it became clear. The song was an old folk ballad about a doomed love affair.

"She went upstairs to make her bed," he sang, "and not a word to her mother said. Oh mother dear, I cannot tell, it's that railroad boy I love so well, that railroad boy, that railroad boy, that railroad boy I love so well."

If Anna could have willed herself deaf, she would have done so, for it was clear that she would carry that song inside her head for however long he let her continue to live.

Cody dreamt of an empty stage. Just the single bare light bulb that had been left on, a practice as old as electricity. Shadows waited in the wings, he couldn't quite make them out but he knew they were there. Ghosts of departed actors, waiting for a cue.

"I'm here," he called out. "I'm ready."

The sound of his own frail voice made him realize he wasn't asleep or dreaming. There was no stage—he was deep in the tunnels, left behind—but the ghosts were really there. He could feel them. So was the light. Light at the end of the tunnel.

He was dying. There was pain, but the pain belonged to someone else and it did not touch him, not really.

In the distance, echoing through the tunnels, he could hear Marlon singing. Mad Marlon with Anna in tow, marching to oblivion.

Get up, Ned. That's your cue.

As a youth, fascinated with movies and with actors, he'd been moved to tears by Ronald Colman's noble self-sacrifice in *A Tale of Two Cities*. Colman as Sydney Carton, trundling off to his doom for the sake of love, a love that transcended death. What was that line? Great stuff, melodramatic and corny as Kansas, but it worked, it made you believe him.

It is a far, far better thing I do, than I have ever done.

That was it.

"Wait," Cody said, getting up to his knees. Rising. "Wait, I'm coming."

When the first shot was fired, she assumed it was Marlon punctuating the song. But almost instantly the mob of mole people melted away, ragged bodies scattering to the sides of the tunnel, and she understood that the bullet had come from elsewhere. From the darkness ahead.

Behind her, holding her tight against his massive chest, Marlon was serene. "How shall I kill a thing of beauty?" he sang out. "Help me count the ways."

Anna strained to see, but the tunnel dark was impenetrable.

"Let her go!" came a voice she knew.

Marlon marched on, frog-stepping her over the railroad ties. A few of the mole people remained lurking nearby, but it was obvious their loyalty did not include exposing themselves to gunfire.

"You can do nothing!" Marlon boomed. "I am the answer!"

Another, unfamiliar voice called out. "Let her go and put your hands up, you crazy fuck!"

Marlon ignored the taunt and kept on marching. "Oh mother dear," he sang, "I cannot tell. It's that railroad boy I love so well."

Humming the chorus, da da da dee, da da da dum.

"He has a gun!" Anna managed to cry, before the hand tightened on her neck.

"Oh, they know that, Dr. Kane," he said. " 'Deed they do."

He fired a quick burst, sweeping the machine pistol from side to side. "Stand aside as history passes by! As time marches on!"

Da da da dee, da da da dum.

They were alone now, just John Chester Marlon and Anna Kane, and voices in the dark to keep them company.

"I can drop you right now, you bastard!" said the unfamiliar voice.

"Da da da dee," Marlon sang, keeping pace. "Da da da dum, the railroad boy has got a gun."

The machine pistol was jammed under her chin, with every step it dug into her neck. She felt a weird exhilaration—whatever happened in the next few moments, she would not be transformed by this madman.

Suddenly a figure emerged from the dark about ten yards in front of them. An older cop Anna did not recognize. A beefy, red-haired guy taking a three-point stance and aiming a pistol with rock-steady hands. "Fuck you think you're going, motherfucker. Let her go."

Another figure popped up, this one much closer. Kevin McRay, mimicking his partner's stance. McRay's hands were much less steady. "The tunnel's closed off from both ends," he said. "Give it up."

Marlon kept on coming, shoving Anna forward, the machine pistol bumping under her chin. "Da da da dee, da da da dum."

"Shit," Jakowski said. "He's out of his fucking mind."

Footsteps skidding on the gravel between the rails. Someone was coming up behind them.

"Hey wait!" Ned Cody cried out. "This is my cue, this is my show."

"They're all of them fucking nuts!" said Jakowski, his aim unwavering.

"Wait!" said McRay. "Back off! We're handling this!"

Marlon swiveled her a few degrees and Anna could see Ned staggering up along the track. Whatever reserve of strength he'd found was fading fast. He lost his balance and collapsed, skidding on the gravel, but he still kept coming on his hands and knees. "I know my lines," he muttered. "I know my lines."

The machine pistol shifted under her chin and she felt the barrel twitch.

A single shot caught Cody in the side. He went all the way down and did not move.

A much louder shot rang out and Marlon grunted, almost losing his grip on her. As he whirled to face the two cops she saw that part of his left ear had been shot away. The smell of his own blood seemed to stimulate him. He grinned with his small, evenly spaced teeth, his eyes so fully dilated Anna thought she was looking into black holes in his skull.

"Da da da dee," he sang, and opened fire on full automatic, catching the older cop full in the chest. He went down slowly, looking stunned with surprise.

"Da da da dum."

He fired again and McRay spun around, clutching his side, dropping his gun.

"Kevin!" she screamed, twisting out of Marlon's grip.

He let her go and concentrated on taking careful aim at McRay, who lay on his side, immobilized by the pain.

Anna, who had landed on her back, tried to kick at Marlon's legs as he went by, but he was just out of reach.

Taking aim slowly, and with great satisfaction. In another heartbeat he'd finish off McRay and then turn to her.

She was looking right into Marlon's face, unwilling to close her eyes. Thinking: *I'm not alone. I'm not afraid,* and it was true, all fear had drained from her. The excruciating fear she'd experienced in the dark closet as a terrified child, the fear of her long-dead father and her living-dead mother, all those fears vanished like moisture instantly evaporated by the heat of her emerging soul, and she knew exactly who she was, and she knew that nothing Marlon did could change or defile that, even if no part of her survived this final moment.

The barrel of the machine pistol wavered. Marlon looked down and saw that Ned Cody had managed to drag himself close enough to grasp the big killer by the ankle.

Cody's wobbly head lifted up and he made eye contact with Anna. He opened his mouth, as if wanting to speak, as if he did indeed have a line to speak, but nothing came out except a small dribble of blood. He smiled, as if expecting her to understand.

Marlon tried to shake his leg loose, but the actor's fingers were locked around his ankle. The machine pistol spit once more and Cody shivered, as if his body had been invaded by ice.

He was dying.

Very deliberately, Cody's free hand reached out, blindly searching along the inside of the track.

"No!" said Marlon, when he realized what the hand was about to do. "No!"

It was as if the dying actor's hand had a life and purpose all its own. As it firmly clamped itself on the dull metal of the third rail, thirty thousand volts of high-amperage power instantly arced through his body and surged up through Marlon.

There was no spark, and no sound. Just the two men motionless, a human sculpture frozen in time, as immobile as one of Marlon's human sculptures.

Not a sound, not a sound.

After what seemed an endless interval, the machine pistol suddenly erupted, emptying itself into the gravel around Marlon's feet. The gun barrel began to glow. Marlon's tongue extruded from his small mouth, swollen and black and steaming, and then he toppled forward, breaking the connection, and crashed to the ground inches from where Anna lay.

She scrambled back out of range, but the killer did not move. She was aware of an unnatural heat radiating from his body as the meat cooked on his bones, and of smoke rising from Ned Cody's blackened hand.

"The fuck happened?" groaned Len Jakowski. His hands plucked ineffectually at the heavy Kevlar. "Am I dead or what?"

Anna crawled over to where Kevin McRay lay curled in a fetal position, blood seeping between his clenched fingers.

She felt for his pulse, found it.

"We're alive," she said.

EPILOGUE

He waited in the rental car, more exhausted than he would admit, even to himself. Two hours behind the wheel and he was ready for a nap. The surgeons who put him back together had said it would be like this, that it might take a year or even two to make a full recovery.

Don't push it, they told him, you're lucky to be alive.

No question about that. The amazing thing was that he didn't feel bitter about anything, and except for an occasional nightmare, he was not haunted by the experience. It was over.

He was a different man, of course. Life went on, things changed, you couldn't escape that. For most of his life he'd wanted to be a detective, unraveling the mysteries of criminal behavior. After the shooting, in those long months of recuperation, watching the doctors and nurses who cared for him, he'd decided to try something new, take a different turn in the road.

He had enrolled in nursing school. Was there any law that said a cop couldn't become an RN? Prior to his rebirth in the underground, he'd never paid that much attention to medicine, or healing, and although he'd known better, somehow he'd always thought of nurses as exclusively female. It wasn't true.

Now he knew better about a lot of things. His head lolled, and he dreamt of smooth, creamy marble. The stone made flesh.

He awoke with a start when she tapped the window. "Sorry," he said. "I must have nodded off."

Anna smiled at him. "We can do this another time."

"No," he said. "I came all this way. How is she?"

"Better, I think. She actually spoke to me. And she stopped rocking. So that's an improvement."

In the sunlight the sanitarium looked a lot like a grand hotel. He was painfully aware that it was not, and that each visit was difficult for Anna. The recent improvement might be temporary. No one knew for sure. This was the first time he'd accompanied her to this place, and his being here was no accident. This was a defining moment and he knew it.

He got out of the car and brushed at the lapels of his jacket. It was important to make a good impression on the mother of the woman he loved, even if the mother was out of her mind. Hey, maybe she'd continue to get better. Why not? Miracles happened.

"Are you up for it?" she asked him.

"I am if you are."

McRay took a deep breath and followed her inside.